LiT
Part IV – Begrimed Harridan
2024 Edition

Maxwell F. Hurley

LiT
Part IV – Begrimed Harridan
2024 Edition

FICTION4ALL

DEDICATION

To all my family and friends.

Special thanks to Matt Weber for all your
continuous support
and
Karen Vetsch for all your help in the past years

PROLOGUE

This past dawn of the season in new life, the Lite Sentry successfully vanquished the Master of the Dark Conduit back into its realm. The cost of this victory left scars among those who stepped onto the battlefield. Loneliness can lure a sorrowed heart into a sinkhole with no chance of escape. Once in, it can consume a being without the knowledge of it happening. It can be pushed away and hidden from those who we love the most. It is a silent killer that tortures the soul. The grief is often hidden by the courier from those they love. Even the Lite is unable to see the growth from this pain.

INTRODUCTION

Alex smacked another bug on her forehead. Which, was pretty stupid, considering she now had insect guts dripping down her pale face. "This sucks." On the other hand, her purple-skinned, gargoyle dog, who also served as a hunting companion, seemed unfazed by the blanket of little creatures crawling on him. The darkness of the jungle helped camouflage Komptin as he walked through the thick foliage. They were on, what Alex assumed, was *somewhat* of a trail. The feeling of tiny little legs creeping up her arm caused her to shiver from disgust. She was almost afraid to see what was crawling on her body. The sensation of a bigger bug slowly moving up on her sent a wave of goosebumps all over her body. It seemed as if time stood still when she saw the stick-looking bug walking up her arm. It didn't seem to care when Alex flicked it off with her finger. The bug just landed on the jungle floor and crawled away.

Multiple life forms made their presence known by releasing an eerie song throughout the jungle. Alex tilted her head back to prevent another creature from scuttling down the back of her neck. The bug was using all its might to dig into her black, weaved-in hair. Fortunately, she was able to reach the back of her neck to grab the black monstrosity. It had a set of curved pinching fangs on its head with a hard shell covering its body. Alex would have opened her mouth in disgust, but she was afraid of something flying into it.

Komptin walked with a confident gait– as if nothing could harm him. Truthfully, there wasn't much besides the supernatural that *could* harm him. Still, she knew him too well; he didn't enjoy this hunt either. Alex turned her head towards the sound of a jaguar in the distance. She casually stepped a bit closer to Komptin. The massive creature turned his head when Alex bumped into him. "What? I just wanted to make sure you weren't scared." There was no chance of her hiding her uncomfortableness from this situation. Fighting Demons or coming in contact with Infiltrators didn't scare Alex as much as the thought of being eaten by wild animals. On the nights she didn't hunt, she started the habit of binge-watching vicious nature channel shows. Her surroundings have now made her think she needed to watch more cuter puppy shows. However, here she was, in this jungle, in the middle of the night.

Alex and Komptin were asked to search for the Infiltrator who killed a Lite Sentry here in Brazil. This walk had given Alex a lot of respect for Juliana. That was her name, and for her to hunt the Dark in such conditions was truly admirable. Alex had never met her, or more shameful, knew her name until she arrived in the small town outside this tropical forest. The announcement of her death was the preamble to her battle at the F.O.R. Headquarters to rescue Anne earlier this year. There was always disgrace and hurt thinking about that night. They achieved their goal of rescuing Anne, which resulted in the Dark Conduit, Vandor, being banished inside the Dark. It was a great win for the Lite, but it came at a tremendous cost. One for which she could never forgive herself.

In the sky above her was one of the brightest shining stars only beings of Lite could differentiate. That star was formed when Ariel, who was one-half of the Guardians of the Conduit, was killed by a Caliginous. Then, another loss happened that night that was difficult for her to handle at times. Roger, who now called himself "Gron," was a Dark Sentry who killed her brother with hate and contempt. His eyes were brimming with satisfaction when he shoved his Dark powered fist through her brother's chest, Kale. Alex wanted Gron dead. There would be a time when Alex could confront him, and then she would show him the true power of the Lite.

Another bug landed on her cheek. Instinctively, she slapped her own face so hard it echoed through the blackened jungle. The remnants of the insect dripped onto her lips. "That's it!" Alex exclaimed. She'd had enough. Even though she'd promised Father Raimundo to find the Infiltrator that killed Juliana, she couldn't take it anymore. It was hot, it was humid, the smell was nauseating, and there was no sense of the Dark.

Alex turned around to go back to the hotel for a nice, hot shower when she noticed something; she stood still to verify her assumption. The jungle was quiet; not a single insect made a noise. A sudden stale sense in the air meant the Dark was ahead.

"Damn it," Alex said out of annoyance. The trail behind her invited a night of relaxation with a topping of being clean; however, she knew there was no turning back now. The path ahead of her was what she needed to trek.

The course laid out before her was barely visible as it had become narrow and overgrown. The only comfort Alex was given now was that the bugs were no longer a nuisance. The combination of sensing the Dark along with the haunting effect of the sudden calm of the surrounding area was something she could not ignore. Keeping her head still, she moved her eyes towards Komptin as he too was on edge. They both instinctively started to walk without making a sound. A clearing was evident on the trail ahead. The two hunters of the Dark both knew something wasn't right in the area.

There was an opening at the end of the trail showing the ruins of a stone building. It appeared to have the layout of an old church. Warmth and security were always present on holy ground, but she didn't sense any here. There was no doubt there would be a confrontation with the Dark tonight. If this were a haven for her, she would not be able to form a weapon. The Dark could not harm anyone on any type of holy land to the Lite. Alex put her fist up and lit it up using the Lite within her. A sense of sadness overcame her as she realized she wasn't in a sanctuary. There was definitely a strong Dark aura engulfing the area.

Komptin didn't move around much. He faced the jungle waiting for the imminent attack. Alex made her way to what looked like an altar at the head of the room. Anybody could see that the amount of blood splattered on the tabletop meant there was a struggle. At the base of the altar, bones were laying mixed with torn clothing. Some light reflected off a piece of metal that was buried underneath all that remained of this poor individual. Alex moved over some of the clothing to pick up a handcrafted rosary. She gently wiped off the dirt to see dried blood covering the crucifix. On the back of the wooden cross, there was an engraving. Alex licked her thumb and wiped off the dirt. There it read, 'Juliana'.

Alex turned to the sky, knowing she was now among those who had perished in this war. There was no doubt; this was the spot the Lite Sentry was killed. A faint sound of tree limbs breaking caught her attention as something of the Dark was emerging. She motioned for Komptin to come with her to hide in the shadows of the jungle floor. Komptin morphed down to his German shepherd state to rest against her. The two of them watched as the noise grew louder from whatever version of the Dark approaching. Out from the blackness of the jungle, an elderly man with long, gray hair emerged. He was using an old, wooden staff with a glass ball on top. Inside was a maroon liquid that almost looked like blood.

The average person wouldn't think twice about the man, but Alex saw something in his eyes. They weren't supernatural. They didn't have the physical presence of the Dark in them, but they were evil.

He grunted as he walked up to the altar, almost giving a smirk of remembrance as he grazed his hand across the bloodstained table. He lifted his head as if to smell the air. "I know you're here, Sentry."

Alex swallowed hard but didn't make a sound. She stared ahead with Komptin at the old man, her body a little more tense. Now, there was a concentrated sense of the Dark.

"Come on out!" he yelled but was facing away from her.

A flash of red eyes came from the jungle; a familiar voice came out from amidst the shadows. "Why couldn't we meet in town?"

Alex's body further tensed as she was now focused on her racing heart. She clenched her fists when Gron came out of the shadows. His red hair was neatly combed as he was on his way to meet the old man. A memory of her brother being murdered by this demon flooded her mind. Alex flashed her eyes and lit her fists from rage as she lunged towards Gron in blind vengeance. She screamed as she shot a beam of Lite at the old man, knocking him over. Roger immediately ignited his fists into a red glow. He flashed his eyes as he easily grabbed Alex to throw her into the wall of the building. The back of her body smashed against the decrepit wall of stone.

Komptin followed suit behind her, now in his gargoyle state, running towards Roger. Komptin yelped as three Infiltrators tackled him from the side. Alex watched him fend off his attackers as she put her hands on the ground to get up. Roger's boot stepped on her hand before she was able to rise. With his fist glowing red, he smacked her on the side of the face, directly on the scar Sanah had given her. The pain was tremendous. She flashed her eyes a neon blue to get back up, only to meet another fist, again to the side of the face. The blow knocked her down onto the jagged floor of the old building.

"Didn't think our next encounter would be this easy," Roger bragged as he twisted his boot on top of her hand.

Alex clenched her teeth. There was no way she would give him the satisfaction of hearing her screaming from the pain. A stone laying on the ground next to her was within her grasp. With all her might, she smashed it against his knee. Roger grabbed his knee as he stumbled backward. Alex was now able to get up with her eyes glowing blue and her fists lit. She punched him across the face causing him to spin into one of the Infiltrators attacking Komptin. That gave Komptin the opportunity to engage in a counterattack.

Roger pushed the Dark bear-like creature out of his way to face Alex. "It was such a satisfaction killing him. You know his blood dripping down my arm, combined with the shock of Anne's and your faces, was something to truly treasure."

"I will get-" Alex started to say, but she was hit in the back of the head by the wooden staff of the old man. The hard ground caught her fall at the cost of blood and scratches.

15

"Go, Sentry, I will see to her," the old man screwed the ball off from the top of his staff to toss it to Gron.

Gron wanted to stay and fight, but he knew he could damage the prize in his possession. "Just let me know if you kill her." Gron held the ball to the light of the moon with Alex in the background.

The old man stared at Alex, "I will kill her, just like the last one." He turned back to his Demon Master. "To his command."

Roger nodded at the old man before winking at Alex who was surveying the situation, "Hey Alex." He blew her a kiss. "See ya around." The minion of the Dark disappeared into the darkness of the jungle with one of the Infiltrators following.

"That only leaves two," Alex whispered under her breath. "And one soon-to-be-dead old man." The sound of an Infiltrator screaming before he was diminished by Komptin brought a small smile to Alex's face. The final Infiltrator took off into the jungle. "Go, don't worry I got this." She went to turn her attention back to the old man. His staff again came swinging at her head. The only part of her body that moved was her hand catching it before it smashed her face. "You're not going to do that to me twice." Alex yanked the staff from his hands to examine it. "I suppose you're not going to tell me what you gave Roger."

"He is Gron. Don't disrespect him with a human name," the old man told her with a sneer.

"I don't want to kill you, but I will," she told

him, breaking the staff with ease with her two hands.

"The last Lite Sentry tried, she didn't leave here," the old man walked up to Alex. "You think you won by locking my Master away?"

"Ah, yeah," Alex gave a snarky reply. "Have you ever thought of using Listerine?" She backed up from his foul breath.

The man snickered, "You wanna know how she died? The mixture of fear and failure in her eyes was truly something to witness." He walked up to Alex as close as he could before touching her. Alex just stared, wanting to punch him. "Are you going to kill an old man?"

Alex remained stone-faced as she felt the Dark behind her, "No." She stepped out of the way as an Infiltrator tried to attack her from behind. The dark beast accidentally ripped apart the old man. After realizing what it had done, it turned to Alex, where she grabbed the bearlike creature by the throat. She tossed it against the wall with a follow-up knee to the stomach. The Infiltrator bent over from the hit, so Alex leapt on the wall pushing herself off with her foot and grabbing the beast's head, driving it into the ground. She cracked her neck before kneeling on the back of its head. Her hands formed a neon blue knife and she stabbed it into the back of the neck, through to coming out the other side.

After it melted into the ground, Komptin joined her. "You okay?" Alex checked a small wound leaking a neon blue liquid from above his eye before scratching his ear. The rosary was undisturbed as Alex picked it up from the ground. She thought about going off and trying to hunt Gron, but she knew she would face him again.

CHAPTER ONE

The clock had just turned to three-thirty in the morning, but sleep was elusive. Kameron laid on his side with the clock face staring back at him. His bed was destroyed from tossing about like a crocodile in a death roll. There was so much going through his mind that night. For some reason, his boss was in his thoughts. Temporary Director Michal Grossman was in line to become the official Director of the FLOTUS detail, which would be beneficial for the organization. Grossman selfishly was instrumental in delivering a blow to the F.O.R. last spring. Only a couple of people knew he covertly planted the explosives in the F.O.R. Headquarters. Besides his selfless act, he was just a good man.

He did have to admit, though, that wasn't all that was troubling him. Alex hadn't contacted him since she'd left for Brazil with Anne to retrieve some records. He flipped over to the empty spot next to his bed. The only sound in the room was from him rubbing his hand on the sheet. It was obvious. He would never know what it'd be like to have her sleeping next to him when he wakes in the morning. "Not every relationship is perfect," he tried to convince himself. A hint of the city lights was peeking through from behind the drapes. Since he was wide-awake, he might as well go for a run.

It was no surprise the temperature was cool during the run. It was expected for this time of day, but the weather was warning of a hot day ahead. He passed an all-night construction crew working on the section of the road a couple of miles from his apartment. He would have to leave for work earlier than usual today. Traffic was going to be backed up, so the alternate routes to work were going to be more crowded. Up ahead on his run, there were some flashing emergency lights. There seemed to be a lot more lights at the scene than for the usual car accident. Kameron's curiosity got the best of him as he found himself heading in that direction.

This was a good opportunity to work on his short-run burst. His legs moved quickly, and the air pressing against his face caused his eyes to water. When he arrived on the scene, he took a moment to practice slowing down with his breathing control. It was relatively easy to control his heart rate and breathing. Kameron stood outside the police tape where he saw police officers talking. On the ground next to them, was a dead body lying on the street. It looked like he was explaining what had happened.

An Asian female police officer approached Kameron, "Can I help you?" She was young-looking, but she gave off the impression she had already seen her fair share of what this city offered.

Kameron smiled to show her that he wasn't a threat. "No, I was just on my run, and I was curious," Kameron felt a little guilty about filling his inquisitiveness with a dead body on the ground.

The police officer obviously didn't care for his attempt at kindness. "Stay behind the tape." She turned her attention to a reporter who'd showed up on the scene trying to get in. "Hey, stay behind the line!" She went off yelling at the belligerent reporter who was trying to get the story.

At that moment, Kameron was awarded with a better view of the body. It was a shell of a dead teenage boy on the ground. The blood on his white sleeveless shirt showed he was shot five times. There was a tattoo on his arm of an upside-down four. Mixed feelings came over Kameron when he saw the symbol on the young boy's dead body. Those feelings had to be pushed away as the alarm on his phone told him that he needed to start heading back to his apartment. There was a sudden chill in the air. Kameron surveyed the surrounding area as if someone was watching him. Although there was no evidence of him being watched, there was no shaking the sensation. Perhaps seeing the F.O.R. symbol just made some bad memories materialize. No matter the cause, this wasn't exactly how he wanted to start his day.

***

Michal was more than happy to hit the stop button on the treadmill. As his experience in life grew, it seemed the price was his body. The left knee had a feeling of water in it, his shoulder was starting to give him trouble, and of course, his eyesight was starting to get blurrier. All qualities he could not afford to give up as a Secret Service agent. Granted, he knew his time on detail protecting the First Lady was coming to an end. It was a bittersweet situation because a possible promotion would be announced today.

The final word of the new Director of the FLOTUS Detail was coming. "Director Grossman" was something he would like to hear. Moreover, he knew he wasn't going to have to be transferred to some detail hunting down some idiotic threat from someone seeking attention.

He wiped down the treadmill before picking up his phone to see a breaking news report of a police shooting that happened downtown. Shame filled him as the first thing he was hoping for was a legit shooting. Was he becoming so callous that it didn't matter if someone had lost a life? There wasn't much about it on the news, but depending on which news outlet one read, the direction shifted on whether they said it was a righteous shooting.

The smell of breakfast cooking from the kitchen lingering in the hallway meant he was already running behind. He quickly bee-lined into the master bathroom to shower. Once he completed his longer and hotter shower than he had time for, he was able to get dressed rather quickly. Michal went into his gun safe to pull out his weapons for his holsters. He stepped out of his bedroom at the same time his seventeen-year-old son stepped out of his. "Good morning, Moses."

"What up?" He walked in front of his dad to the breakfast table. The music from his headphones were so loud that every word could be made out.

"Really? 'What up?' Is that all I get?" Michal watched his son, who wasn't giving his father any time this morning, just walking in front of him. Moses had the potential of being such a good boy. He was athletic and smart, but his attitude as of late was something Michal couldn't get over. His clothing had become more of something of a high-class gang member. All he did was hang out with his friends or in his room, listening to music. The only time they said more than a sentence to each other was if they were fighting, which seemed to be a lot as of late.

They both sat down at the table. Michal sat in his normal spot facing the door but away from the window. Moses sat as far away from him as possible with his phone, and the only movement was from him bobbing his head to the music or answering a text message. "Moses, you know there are no headphones at the table." His son just continued to listen to music. "Moses," Michal said a little louder.

"Listen to your father," his wife, Talia, said as she came up behind him, smacking him in the back of the head. Moses took off his headphones as she placed the plate full of food down in front of him. Michal loved Talia's breakfast; it was something she always put her generous heart into by making a hearty meal to start the day. Talia calmly put her hand on her son's phone to tell him to put it away. "Not at the table."

"Sorry Moms, there was another shooting by some saltine pig early this morning," he told her. He started to scarf down his breakfast.

Michal sighed at his son's ignorant comment. "Moses, you don't know the facts of the case yet. The body cam hasn't been released." His wife brought him his plate. Michal couldn't help but admire the beauty Talia still had after all these years. Even though some gray hairs were starting to peek through, her presence still made Michal feel like a thirteen-year-old boy with his first crush. "Thank you, honey."

"No problem, but do we have to have this discussion, now?" she asked him, trying to prevent a fight.

Moses just shook his head. "What? How can you say that? You know it's just another cop trying to use any reason to eradicate another brother. Black people keep falling victim to these so-called protectors. Yah, they're protectors all right, to the whites."

"Where do you think we should go for our family vacation this summer?" Talia tried to dissolve the situation before it started to snowball. She sat down to drink her coffee before biting into her breakfast.

"Really, do you think all law enforcement are trained just to shoot people with dark skin?" Michal was trying to get through to his son. "I've been in law enforcement for twenty-five years; I don't remember any training like that."

"You're an over-glorified security guard." Moses' annoyed demeanor towards his father was evident. "All you do is protect people who write laws to keep black people down."

"Hey, take a look around." Michal started to get angry. "You're not exactly in the projects." The appreciation he lacked for what his father had provided for his son didn't make Michal angry. It was more coming from hurt.

"You're just an Uncle Tom sell-out with a gun," Moses said underneath his breath as he got up.

Michal stood up as well. "What did you just call me?" He threw down his napkin.

Talia put her hand on Michal's. "Calm down." She turned over to Moses, who was now getting ready to head out the door. "Where are you going?"

"School," he forcefully said. "Hopefully, I make it before some bacon decides to shoot my black ass as well. Later Moms." Moses grabbed his backpack. "Dad," was all he said before shutting the door as he left.

Michal sat down, shaking his head before rubbing his face with his hands. "So angry. We didn't have this problem with the first one."

"He's just a teenager trying to figure the world out," Talia tried to comfort her husband. "Your mother told me some of the stuff you did when you were his age."

"I was an angel," Michal playfully told her.

"Really? What happened with you? Was it Madison?" She smirked as she drank her coffee.

"She told you about that?" Michal got embarrassed. "I gotta go to work." He was up out of his chair to put his suit coat on. He kissed her goodbye. "Love you."

"Love you, too, honey. Good luck today." Talia adjusted his tie. "You know, maybe we can try that sometime. I bet I'd be better at it than Madison."

Michal grabbed his keys. "I'll be home before Moses gets back from school." He gave her a kiss goodbye before heading out the door.

***

Father Raimundo was reluctantly going to pack up the last container of records. This box was the one he was neglecting to do, the one he didn't want to do. The stairs leading down to the basement seemed to creek with sadness, almost a sorrowful cry at every step. There in the corner was the empty desk in the basement, Juliana's desk. He just took a moment to stare at it. The lights weren't turned on for some reason but the dark was just a fitting tone for how he was feeling. The only light was from the window of the basement which God had shining on her desk. It was as though it was a last tribute and an understanding, that He was giving a moment of honor   to the fallen Lite Sentry.

He took a deep breath before going to her work area. It seemed the desk itself had the impression of mourning her death.   The elderly Latino priest grazed his fingers across the desk to a picture she had framed. It was of her and Lucas, a young man who had started to court his young Juliana. It was rare that she dated, but the excitement in her voice when talking about him was evident.   The background of the picture was at a nearby waterfall, just across the field. The mist generated from the water crashing had a small rainbow that emphasized the happiness of the couple. The hurt on Lucas' face when Father Raimundo had to tell him about her death was something he will never forget. The glass of the picture reflected the image of the sad old, gray-haired man. He gently put the picture down into the box to make sure it would not break.

The rest of the stuff was just basic memorabilia. There was a small piece of cloth given to Juliana from the Conduit of Lite. That too went into the box. As he was putting the rest of her desk items into the container, he found a picture of Juliana and Sanah with his family. This picture brought him back to the last time he saw Juliana alive.

Father Raimundo was closing up the church. It was particularly hot and a storm was not far off in the distance. In the back of the church Juliana was on her knees, her hands folded together tightly with her head down. "Juliana?" He could tell she was holding a heavy burden.

She lifted her head with tears streaming down her face. "Father."

"What's troubling you?"   There was an old handkerchief in his pocket, which he handed to her.

Juliana took it with one hand because the other was holding a picture of her with Sanah and his family. "Thank you," she blew her nose. "I'm having mixed feelings, and I'm ashamed of them."

"It would help to talk about them," he offered before sitting down on the pew next to her.

Juliana got off her knees while hanging her head in shame. "I have such anger and guilt."

"Directed at Sanah?" Father Raimundo attempted to pinpoint what was upsetting her.

"Partially," Juliana looked at the picture. "You know, when I was in the Holy Land being trained by Sanah; he took me in as part of his family. He loved his family so much. Laughter was common in that house. His little boy used to beg me every night to tell him a story, even if I made it up." She smiled at the memory. "His wife and I used to go shopping in the market every week. Even if we didn't need or buy anything."

"Sounds like it was a happy time in your life," Father Raimundo observed. "Cherish those memories. Don't focus on anger at Sanah for his actions."

She turned to Father Raimundo with additional tears running down her face, "That's just it, Father. I have guilt for not being there for him. My anger is misplaced, but I know I shouldn't feel this way."

"What way is that?"

"I have such strong animosity towards that new Sentry, whatever her name is," she gritted her teeth. "I know it's been about two years since Sanah died, but I thought this was something I could handle myself."

"Are you sure you are angry at her or just confused because you don't want to be angry at Sanah?" The Father could see that Julianna was showing signs of struggle with an internal conflict.

Juliana got up and moved around the pew to turn around and face the father, who was sitting down. "No, he was a good man, a family man. His dedication to hunt, to God, was unbreakable. She should have tried to reason with him! Instead, she tried to kill him, and I will never forgive her for that."

"I'm sure there is more to the story than what the Muslim Council told us," Father Raimundo tried to calm her down.

"That selfish brat was more interested in her life than what was going on around her. I swear if I ever see her..." Juliana stopped herself when something caught her attention.

"What is it?" Father Raimundo asked her.

"The Dark, someone just got infiltrated. I have to go," she told him. "Do you mind?"

She handed him the picture. "Thank you."

"We will talk when you return. I will put this on your desk. God Bless, Juliana,"

Father Raimundo signed the Holy Trinity.

"When I return, Father." She turned to go on her hunt but then suddenly turned back to him to give him a big hug.

He returned the hug. "Go, go and ensure the balance is kept for mankind."

That was the last he saw of her. On the night of her death, Celestial herself came to him to deliver the message in the middle of the night. She was even so kind as to show him what star she was. He closed his eyes and prayed nothing in particular, but just prayed. The picture was placed in the box, and he turned with a startle. Behind him was the young Catholic Council Historian who was here to help package and escort the records to DC before they went to the Vatican. "Oh, Anne, I didn't know you were there."

"I apologize, Father; I came down to see if everything was ready. I didn't want to disturb you." Anne cautiously approached. Her wavy, brown hair was tied in a tight bun. Her black-rimmed glasses supported by her high cheekbones. "Are you okay?"

"I'm fine, thank you," he told the sweet, young lady before him. "Just a little harder than I thought it would be."

"I get it." She rubbed his arm. "Do you want me to leave?"

Her caring smile provided him some comfort. "No, no." He patted her hand. "I think it's good you're here." He closed up the box and handed it to her. "Take care of this one."

"I will personally treat it as if my life depended on it." She grabbed the box. The two of them walked up the stairs to the back room of the church where the rest of the records were ready for shipment. "Tell me about her?" Anne requested.

Father Raimundo smiled at the memories of Juliana. "She was so kindhearted and full of life."

**

The walk back after a hunt was always the most relaxing part for Alex. It was the time for her to wind down. She felt as if she provided a good deed when she avenged the death of the Lite Sentry assigned to this area. It would have been nice to have known her; Alex thought they would have hit it off. The host church was on the other side of this little town. It was a small little village, a hidden jewel for tourists. It was quaint, but it didn't have her favorite energy drink or a decent burger. Komptin was at her side as usual. He didn't look happy as the humidity was getting to him. It just added more stress to this trip. There seemed to be animosity from Father Raimundo when she arrived. As if she personally did something to make him not like her. She didn't really care, though he wasn't the first priest that didn't like her.

There was a small little track and field to her right on her way back to the church. The coach was yelling at some kids running. It reminded her of Mole, but then again, every time she saw a biker or runner, it represented her lost brother. That, and seeing Roger again, wasn't something she was expecting. That one seemed to come out of nowhere. The anger, the pain she felt when she saw him. It was pure rage. The fact that he was able to manhandle her by throwing her into the wall so

31

easily was something of a painful surprise. He had grown so much stronger and would have been able to overtake her, but he was more interested in that ball filled with some sort of liquid. She didn't know what it was, but it wasn't going to be good.

The vendors started their morning routine to market their goods. An attractive man selling fruit caught Alex's eye. His smile was proof that she too had caught his eye. "Good morning," he said in a Spanish accent.

Alex caught herself checking him out. She immediately recovered herself. "How'd you know I spoke English?"

He smiled at her confidently. "There are not that many white-faced girls with long, black hair here," he told her. "Especially one who is so beautiful."

Alex tried to keep herself from blushing from his kind eyes. It was cute the way he got embarrassed when Alex caught him checking her out. "Well, I've never seen a fruit vendor with so much to offer," she flirted back. Komptin gave a loud bark at Alex as if he was agitated with her. "Quiet," she scolded by waving him down.

"Would you like to come in for some breakfast?" He showed her into a little eating establishment.

"I could eat." She smiled as she touched his arm. Komptin barked again. "Stay out here if you can't be good," she scolded him as she tied him to a bench. The massive German shepherd laid his head down on the ground in shame.

The attractive Latin man gave her a small pastry with a cup of coffee. "I'm Javier. I have seen you before. I've been trying to think of a way to talk to you."

"I'm pretty easy," she told him. Then she quickly recovered, "To talk to, that is. My name is Alex." The pastry was flaky as it crumbled onto the table. She laughed. "I'm so messy."

Juan reached over and wiped off some of the pastry that was on her face with his thumb. "Not at all," he smiled. "Are you in town long?"

"No," she told him, staring into his eyes. "I am leaving soon." The coffee she sipped tasted so good.

"Then I guess I should move fast," he teased. He said something in Spanish to his co-worker.

Alex so wished she knew what he was saying, but there was a sensual mystery to not knowing. "Fast has its advantages." She realized she had put her hand on his arm before quickly pulling it back. "I should get going." Alex stood up to leave. "Thank you for the pastry."

Javier followed her out and handed her a luscious apple. "Perhaps, you would like to tour the field with me tonight? There is a wonderful waterfall that is truly breathtaking when the moon shines upon it," he offered her a tempting night ahead of them. "This night could be yours." He watched her as she took a bite of her apple.

Komptin barked again with a subtle growl to it. "Hush," she said, tapping him on the nose. "I'm sorry, but I have to leave today."

33

"Another time perhaps," he offered with a glisten in his eye. "If the fates allow it, we will cross paths again."

A rush of guilt hit Alex. "I'm sorry, but I really need to get going. Thanks for the apple." She continued to the church, her walk a little brisker. "Stupid," she thought to herself. "What the hell was I doing?" The church was now in sight. Anne's enclosed delivery truck was already there, which meant they were getting ready to pack the sealed records to ship to the Vatican. Alex made it to the automobile, where it offered a place to lean as she ate her apple, when Anne came out carrying a box. Alex went to go help her, but she politely declined.

"I got it, sweetie." Anne gently put it on the bench seat as if it was the most precious one. She closed up the truck and secured the records.

"How many do we have to carry?" Alex finished her apple. She examined the apple's core before throwing it away in a nearby garbage.

"There are a total of fifty-three," Anne told her. "I will help Father Raimundo get the rest of the boxes if you don't mind keeping guard."

"I am a Sentry." Alex put on her mirrored sunglasses in a playfully dramatic fashion. She watched Anne give a smile before heading back into the church. Anne amazed Alex. The strength she portrayed since Kale's death has just been astonishing. She took her two weeks off after the funeral to mourn and get everything in order. When she returned, she looked as if everything was just as fine as always. Even when Alex talked to her about

Kale, it seemed to never really bother her. Alex shed so many tears over the death of her brother.

Alex felt as if there was a cold dead stare facing her direction. There was a small amount of Dark present, but that was expected. It wasn't that, this was something else. There was no one behind her; she saw there was nobody on the rooftops. She wanted to see if Komptin sensed anything and then it was evident. He was the one staring at her. His eyes were not glowing, but she knew he wasn't happy. "What?" He barked at her in return. Alex was shocked that he actually shook his head in disgust before laying down in the shade next to the church to sleep.

They had to get moving, but as Anne was saying goodbye to Father Raimundo. Alex thought this was a good time to approach him about Juliana. "Father," Alex walked up to him.

"Yes," he replied to her, a little guarded.

Alex reached into her pocket to give him the rosary with Juliana's name on it. She gently placed it in his hands. "I'm sure she died in a way that would make you proud."

Father Raimundo held in his tears as he grabbed the rosary. He examined the bloodstains on the crucifix. His eyes closed to give a prayer. "Did you find out how she died?"

Alex nodded with no expression.

"Was it quick and painless?" He asked her.

Alex didn't know how to answer it. She knew how she died. The thought of laying on that sacrificing altar, watching the blade coming down into you, helpless. "She fought til the end," was all Alex could think of so she wouldn't have to lie to a priest. It seemed the father accepted her answer. "And I found the ones who killed her; they will not have the chance to take anyone else's loved ones."

Father Raimundo just gave a small smirk of understanding. "Well, I guess this is it."

Anne's interest peaked at the tone of his statement. "What do you mean, Father?"

"I can't do this anymore. I've put in my notice to the Council," he told her. "I've asked to be transferred to another church. I need a break from all this."

Anne just nodded. "Yes, I can imagine. What about the mission here?"

Father Raimundo replied, "A non-Council priest will take over. There aren't that many Council priests out there. Plus, there is no way of knowing which council will have a Sentry activated."

Alex didn't understand. "What do you mean which council?"

Anne answered for him, "Remember, not all Sentries are Catholic. There are Muslim, Jewish, Lutherans, Baptists, and so on. There is even talk to bring the Church of Jesus Christ Latter Day Saints into the Council of the Religions."

Alex felt like an idiot for forgetting that. Besides dealing with Sanah a couple of years ago, she hadn't had any dealings with any other Councils. "Yes, of course." Alex flipped her long, black weave to her back. "Komptin, let's go."

Komptin jumped into the moving truck to get ready to go back to D.C.

***

Gron held the smooth, round container with the thick, red liquid in front of the private jet's window. It moved like a lava lamp as he moved it around against the sun. Collecting these orb balls was a strange custom the Dark kept. The Dark was austere about maintaining the tradition. Gron thought it represented that no matter what happened, they would triumph over the Lite. There were sets of these containers in his office sitting on a shelf. Each one was a Sentry from a different religion. The collection was almost complete. He thought the only ones he needed was Buddhists, Methodists, and Jewish.

"Is there anything I can get you?" A very attractive flight attendant approached him with a hot towel on a tray; next to it was his favorite drink.

Gron grabbed the drink and shook his head.

"Very well, if there is *anything...*" she emphasized, "...I can do for you; I will be right up front." Her gaze upon him was well received when she grazed her finger across his leg. Gron was powerful and held tremendous respect, not just within the F.O.R. but in the Dark as well.

The Dark Sentry watched her saunter away in her short, sky-blue skirt with a white button-up short-sleeved shirt. The color of her uniform reminded him of Alex's power. There was no doubt he was shocked to see her in the depths of that jungle. Her beauty was not to be ignored, but she was just as deadly in her anger towards him. The last time he'd seen her, they were exchanging blows in front of the burning F.O.R. Headquarters building. The Lite paid for their interference with Vandor's feeding. The Conduit of Lite lost one of her Guardians but most satisfying of all, Gron himself killed the Sentry's brother, Kale. Although, they also had to pay for that night. The Lite managed to banish Vandor into the Dark with multiple Demons being killed. Even a Caliginous perished that evening.

He needed to get Vandor back; he needed to open the Conduit to the Dark. The biggest obstacle was that he didn't know how. The Dark Myst, Salamor, had the knowledge to bring their master back. There was no sign of him, leading to one of two conclusions: he was sucked into the Dark with Vandor or the Lite Sentry found a way to kill him. There was no other explanation.

The only option that seemed feasible was to grab the Dark Texts from the Catholic Church, where the Pure of Heart had them locked up. Megan was trying her best to get them, but she told him that Anne is relentless in the security of her files, especially the most important ones. Megan couldn't attempt to steal them because the risk of her breaking her cover as a Dark asset wouldn't be worth the gamble. The only bit of information she got was Anne's return from Brazil. She was going to take them to the airport the next day for transport to the Vatican. Then, they would be near impossible to get. Not to mention the fact the Lite would hold one of the Dark's most valuable possessions was disgusting enough.

Gron took a sip of his drink when some breaking news caught his attention coming from the television. It seemed as if there was a police shooting by a white officer when a black teenage male was stopped on an expired license plate tab at a traffic stop. Gron grabbed the remote to the television to turn the volume up.

A male who must have been in his early thirties was speaking to a reporter. The caption below read, "Qawi, Community Activist." There was much anger coming from this man's voice. "This is just another instance where our government, our government in power over our black brothers and sisters, disregards what is right, what is correct, trying to keep us under control. They teach this country that black people are the enemy, that all blacks are evil. Why? They fear us. Look at it. We are strong, strong, proud people. We bond like no other, why? Because the government fears what we are capable of. The white controlled government pays the Jewish run media to slander whom they fear the most, a powerful black community. This young boy, Darius King, is the soul who pays for such ignorance and fear."

The news anchor started to back his ranting. "Such hurt and anger over the travesty of this poor boy killed by a white, male police officer. We still have no word from the DC Metro Police

Department. The Public Affairs officer for the Police Deputy Commissioner stated they will give an official statement once the body-cam footage has been reviewed."

Gron shut the television off as he gave a devilish grin. He flashed his eyes with neon red as he threw the ball filled with the red liquid in the air and then caught it. The stewardess promptly came to Gron when he pushed the button for her. When she approached, all he did was nod. The beautiful, blonde girl smiled as she put her hands on the leader's legs.

CHAPTER TWO

"Something on your mind, sweetie?" Anne leaned over to talk to Alex, who was on the other side of the aisle of the small plane. It didn't take a detective to see something heavy was on Alex's mind. She had let her hair down to relax a bit as she read one of her religious history books. Anne knew if Alex was that deep in thought, she might not get it out of her, but she had to try.

Truthfully, there was a lot on Alex's mind. She knew she couldn't tell Anne that she had run into Roger while in Brazil. Anne had been so strong since Kale's death; she didn't want to hurt her feelings. Then, there was the fact that her mind kept racing back to that guy from the fruit stand. She was so confused why she flirted with him the way she had. It was evident that Komptin didn't approve, and truthfully, she didn't either. That situation was heading down a path she shouldn't have even set foot on.

Kameron was a gift in her life. He had been nothing but supportive when Kale was murdered by a demon-possessed Roger. Alex accepted Kameron's shoulder to cry on more than one occasion. Bless his heart– he never said a word to try to comfort her. He just kept quiet, holding her, and the sex. There were just no words for that.

"Alex," Anne spoke a little louder.

Alex jumped when she heard her name. "Huh? Sorry." She got up to go into the small fridge on the plane, where a supply of Apollo energy drinks was waiting for her attention. It was a taste of Heaven. Komptin lifted his head when Alex returned to her seat. The monster of a German shepherd stretched before walking over to Alex to put his head on her lap. It was as if he were telling her that no matter what, he'd still love her. She smiled at him as she scratched his ears. "I just had some things racing through my mind."

"Anything you want to talk about?" Anne took a sip of water with lemon.

Anne's heart was just so big and caring. There were times Alex wished she could be more like Anne. Alex felt sick to her stomach the way she'd acted in disrespecting Kameron by flirting with another guy. "Nah, you know those times where you think of everything while thinking about nothing."

Anne looked back at the boxes to make sure nothing had happened to them. "I get that." She gazed at her watch.

One of the pilots came out from the cockpit. "We should be landing in about an hour. We just got word the Vatican Record Keeper's representative had some minor maintenance issues with their plane, meaning they won't be in until tomorrow."

Anne sighed, "That means we have to transport them back to the church for storing." She looked back at the boxes with Alex simultaneously.

"We've got to move all those boxes again?" Alex wrinkled her nose.

"Yes." Anne got out her phone. "I'll call Father Richard. He'll have to meet us at the airport with a truck. Hopefully, Declan can escort us."

Declan was the new bodyguard for Cardinal Joe. He was nice enough, a little naive but seemed like a good person. When Alex found out Kameron was offered the position and didn't take it, she was upset. She couldn't fathom why he wouldn't want to work for the Cardinal.

***

Kameron got into work and headed straight into the Director's office to congratulate Grossman on the promotion. He peeked in to see Grossman packing up the office into a box. "This isn't a good sign."

Grossman was upset. "I just got word that I didn't get the Director's position."

Kameron was shocked but didn't show it. "What was the reason?"

"Honestly, I don't know. But a buddy of mine up at HQ told me they want to bring in somebody who wasn't involved with F.O.R.," Grossman told him. He paused as he looked around the office as if he was saying goodbye.

"I thought the investigation cleared that you weren't involved with the destruction of that building?" That was the only time Kameron had lied on a report. When he was under investigation for involvement, he left out the fact that Grossman helped him bring down the F.O.R.

"That never came up. They said I was a potential security risk since my access code was used in your rescue." Grossman tapped the desk.

"But we told them you got me out of there." Kameron made sure no one was behind him. "There were no video security feeds inside, so there was no evidence of Alex."

"I know, but they said I was too close to the situation, and if I go peacefully by the end of the month, I will get my full retirement with benefits," Grossman stared at a plaque with his name on it.

"They are forcing you to retire?" Kameron couldn't believe what he had just heard.

Grossman just gave a somber nod. "Kameron, you really need to ask yourself if she's worth it."

"What do you mean?" He was almost afraid of the answer.

Grossman followed him out of the office. "They are forcing me out. Who knows what's going on? Is she going to be worth all this potential trouble?"

Kameron turned his attention to a pair of pigeons sitting idle outside of the window. Hearing this was not what he was expecting. "I would do anything for her." This conversation quickly turned into his relationship with Alex.

"I know. Look, it's no secret she scares the living hell out of me, but you have to ask yourself; what is your future with her?" Grossman advised his friend. "I know you love her. That much is obvious. But the fallout for helping her is going to catch up to you sooner or later."

Kameron couldn't help but think about it. Maybe he should have taken that position with the cardinal. "How about letting me take you and your family out for dinner? Since they aren't even allowing you a proper retirement."

"I want it good, expensive, and all on your bill," Grossman teased.

"I'll make it happen," he assured him. "Come on. I'll walk you out."

Kameron usually lifted weights in the afternoon at a local gym. He liked to do it in the afternoon versus the morning. The only times he lifted in the morning was with Kale, when he was alive, because it was the only time he could make it. Usually, the morning was for his run, but this afternoon he wanted to run; and run he did. By the time he made it back home, he realized that he had run half a marathon.

There was frustration he needed to run off. He wasn't mad at Grossman for what he'd said. He was more upset that he might have had a valid point. Alex was coming home around five today. He wanted to surprise her at the airport but he thought it would be best to greet her at the church. The weather outside was tranquil; he wanted to soak it in before heading up to his apartment. On the way up to his apartment, he ran into Ms. Claire. She was a sweet widow that was always pleasant every time she talked to him. "Good morning, ma'am," he greeted her.

"Well, hello, Kameron. How was your exercise?" She went to pick up a box that was left outside her door.

"Let me get that for you." Kameron wiped his sweaty hand on his clothes before picking up the box. "Heavier than I expected."

"It's my cat food." She invited him in. "Could you please bring it to the closet?"

"No problem." He brought it next to her closet.

"You remind me a lot of Bradley when he was your age." She smiled as she thought of her late husband. "You want some water?" Ms. Claire walked into the kitchen to get him some water.

"Please." He felt her orange cat rubbing against his leg. The cat was enjoying Kameron petting him behind the ears. "Thank you."

Ms. Claire handed Kameron a glass of water. "Oh, Zoey, you're going to get hair all over him." She made a small grunt, as she was a little stiff picking up her cat. "I'm not as flexible as I used to be. This kitty is just so friendly to everyone." She gave her a quick snuggle before putting her in her cat bed next to the window. "How's that little girlfriend of yours?"

"Alex? She's fine," he told her. In honesty, he didn't know. There was a chance that she could have been killed, but there was no way of knowing. That reminded him that he should get with Anne on establishing a code of some sort to text him in case the worst happened.

"You know me and Bradley, God rest his soul, were married with a baby on the way at your age," Ms. Claire recalled. "He was such a good man."

Kameron took a sip of the water. It had a strong city water taste to it, but Kameron hid that from his sweet neighbor. "You were lucky to find the right one so young."

Ms. Claire sat down at her table. The cat jumped up on the table to be petted. "She must work a lot. I don't see her around in the morning."

Kameron's thoughts went straight to the empty bed this morning. "She's dedicated to her work."

"Can I be blunt?" Ms. Claire got some iced tea to put into a glass.

"Of course," he gave her permission knowing she was going to give relationship advice.

"Kameron, you have been dating this young lady for a while now. I know you met each other's parents, but; if she's not spending the night, there's no commitment," she advised. "Even when I was young, I stayed at Bradley's overnight. There's nothing like waking up next to the one you love."

"It's complicated." He finished his water.

"Is she married or involved with someone else?" she flat out asked.

"No, ma'am." Kameron showed her the empty cup, asking her what to do with it.

Ms. Claire pointed, "Dishwasher, please. Well, I have a beautiful granddaughter that would be perfect for you if things don't work out." She got up and showed Kameron a picture of her. She was a beautiful girl in a cheerleader outfit for the

University of San Diego. "She's in her senior year."

"She's very lovely," he assured her. "But things with Alex are fine."

"Okay, Kameron." Ms. Claire smiled out of disappointment. "But why settle for fine when they can be great?" She put the picture down, giving it a moment of endearment.

A message came in on his watch from Alex stating that she'd just landed. "Thanks for the water." He opened up the door to go to his apartment.

"No problem, she is coming home this fall if you would like to meet her," Ms. Claire informed him.

"I'd be honored to meet her, but everything between Alex and I are just where they need to be." He let her know. Kameron said his goodbyes to Ms. Claire before replying to Alex's text message. He replied, "Can't wait to see you."

She sent him a picture of herself blowing a kiss at him.

Kameron grabbed some orange juice in a glass and walked out on the terrace before heading into the shower. He knew what Ms. Claire said was out of care, but it still bothered him. It was troubling because on some level, she too was right. What kind of life was he expecting from Alex? Even on nights she didn't hunt, she wouldn't be in bed with him. Is he just being selfish or just delaying the inevitable?

***

It was hot on the tarmac at the airport as they carried the boxes into the back of the suburban. Alex had to be careful not to carry too many boxes to not raise suspicion of her powers. There was one moment Father Richard had to remind her when she picked up five boxes with ease to put them into the van. Normally, she wouldn't have any trouble keeping things under wraps, but her mind was elsewhere. It was obvious she was thinking of Kameron.

Earlier, when she got off the plane, she found herself relieved but disappointed he wasn't there to greet her. Being apart because of travel for work was common, especially on Kameron's end, but this one was different. There was just so much that'd happened. Seeing Roger again just emphasized the dangers her loved ones could face. The guilt of putting Kameron in danger was something that still ate at her, or maybe that was just another excuse.

"Alex, we're all packed up and ready to go," Father Richard tapped on her shoulder. "Alex."

"Huh, what? Oh, sorry, Father. Yes, of course, there's a lot more to know, but we'll figure out what the Dark is up to." Alex turned back around, half-way hoping she would see Kameron coming to greet them.

Father Richard took a second to think about what she said before blowing it off. "Is there something out there we should be worried about?"

The middle-aged man took off his hat to wipe the sweat off his shaved baldhead.

Alex was always amused at how shiny it was. Sometimes she wondered if she could see her reflection. "Oh, no, not at all." She shook the cobwebs out of her head. "Are we ready to go yet?"

"Anything you want to talk about?" He wiped more sweat off his head. Father Richard seemed to be a good man. Cardinal Joe asked the council for him to be the Administrative Priest when he took over. Alex guessed they met each other sometime in the past. He wore rimless glasses when indoors but when he was outside, he wore prescription sunglasses.

"No," Alex made sure she had her hair into a tight bun in case she ran into the Dark on the way home. Maybe tonight, she should go for a hunt. Maybe see if Roger was in town. There was a faint sense of the Dark, but nothing out of the ordinary. The Washington DC area was so heavy with Dark activity that the sense of stale air seemed permanent.

Anne approached the two of them. "Declan just said we are cleared to get off the tarmac."

Alex noticed she maintained that particular box with her throughout the trip. Alex wondered why that particular box was getting such extra attention. "Good, I want food." Father Richard joined Declan in the front of the vehicle.

Alex and Anne both walked to the back of the vehicle. Anne double-checked the backdoors to make sure they were secure. "You okay? You seem

50

distracted," Anne asked her. She quickly scratched Komptin behind his ears.

"I'm just hungry," was all that Alex could say. "Food," she emphasized.

"We need to get these to the church. Then we can get something to eat," The two of them got inside the van, where Anne did a final count of the boxes for the fourth or fifth time. "We're all good, Declan." Anne buckled herself to the other side of the bench seat. "I'll feel safer once they're secured back at the church."

Alex reluctantly agreed. She would argue the fact they could go through a drive-thru but Anne would quote the Vatican Record Protocol. She was pretty laid back on a lot of things, but the security of her records was somewhere she never bent nor wavered. Just before Declan started the truck, Alex's stomach rumbled loud enough for everyone to hear. Father Richard and Declan both turned around to look at Alex. "Hey, it wants what it wants."

On the drive back to the church to drop off the records, Alex could feel the Dark a little more in spots as they passed by. They passed a F.O.R. bulletin board showing that they are still active and strong. It didn't surprise Alex that she sensed the Dark. One time, Komptin raised his head to look around, but then he went back to sleep. It wasn't anything to be worried about, they weren't close enough to sense her, but she knew that she should hunt tonight, or at the very latest tomorrow. It was hard to concentrate because all Alex could do was think about food.

Traffic had been backed up due to an accident on the freeway. Declan even shut off the engine because they weren't going anywhere. Alex was off staring at the local government buildings in the distance. The Capitol was so impressive, almost majestic. Kameron had taken Alex on a tour of the building and White House. She had senses of the Dark in the buildings, but she couldn't go around roaming the halls looking for Demons. Kameron could tell she sensed them, but when she looked at him, he just remained stoic.

Alex felt Anne move over closer to her. Alex smiled and turned back out the window. "What?"

"Are you going to tell me what's wrong?" Anne asked. Declan started the truck back up because traffic was starting to move up ahead.

Alex whispered to make sure no one heard. "I think we're barely moving, and I'm hungry." Alex tried to play it off, but she saw Anne wasn't having it. She moved over closer to Anne so only she could hear her. "I almost cheated on Kameron."

Anne's eyes got big; there was no doubt she was in genuine shock. "Oh, Alex, I... but you didn't?"

Alex wiped a tear before shaking her head. "The temptation was there, but I didn't do it." She wiped another tear. "I don't know why I would do that? It was just stupid."

"What happened?" Anne leaned in closer, grabbing her friend's hand.

"I ate breakfast with some random guy. We ended up flirting with each other. He then offered to show me around, but I knew where it was going to lead." Alex was ashamed of her next words. "And if it wasn't time to head back, I'm afraid I would have done it."

"Sweetie, it sounds like you just got caught in a moment of flirting," Anne tried to calm her down.

"How do I know that? What if I don't love Kameron anymore?" Alex's tears were falling freely. "You know how I was before him."

The two of them saw the church get closer as they approached the back parking lot. Kameron's BMW was parked in the far corner. "I guess we'll find out soon," Anne told her.

The truck was parked behind the church, where Kameron, in a full suit, walked out to greet them. Cardinal Joe and Megan came out right behind Kameron. Alex made eye contact with Kameron, and he held up a greasy brown paper bag with an Apollo. He mouthed, "Hungry?"

Alex laughed as she saw him with a glowing smile. Anne leaned over to her, "I think you're okay, sweetie." She patted her on the leg.

Alex opened the door in a full out sprint. She leaped into the air for Kameron to catch her, causing the burger and Apollo to fall to the ground. She kissed him and didn't care who was watching.

"Miss me?" Kameron laughed.

Cardinal Joe walked by Alex and Kameron kissing each other. "Just remember, we are still on

His ground." He gave them a little chuckle as he patted Alex on the back as he walked by.

Megan shook her head. "Hello, Alex," she said in a cold, distant tone. "You think you would have gotten some sun while you were down there."

Alex stuck her tongue out at her. Kameron gently turned her face back to him and pushed her tongue back into her mouth before giving her a small kiss on the nose. Both of them laughed before he put her down. "Come on. Let's help get these boxes done."

***

Locking up the records in Anne's office was a bit faster than expected. It looked as if Alex and Kameron had some unspoken plans because the two of them took off as soon as they could. Anne parked her car underneath the carport assigned to her. For some reason, she found herself staring at the apartment number in front of her. Her mind was racing on how she was extremely disappointed in Alex. How could she think about cheating on Kameron? He was perfect for her; he was a good balance for her impulsive nature. Although, it did seem like she came to terms with her feelings when she saw him. It wasn't fake or forced. Anne knew Alex, that was genuine.

"Good for her." Anne was startled when she actually said that aloud. She grabbed the keys from her purse. That was as far as she'd gone before she found herself not wanting to go up to her empty apartment.   The night ahead of her was no doubt going to be one of emptiness.

A tap on the window startled Anne. The night watch woman was holding a flashlight in her face. "You okay, Ms. McClure?"

Anne raised her finger and stepped out of the car. "I'm fine, how are you, Laila?"

"Oh, I couldn't be happier." She was a bigger woman with dark skin but her smile was something that could make anyone's day. She cared for almost anyone who crossed her path but was not afraid to be stern when necessary.

"How's Ralph?" Anne made sure her car was locked.

Laila surveyed the area as they started to walk towards the complex.   "He was asked to manage another restaurant."

"That's great," Anne congratulated. "Does he still get free food?"

Laila laughed. "That was the only reason he stuck with that franchise. Maybe he won't be coming home smelling like grease every night. Always making me hungry." Laila escorted Anne to the stairwell of her apartment. Laila walked up the stairs to make sure Anne found her apartment without incident.

Anne saw some lights on in the apartment next to her. "Somebody moved in next door?"

"Yes, a married couple, they seem nice. Theodore, who goes by 'Teddy', is a professor at Georgetown University and his husband is a graphic designer of some sorts," Laila informed her. "They seem pretty nice, low-key, quiet...which is good."

"Laila," a voice came from her radio.

"I told you to call me by my call sign." She winked at Anne.

With clear annoyance, the man on the other end replied, "Mother Bear, there's a noise complaint on the other end of Complex B."

"I hope it's not 4F again...so sick of those kids," she told Anne. Laila held up the radio, "Roger that. I'm on my way."

"Good luck." Anne walked up the stairs to her apartment. She went to put her keys into the keyhole, but they dropped. The door from down the walkway opened. Out came a big man with a beard. He was wearing a Mickey Mouse tank top and white shorts, holding a glass of wine. She gave him a smile and waved. "Hello."

"Hi there, honey," the big man approached Anne with a soft, gentle voice.

"I'm Anne." She put her hand on her chest.

"I'm Teddy." The big man came over and gave Anne a tight hug.

It took Anne by surprise as she returned the hug.

"I turn my back one second, and you go straight on me," another man said from the doorway.

"Oh, mish," he playfully waved off his husband.

"You must be Anne, I'm Elias," the man approached her. He was an average-sized man, clean-cut, with a presence that reminded her a bit of

Kale– then again, almost everything reminded her of him.

"How'd you know that?" Anne picked out the key for the apartment.

"We have a package for you, it was brought to our place by mistake and we just kept it for safekeeping." Elias turned back to his apartment to retrieve her mail.

Teddy took another sip from his glass. "Oh, that's right, would you like to come in for a glass of wine?"

Even though Anne was tired, a nice glass of wine sounded appealing. "I would like that, thank you,"

"Come on, honey." The man put his massive hairy arm around her. For a split second, Anne felt so secure and content. It had been a long time since she felt such security. He led her into their apartment where there were boxes scattered everywhere. "We're still unpacking."

Anne sat down on the couch after Teddy offered her a seat. Elias came out with a small box. The package came from Kale's mom, Kate, who was sending her stuff that once belonged to Anne's husband. These boxes were so hard for her. It usually took Anne a couple of weeks to get the courage to open them. The wine Elias had given her was exceptional. Teddy had to take a phone call in the other room. There was about a quarter of it left by the time Elias was done talking about some of the graphic designs he was creating for some low-budget movies.

"Elias, are you still talking about those posters?" Teddy came out. "Sorry about that phone call, but sometimes work never stops."

"You are so right, honey. I can lose track of time talking about work. So, tell me all about you," Elias said.

Teddy got situated on the couch.

Anne smiled out of embarrassment now that the focus was on her. "Well, I'm a registered Catholic Historian. I come from a small town and moved to DC to support my sister-in-law in her job."

"Your sister-in-law? Not many people would move to support their brother's wife. You must be close?" Elias asked her, grabbing himself another glass of wine. He offered Anne a refill but she covered her glass.

Anne regretted answering but she didn't want to lie. "We are, but it's actually my husband's sister," she informed them.

"Is your husband out of town on business?" Teddy motioned to Elias to refill his glass as well.

There was a pause before Anne spoke. "He was murdered earlier this year."

The stunned look on both their faces was enough to make Anne realize they were taken off guard. "Oh honey, I'm so sorry," Elias sat next to her to give her another hug. "Would you like to stay for dinner? It's not going to be anything fancy. We ordered Thai, but we'll have plenty."

"I really should get going. I have a lot to do tomorrow." Anne finished her drink. "But I promise to take you up on dinner on a later date."

Anne returned to her empty apartment. Even though it was summer, it seemed cold there. A shiver overcame her body for a moment when she turned on the light, but a sudden burst of light followed before it went dark. Moments like this, she often wished Alex were here with her.

Luckily, her phone was close enough to be fully charged to use the flashlight. The kitchen door squeaked when she walked in to turn the light on, but that one too was out. It would seem the entire apartment was out of power.

She called the super to tell him it was out. He said that he was out to dinner and wouldn't be able to get to it for at least another ninety minutes. Anne thought she should hurry to shower to use the hot water before it went cold, even though the only light in the bathroom would be her phone. After her shower, she lit a candle in her bedroom. It was illuminating enough to see the outlines of the room. In the closet, she grabbed her maroon bathrobe. Then there it was. The sweatshirt Kale had given her that night on the lake. Anne gently took hold of it and crawled into the bed, clenching it as she was surrounded by darkness with tears running down the sides of her face.

**

Gron sat at his desk in an unbuttoned, maroon dress shirt. The news continued its coverage of the Darius King shooting right after a report of the body of a missing flight attendant was found. Without them knowing, they were playing right into the plan Gron was laying out. It was obvious the city was becoming divided over the issue of this police shooting from the news outlets, which was exactly what he needed.

The door from his private bathroom opened. Megan, in her short mini-skirt, walked over to the couch to sit down. She crossed her legs and turned her body to make sure to show them off to him. Gron couldn't help but admire how evil she was for a primate. "They had to store a bunch of records in the church overnight before bringing them to the airport. When they get there, to the Vatican, they will go. I'm pretty sure she is going to be transporting the Dark texts tomorrow."

Gron got annoyed, "If Salamor was here we wouldn't need to do this. It looks as though this will be our only chance to get them." He turned to Megan who was wearing a dark-purple wig with a hint of black streaks in it. "I need you to get them, but not at the expense of your cover. You're the first to be a member of the Dark and be so close to the Council."

"They have no clue of my intentions. I'm hoping to gain their trust enough to become a member of the Council; but getting those records– short of torturing and killing Anne, I don't know how to get them," Megan confessed. "I can get her here if you wish."

Gron thought about it for a second but then shook it out of his head. "No, that didn't go too well the last time we kidnapped her." Megan got up to get a drink from the bar. "Besides, I already have an idea how to get them and perhaps nudge you closer to becoming a member of the Council," he sneered. Megan swallowed her drink with in one go before jumping onto his lap causing him to drop his drink. "You spilled my drink."

"Punish me." Gron picked her up with ease and threw her into the air. The couch caught her and hit the wall from Megan being tossed onto it. The room was filled with her evil, seductive laugh as she bit her bottom lip.

Gron couldn't believe it. "You are one sick primate." He stood over her before picking her up by the arm forcefully.

Megan's hand grabbed his hair as she pulled him closer to her. Her tongue licked the outside of his lips in a teasing play. "I've only just begun." Excitement overcame her body as Gron flashed his red eyes. "The teeth," she commanded. "I wanna see the teeth." Megan slowly went back to the couch not taking her eyes off her prize.

The Demon's teeth grew as he walked over to Megan. A low growl emanated from his body. Gron thought how unexpected it would be for him to tear Megan to pieces. The shock of him ripping her body would be something she would not expect. He loved that unexpected expression on a primate's face when he tore into them. That flight attendant's face when he tore her body open was especially noteworthy. Nevertheless, he needed Megan. She was the only one who could put the Dark Texts in a place he could steal them. For now, he would just have his way with her. He approached her slowly, until the intercom buzzer sounded.

"Bummer," Megan pouted as she banged her head against the wall.

Gron angrily pushed the button on the intercom. "What?"

"My leader, Qwai has arrived," a young woman announced over the intercom.

Megan seductively smiled. "You get me a toy to play with?"

Gron turned to her. "This is work."

Megan bent her lower lip with a sad face. "I want a toy."

"Work first, playtime later." Gron grabbed an extra tie from his desk drawer while answering the intercom. "Give me ten minutes and send him in." Gron put on his pants. "Go freshen up a bit. Get it ready." Gron walked over to the mirror as Megan went to the bathroom to play her part. His shirt was now neatly buttoned and he made sure the tie was straight before he was going to talk to Qawi. These types of meetings were so much easier with Salamor floating around. He could sense their frustrations, feed it, and use it to manipulate them for the Dark.

Gron splashed on some cologne before sitting at his desk. He ordered the secretary to allow Qawi into the office. The young, caramelized-skinned secretary opened the door to the office. She was wearing a short skirt, with a red-tank top. "Qawi, sir."

"Thank you, sista." Qawi was a lot smaller than he would have thought. A bit skinnier than on television. The media seemed to film him to make him appear much bigger than he actually is. Qawi stood in front of Gron's desk, without budging.

Gron just nodded as Qawi studied him. "Get you a drink?"

"Don't offer me a white man's poison for the black soul. That's how you manipulate us brothers and sisters. You poison us with your mind-control nectar, you-"

"Stop," Gron gave a low laugh as he put up his hand. "Just stop. I get it, I'm white, but trust me when I say this. I'm not the Devil."

"That remains to be seen," he told the leader of the F.O.R. with a cold stare.

"I actually want to help you," Gron told him, setting down his drink. "Please, have a seat." He pushed the button again to the intercom.

"Yes, Mr. Somberson," the secretary answered.

"Can you please get Qawi a ginger ale with a twist of orange?" he asked, even though she should know it was more of a command.

Qawi tried not to be impressed with his reaction but failed. "How'd you know?"

"Lucky guess." Gron came around to sit on his desk facing the activist leader. The sound of ice hitting glass was all that could be heard as Gron sat on top of his desk swirling his drink. "You're not a fan of white people, are you?"

"You can't be trusted," he explained. "There are too many times that you-"

Gron put up his hand, "Just stop– really, stop."

The secretary came in with Qawi's drink. She smiled at him as she handed him his drink. "I see you still have black people doing your bidding."

Gron watched her walk away, enjoying the view. "She's well paid, plus the benefits, if she's a loyal employee, truly life changing." He noticed Qawi studying his every action. "What is it that you want?"

"To lead our people to true freedom." He was about to start a speech but he knew it was going to be ignored.

"That's not what you want," Gron told him. "I know what you really want."

"What a surprise, the powerful white man knows what a black man wants." Qawi was showing signs of agitation.

"The freedom you speak of, for your 'people'," he finger-quoted. "You want to be their leader, to provide for them."

"I know what they need, what is happening to them, the in-justices. I can make sure we are free with my leadership," he preached.

"So, what you are looking for is power." Gron took a sip of his drink. "Enough power to accomplish what you need to rule. Do you want this power?"

The side bathroom door opened to Megan coming out putting her arm around Gron. "It's ready."

Gron bit the arm of Megan causing her to shiver with excitement. "What if I told you that I can get you enough power to lead your cause to a whole new level?"

Qawi was studying the man in front of him. "What's the catch?"

"Just absolute power for your cause and the complete financial and influential power the F.O.R. has to offer," Gron tantalized him. Gron didn't need Salamor. He knew Qawi was hooked on what he was offering. "I want you to promote the F.O.R. You can even start your own chapter. One that you tailor to what you think you would need. Think what you could do with that power. With us, you will have the ear of people in congress, senators, lawmakers..." Gron was going to go on but there was no need.

Qawi turned to Gron. "Let's see what you got."

***

Alex turned her head to the window in Kameron's bedroom as stale air came across her senses. She took in a small deep-breath knowing that another infiltration had taken place. Above the city, Osiah's purple star was shining bright for only beings of Lite to see. Below the stars was the darkness of the city being illuminated by artificial light.

She turned to watch Kameron sleep next to her. It seemed that even in sleep, his light-brown hair was never out of place. She was lucky to have him. Time seemed to stand still in this moment while watching him. There was no doubt she loved him.

Her flirting with that man in Brazil was something she could never forgive herself for. There was a time during dinner she was going to tell him what she'd done, but her body wouldn't allow it. He put his hand on her waist as if making sure she was still there while he was in a deep sleep. Times like this she felt guilty that he would always wake up to an empty bed. She would never sleep next to him; she would never know the feeling of waking up in his arms.

It was close to midnight when Alex got out of bed without waking Kameron. Kameron so enjoyed having her in bed next to him. He seemed to sleep more soundly. Alex had her headphones in her ear as she went through social media videos. She came across one with Scarlett Roberts promoting F.O.R. life. This got her more motivated to start her night.

She had taught herself to keep her hunting clothes in the spare bedroom so she could change without disturbing his sleep. It only took a couple of minutes for her to apply her makeup in the guest bathroom. Alex was a bit surprised to see Komptin in his Gargoyle state, snoring underneath the window in the living room. She quietly walked past him to grab an Apollo from the fridge. The appliance light made Komptin open one eye to see what was going on. The sounds of a gargoyle dog stretching were quite intimidating even though Alex knew he was just a big teddy bear.

The sound of the can opening was a bit louder than Alex expected. She nonchalantly glanced down the hall to make sure she didn't wake

Kameron. Alex opened the refrigerator to see if there was any junk food before she went out. All Kameron had was raw vegetables and fruits. There was hope there was something in a brown bag. She opened it up to see a plastic container full of little plants. "Sprouts?" Alex read it aloud. "Seriously, Kameron?" Alex did one final look through some cupboards before giving up. "This guy needs to get introduced to some...Oh my God!" Alex couldn't believe it. Behind some nuts, sat a box of Hostess Cupcakes. "Oh, he is never going to live this one down." She opened one of the individual packages. "This is exactly what I needed, ready to go?" Alex asked her hunting companion. Komptin flashed his eyes telling her that he was ready to hunt the Dark.

Alex walked out of the apartment complex on such a nice night. She took about three steps before stopping. "You know, I know you are there."

The former Guardian of the Conduit dropped out of a tree. "Lite Sentry." She was in her angelic battle armor. The misty wings and halo emphasized her strength. She walked up to Alex as her armor turned into a pair of jeans and a neon-green, button-up shirt. It was no doubt paying homage to her fallen sister, Ariel. The angel put her hand on Alex's shoulder. "Good evening."

"What are you doing here?" Alex took another sip of her drink.

"The Conduit of Lite has new guardians, so I am not needed. All other positions within the Lite are currently occupied." Devine turned her head to the sound of a horn blaring in the distance.

Alex gazed in the direction of the car horn. "So, you're bored."

Devine turned back to Alex. "I am without a job."

"Well, I'm off to get into trouble with the Dark." Alex could see that Devine was jealous of the battle Alex was searching for. "You wanna come?"

"If you need me to assist. I will join you." Devine joined Alex on their walk throughout the city. Devine was on guard while Alex was finding amusement in how intense she was.

"Have you ever hunted before?" Alex was watching Devine turn her head at every sound.

"No, this is my first," the angel told her.

"How is that possible?" Alex was confused.

"I was a guardian, purely defensive. The Conduit was my priority," Devine explained to her as she turned her head to a noise. "Is that the sign of the Dark?"

Alex rubbed her head. "No, that's the sound of a motorcycle." Alex knew she wasn't going to get to the Dark tonight. Devine was a great Guardian, but her sense to hunt was something that needed to be worked on. However, her surrogate older sister was in need of some company tonight so she wasn't going to abandon her. "Come on, this way."

The two of them stopped off at a local convenience store so Alex could purchase an Apollo. The man behind the counter was in his sixties with a gentleness in his eyes. Alex smiled at him before grabbing an Apollo from the cooler.

Out the window were three young prostitutes out underneath the lamppost. Alex couldn't help but feel sorry for them. She gave the man her card as he ran it through the machine.

Devine approached the counter with multiple candy bars and snack cakes. "I would like to consume these."

Alex shook her head, "I guess these as well."

The man was nervous of Devine who was studying him. "Is there anything else?" he asked.

"You are the protector of this establishment?" she boldly asked him.

The man continued to scan the items. "Until seven in the morning.

"You truly are a noble warrior to protect the food of the people, I commend you," she told him out of admiration.

The man looked at Alex.

"Cosplay," Alex covered Devine's innocent views on human society.

The clerk shook his head out of disbelief. "I get them all on my shift." He handed them a bag full of the items. "Have a good night, ladies."

"Serve with honor," Devine gave him an approving nod of respect.

Alex walked out with Devine who was eating one of her candy bars. She looked over toward the three young-looking prostitutes. "Sad, isn't it?"

Devine looked up with a mouthful of caramel and chocolate. "What is that?"

Alex motioned with her head. "Those girls. They are sex workers."

"I thought you humans enjoyed mating rituals." Devine was interested in the bag full of candy.

Alex watched the girls. "Oh we do, trust me. Although, when it's forced on a person, it can be quite the opposite."

The two of them watched as a sketchy male came up to them. The girls were giving him money from their purses. He was yelling at them before slapping one of the girls across the face with the cash.

"Sometimes I wish I could get involved, but there is no evidence of the Dark," Alex told Devine.

"That is the rule for Sentries." Devine watched as she started to eat her second candy bar. "Although, I am not a Sentry."

Alex turned her head to Devine. "Won't you get in trouble for interfering with us?"

Devine watched the man continue to belittle the girls. "We are allowed to lend a hand at random, as long as we are discreet." Devine handed Alex the bag of candy. "I do believe I can be discreet." The angel confidently marched across the street toward the man and the girls.

There was a table and chairs outside the store. Alex sat down with her feet up on the other chair. She opened the Apollo and stole one of Devine's candy bars. Komptin sat down at Alex's side to watch. "This should be interesting."

Devine approached the girls with the man still yelling at them. "Excuse me."

"What?" The man turned around. "Oh, hey. You looking for employment?"

"I am currently without a job," Devine innocently told him.

"I can take care of you," the man approached her. "But first, I need a preview of the product." He put his hands on Devine's waist as he started grazing his hands up her body.

Devine took his hands off her body. She easily pushed him out of the way so she could talk to the girls. "Do you wish to leave his employment?"

The girls quickly nodded their heads. One of them spoke. "I want to go back home to Oklahoma."

"I have nowhere to go," one of the others said.

The smaller one sobbed, "Me either."

The man stepped in front of Devine to get in between her and the girls. "They are my property."

Devine rolled her eyes. "Move." She pushed him to the other side causing him to fall to the ground. "What do you need to do to go back home?"

"Our money, he has it," the Oklahoma girl told her. "With it, I can take all of us back. Start a new life."

Devine nodded. "I will get what is yours." She took a step before turning around. "How much is yours?"

The girls looked at each other. "I don't know, about five thousand."

Devine turned to the man trying to get up, but she pushed him back down with her foot. "Do you have their money?"

"Go to hell!" he yelled at Devine.

Devine picked him up with ease, threw him against the wall and held him up with one hand. "Hand me your money." The man gave her the wallet. "Count out five thousand." The man counted out the money. "Give it to the girls." He handed the money to the girls. The girls took the money and counted. Devine turned to the man. "You smell. You should really bathe." She let him go.

"Thank you, thank you." The girls ran to Devine.

"Promise to take care of each other," the angel instructed the three girls. "You can go. He will not harm you."

The group walked out together as if a huge weight was lifted off their shoulders. Devine started to walk back to the Lite Sentry when she saw Alex point to the man behind her. The angel quickly turned around before being stabbed. She fluently grabbed the knife and threw the man into the street. The man got up and pulled out a gun. Devine grabbed the gun out of his hands with lightning speed.

The man put up his hands. Devine stared at him before he took off running down the street. She grabbed the pistol and knife and bent them together. She tossed what was left of the gun and knife in the garbage next to Alex.

"Feel better?" Alex finished her can of Apollo.

Devine grabbed the bag from the table, she looked in the bag, and then at Alex. "One is missing."

***

When Kameron got up in the morning, it was the same as all the other mornings. He woke up knowing Alex wouldn't be there, but it didn't stop him from wishing. His hand went over the spot she'd been as he fell asleep. This morning was just as the others: he went for his morning run, showered, and got ready for work. A smile grew as he saw three wrappers of Hostess Cupcakes in the garbage. Kameron had bought those the day after his third date with Alex. He was curious how long it would take Alex to get comfortable enough to look through his cupboards for something to eat. It made him feel good that she did.

He sat on the couch with his tablet to open the news about Darius King. The orange juice he was drinking was thick with pulp, just as he liked it. The news article he was reading was spinning that it wasn't a legitimate shooting. The reaction comments to the article would appear this was escalating quickly. There were a couple of people with F.O.R. banners on their profile pictures asking for a resistance march.

Kameron's reading was interrupted by a knock on the door. Kameron got off the couch to open the door. Grossman was on the other side, and he didn't look happy. "You okay?" Kameron invited him in.

"Just when it rains, it pours," he told him. "My kid is all up in arms over this Darius King shooting."

"It's really hitting the airways hard arguing both sides of the issue," Kameron added to the conversation.

Grossman turned to Kameron. "The problem is that people won't veer from the source of their information."

Kameron couldn't fault that statement. "What are you doing here anyways?"

"I thought I would give you a ride to work," Grossman offered.

Kameron could tell that his friend just wanted to have somebody to talk to. "Actually, that would work, but I need to stop at Alex's work. She forgot her cell phone." Kameron finished his orange juice. He rinsed out the cup before putting it in the dishwasher. "I gotta shower. The remote to the TV is in the drawer in the end table."

The car ride over was quiet. It seemed as if Grossman's mind was somewhere else. He was contemplating something, like something he needed to tell Kameron. "FLOTUS wants to go to Michigan to help with the polling in Detroit."

"Didn't the POTUS detail say it was a logistical nightmare?" Kameron was reading about the shooting from another news agency. "This is saying that Darius King had a felony arrest warrant for beating up some teenagers for some drugs they had on them. This is getting ugly fast."

"It won't be that bad," Grossman told him. "Once she's at the hotel, the fundraiser is just down the block. She wants to stay a couple of days to promote a humanitarian look for POTUS."

"She's going to need to stay a month," Kameron cracked a small joke.

Grossman laughed. "True, but we don't have that privilege of having a political opinion." A phone call came over the car. "Yes, honey."

Grossman's wife spoke, "Just got a call from Moses' school. He skipped school today. One of the teacher's saw him in the parking lot but then saw him take off with a group of friends."

"Ugh," Grossman had disgust in his voice. "Let's see what he tells us after he gets home. I'd like to see what he says when we ask him how school was."

"Okay, well I have to get going to work. Love you," Talia's voice said over the speaker of the car.

"Love you too," Grossman hung up the phone. He turned to Kameron, "Birth control, double up on it."

Kameron smiled. "That's one discussion that Alex and I don't need to have."

***

Alex walked into Anne's office as she was filing some papers in a metal cabinet behind her desk. She leaned on the doorway of her office watching her while holding a cold Apollo Energy Drink.

75

Anne jumped and caught her glasses when they fell. Anne wasn't expecting to see Alex standing there. "You scared me. You okay?" She finished filing her papers before locking the cabinet.

"Not a good hunting night, but it was entertaining." Alex had to switch hands because the can was too cold to hold onto. She sat down on the chair in front of Anne's desk and propped her feet up.

Anne smiled as she lifted Alex's feet to grab a piece of paper. "If you don't mind, could you escort me with the records to the airport? It won't be that exciting either."

"Yah, I figure we can go to lunch afterwards." Alex picked up the bronze flower Mole gave Anne when he asked her to marry him. Alex saw Anne looking at the flower. The sadness in her eyes was evident so she put it back where she'd found it. "Is everything set at the airport?"

"Yes, Father Partinello and Father Grecko will meet us at the airport for the exchange. It shouldn't take that long." Anne reviewed the transfer paperwork one last time. "Looks like all is in order."

"Well, the good news is that Megan will be on vacation this week, so party time for me." Alex gave a little dance in her chair.

"Ever think of giving her a chance? She may surprise you," Anne offered a piece of advice. She walked around her desk to hop on it. Anne looked out to make sure no one was listening. "Rumor has it that the Councils are extremely short handed.

They are actively searching for Council Priests, Ministers, and Support Personnel."

"Do you think the Council will hire her?" Alex shivered at the thought. "She's such a manipulative witch."

Anne laughed but then got a bit serious as she looked at the time. "Come on, sweetie, everybody has some good qualities." Anne hopped off the desk to open the safe to get the Dark Texts. She placed them in a locked briefcase. "Let's go."

The two of them walked upstairs to see Father Richard and Cardinal Joe talking about the shooting of Darius King. Cardinal Joe turned to them. "Good morning girls."

"Morning." Alex tossed her empty Apollo can in a garbage can next to the wall.

"Good morning, Cardinal, Father." Anne held onto the briefcase.

"Is everything good to go?" Father Richard saw what time it was from his watch.

Anne showed them the briefcase. "Yes. Declan is watching over the records trailer attached to the van."

"Why a trailer?" Cardinal Joe asked her.

"In case the van breaks down, we can just move the records with the suburban if needed," Anne said. "Just in case."

Father Richard chuckled, "Covering all bases."

The sound of the door turned their attention to Kameron and Grossman coming into the church. Alex hadn't seen Grossman since the night they took down the F.O.R. building. "Hey," she smiled at Kameron. "Grossman, long time."

"Alex." Grossman seemed to be looking around.

"He's sleeping at my desk." Alex turned to Kameron. "You look happy."

"I couldn't have a better morning, cupcake," he winked at her. "You forgot your phone." He held it up to her.

"Oh thanks, I thought I lost another one." Alex smiled at how wonderful Kameron was to her. "Oh, you even charged it for me."

"Alex, your next phone is going to be a flip phone," Father Richard teased.

Cardinal Joe got a phone call. "Excuse me, Anne. Give me a minute before you leave."

"Yes, Cardinal," Anne agreed.

Father Richard turned to Kameron. "Any thoughts on taking us up on our offer?"

Kameron got a little uncomfortable with Alex right there. It was as if he was afraid it would turn into a fight. "No."

Grossman turned to Kameron. "What offer?"

Alex crossed her arms and tapped her foot. "Yes, Kameron, what offer was that?"

Kameron knew he was busted. "They offered me the job to be the Cardinal's driver, but I turned it down." He looked over at Alex who was just staring at him with her arms crossed, tapping her pinky finger.

Alex returned with a glare, playfully telling him that she knew but she wasn't happy with his decision. "Oh, we'll talk about this later,"

Kameron could tell Alex wasn't going to hold back her feelings about that when they talked.

"A driver. Is the Jewish council hiring?" Grossman chimed in enthusiastically.

Father Richard answered, "I can make a call, if you want."

"I would, really I would," Grossman had hope in his voice.

Alex looked to Kameron for answers but all she got was him mouthing, "Later." She got the message that it would be a long conversation.

Cardinal Joe returned. "The Catholic Council just informed me that there is an impromptu CR meeting that Father Richard and I have to get to."

"Meaning Declan can't bring Anne to the airport." Alex's body shrunk with disappointment. "I hate driving that thing."

Grossman jumped in, "We can help."

"I'll take all the security I can get." Anne said relieved.

Cardinal Joe looked at his watch. "Oh, Father, we have to get going."

Father Richard started following the Cardinal when he snapped his fingers. "Oh man, I told Megan I would bring her to the airport."

Cardinal Joe and Father Richard both looked at Alex. "Oh man, are you serious?" she complained.

"It's on the way and you're going there anyway," Father Richard told her. "There's room in the van."

Alex just rolled her eyes as she went to the back to relieve Declan from guarding the records. "You're driving, Kameron. I hate that thing. Plus, you'll be safer from her clutches." The group started walking out of the church. Alex gave a sharp whistle for Komptin to join them.

They arrived at the apartment complex where Megan was to be picked up. "How much does the Council pay?" Grossman looked up at the apartment. "This is nice." The group of them was amazed how she could afford such a nice apartment.

Alex quickly interjected, "She is not..." Then she said it a little louder. "She is not a member of the Council." There was definitely a bit of animosity in her voice.

Grossman gazed behind. "Does she know anything about you?"

"Oh, God, no," Alex went back to her phone.

They only waited a couple of minutes when Megan came to the van. "Thank you for picking me up." She saw that Kameron was driving. "Kameron, what are you doing here?"

Megan jumped in the front seat next to Kameron, so Grossman was put in the seat next to Anne. "Taking Alex to lunch after we drop you off at the airport." Alex had to sit in the back row of the van with Komptin. Kameron watched her roll her eyes in the rear-view mirror. "Where are you heading?"

"I'm just going to Florida to get out of town for a bit." She was digging in her purse making sure she had everything.

Grossman chimed in, "What are you going to do down there?"

"Beach, and relax," Megan replied to him. "Oh Kameron, I'm excited to get into this new bikini that I just look great in."

They continued to drive down the road trying to get to the freeway when Komptin lifted his head. Alex knew what he was alerted to because she felt it as well. The Dark was definitely nearby.

"Hey, what's that?" Grossman pointed in front of the road.

Anne looked up from reading her book. Her nerves shot up. "I don't like this."

On the road ahead was a mass gathering of people with signs demanding justice for Darius King. Up on the stage was the leader of the group, screaming something.

"See any way around this?" Grossman asked Kameron who was surveying the situation as well.

"No," he answered. "We have a bus behind us and all other routes are blocked by people."

Anne started to look around, holding tightly to her briefcase.

"You okay, Anne?" Megan looked down to the briefcase that she was holding. "You look nervous."

Then a bunch of people started to unload off the bus. Alex looked behind her to see a bunch of people with patches showing a "U" with a "1" inside of it. "Who are these people?" Alex said. The group marched angrily towards the Darius King crowd.

The leader saw them march towards them and started calling them out, "Here comes the United Won. These fascists, these government supremacists, are here to silence us!"

The United Won leader turned on his bullhorn, "Darius King was a thug! Shooting justified."

"This doesn't look good," Alex said as she started unbuckling her seat-belt.

"Alex, you can't involve yourself in this," Anne reminded her. "This is not an issue for you."

Kameron looked to Grossman who was dialing his cellphone to law enforcement. Then something caught his attention; Grossman stopped his phone call, "Moses?" Grossman threw Kameron his phone. "Kameron, call this in." Grossman got out of the van.

"Don't get out of the van!" Alex could feel the air escalate quickly.

Kameron tossed the phone to Megan, "Call the police." He got out of the van to chase Grossman down.

"Damn it, Kameron." Alex followed him out of the van.

"Moses!" Grossman yelled. He could see his son throwing a glass bottle at the United Won crowd while yelling at them.

Alex watched the event start to unfold. "Oh my God." The crowds started to run at each other. Kameron, Grossman, along with Alex and Komptin, were stuck in the middle. She nudged Komptin. "Don't kill any of them." Then Alex felt the presence of a Demon. She looked at the crowd to see if she could locate the foul creature. She caught a glimpse of a man staring at her. He flashed his eyes and took off running away from the crowd. "Go, get him, I'll stay here!" Komptin took off after the Demon in full stride. Then, the crowd collided with each other. Multiple people from each group were fighting with one another. Alex was defending herself in an attempt to get to Kameron and Grossman.

Kameron started fighting the crowd the best he could. Grossman appeared to be fighting to get to someone in particular. Kameron blocked a punch that was heading for his face. He quickly grabbed the arm and broke it. Then he punched the guy in the ribs and tossed him aside as he was no longer a threat. He grabbed a teenager and threw him to the side as he was trying to get to Grossman. The young teenager took out a switchblade and stabbed Kameron. The pain caused him to drop to his knee onto the ground. There were still people he was fending off.

Alex turned in time to see a kid with a knife stab Kameron in the side. Alex was fighting people on both ends to get to Kameron. She had never fought this many people at once, but she had to watch herself and be careful not to kill any of them. Alex took hold of one arm of the people from the United Won and swung him into a group of kids that were attempting to light a bottle with a rag in it.

Her eyes flashed blue as she quickly busted through four other people to get to that kid. She grabbed that kid and lifted him up in the air, about to throw him onto the ground.

"ALEX!" Kameron yelled. "DON'T!"

Alex stopped herself from slamming the kid into the ground. It wasn't the gentlest she ever put something or someone down, but the kid managed to limp away. "Are you okay?" She came up to him. "Come on, we got to get Anne and Megan out of here," Alex told him. "How bad are you hurt?" She blocked a punch from someone trying to attack them. She returned a punch of her own, sending him to the ground.

"It's not bad. It got deflected off my vest," he told her. "Where's Grossman?"

They both turned and found him. "Moses!" he was yelling. They looked to see a kid turn his head to see who was yelling. The shocked look on the boy's face meant he knew him. He didn't know what to do. The boy just took off running away from the crowd as Grossman followed him. Anne was full out scared when the van started rocking from the crowd. Someone threw a rock at the windshield. Anne screamed, but then it turned to pure fright when the van was being tipped over. It came crashing down on its side. The sound of breaking glass from the windows of the van intensified the situation. Then a different kind of breaking glass was heard followed by a sudden rush of heat and smoke filling the van. The door ripped open as a Demon with glowing red eyes jumped in to grab the briefcase.

"Oh, no you don't," Alex said as she grabbed the Demon. She was glad she could throw this one onto the ground as hard as she could. The two of them started to fight. Alex felt herself be pulled off the Demon by three other people. Alex didn't know if they were provisionaries or part of the riot.

Anne tried to reach the briefcase but it was taken by a random person. Anne felt her whole world disappear as it left her sight. "NO!"

"I'll get it," Megan said as she opened the door to the van and hopped out.

"Megan don't!" Anne yelled. Anne struggled to get herself out of the van as it was filling with smoke and fire. "Alex!"

Alex picked a man up and threw him into a man hitting Kameron. "What?"

"The briefcase!" She pointed to a man running down the street with Megan chasing him.

Alex cracked her neck as she charged through the crowd. She punched and tossed anyone in her way.

***

Megan met up with the Demon that grabbed the briefcase in a local after-school kids club building. "Give them to me," she demanded excitingly. Brovish gave her the case that held the Dark Texts. "It's locked."

"Not a problem." Brovish broke open the lock.

Megan eagerly opened the case to see the Dark Texts. "We did it. We actually did it." She couldn't help but smile. More importantly, now they would be able to bring Vandor back.

The sound of Komptin's bark was getting closer. "The mutt has already destroyed Jeldrok," Brovish stated. "The Sentry will not be far behind."

"They can't find the texts. Take the briefcase, make sure they see you and run," Megan said as she gathered the texts.

He started running towards F.O.R. Headquarters. Megan heard Alex call out her name. Megan ran, turning each corner trying to hide from the Sentry, but each of the corners led to another dead end. There was nowhere for her to go. She ran into the bathroom as Alex was loudly calling for her. "Why the hell isn't she chasing Brovish?" Megan anxiously thought. She was about to be caught with the Dark Texts. She opened up the utility closet in the bathroom and found an extended lighter they must use to light the hot water heater. Megan couldn't be caught with the texts because her cover would be blown. She had to get rid of them. The lighter easily ignited to start burning the texts. The Dark's only hope to get the information to bring Vandor back would be to find Salamor. All hopes of bringing Vandor back were about to go up in smoke.

Megan was shocked at how quickly the pages were lit. The burning of the texts created a red smoke that seemed to get closer to Megan. She couldn't avoid it; it was as if it was chasing her. It had no smell, no heat. The smoke entered her mouth, nose, ears, and eyes. Megan's body started to be overcome with a burning sensation that turned to a sharp sting. She cried out in pain as her body flew across the bathroom into a stall. It then flung onto the ceiling followed by smashing into a mirror.

Alex came barging in to see Megan on the ground with blood dripping from her mouth and ears. "Megan," Alex came running up to her. "Are you okay?"

"I'm fine, Alex," she tried to get up.

"What happened?"

Megan thought of a quick lie. "Anne's case, she seemed so worried about it. I don't know what came over me. I just knew she had to get it back." She wobbled a bit. "Whoa. Head rush."

"What were you thinking?" Alex helped her up and brushed her off.

"I had him cornered with it but then he heard Komptin and for some reason, he really got scared," she continued. "He threw me into the mirror and took off."

"You're lucky he didn't kill you," Alex slightly laughed out of amazement. "Come on." Alex shook her head, "I can't believe you did that." She patted her on the back in support. "Let me check to see if the coast is clear."

Megan stood up straight. She saw the Lite Sentry leave the bathroom. Everything was so clear, so easy. She knew exactly how to bring Vandor back, now that she was the Dark Harridan.

CHAPTER THREE

Gron grabbed Brovish by the throat with his red-lit hand. With all his anger, he threw him through the door from his office. The pieces from the door were scattered about, some of them lodged in Brovish's body. The scream from the secretary echoed in the hallway. "Shut up!" Gron scolded her. The movement from Brovish trying to stand up turned Gron's attention to him. "You left them there?!"

"My leader, the Sentry, didn't go after me. She went to make sure Megan was all right," he explained.

Gron's eyes were glowing with hate. He again manhandled Brovish by throwing him into the conference room. The sound of his body hitting the conference room table had other provisionaries peering out of their offices. "And now she is nowhere to be found!" Gron continued his assault on Brovish by continuously punching him in the face.

The Demon tried to put up his arms to defend himself, but the force of Gron's blows made it a weak effort. Black blood started to splatter about, some of it landing on Gron's face and chest. The Dark Sentry formed a knife and thrust it into the chest of the Demon. Brovish's body disintegrated into the table. Gron stood over his kill, panting more from anger than physical exertion.

"Was all that for little ol' me?" a familiar voice came from behind.

Gron turned around to see Megan in the doorway. Her eyes were cold with evil. She now had real, long, red hair with black streaks. She seemed to flow as she walked towards Gron. "Megan?" Gron asked in confusion.

"That's a human name," Megan said out of disgust. She walked up to Gron and licked some of the black blood off his face. She bit her bottom lip. "How about Mistress Luna?"

"Misluna." He playfully smirked, running his sharp fingernail up the battered arm of Misluna. He picked her up and threw her on the conference room table with force. Misluna bellowed an evil laugh as she dug her fingernails into Gron's back. She bit him on the neck, causing him to bleed. The taste of Gron's blood when she licked her fingers was more than satisfying.

Misluna ripped open Gron's shirt to expose his chest. Gron picked her up, and she wrapped her legs around his body to hang on. With full force, he ran her body into the wall. The collision caused an indentation in the wall. Misluna smiled with pain.

***

"I couldn't believe it," Alex confessed to Cardinal Joe. "She went after those texts like her life depended on it. I hate to admit it, but I was impressed. I wasn't expecting it." Even though Alex told him what had happened, it was the first time Cardinal Joe was generally angry. She knew it wasn't at any of them in particular, but at the entire situation.

Anne just sat there in her chair, quiet, not saying a word. Her face was as lost as when she had lost Kale.

"Anne," Cardinal Joe recognized the signs on her face. "Anne." She slowly and shamefully made eye contact with him. "This wasn't your fault."

"Anne, you did everything within your power," Father Richard tried to comfort her.

Cardinal Joe tried to ease her burden. "Father Partinello even told you that at the airport."

"They were my responsibility." Anne just shook her head out of disbelief at the situation. "All that history, the Lite history, was destroyed … lost." Anne wiped a tear dropping from her face. "All the recordings of Juliana are lost forever. Another promise I broke."

Alex peered at Anne with sympathy. She knew something else was on her mind. Alex put her hand on Anne's arm in support, but it felt like she was too far in her thoughts to feel it.

"Alex, could you please give us a minute?" Cardinal Joe asked her.

With a moment of hesitation, because she didn't want to leave her friend, Alex got up anyway. She walked into the office to notice that Megan hadn't been in yet. She didn't know what to do. She wanted to be here for her friend, but she also wanted to be at the hospital with Kameron. When the cops finally broke up the riot, one of them transported Kameron to the emergency room. Kameron had called her while she was escorting Megan back to her apartment. He said that he was fine, only getting stitches.

Alex sat at her desk. The phone rang, and she saw it was the Council on the other end of the line. Cardinal Joe picked it up from his office before she could answer it. Of course, she waited until the last possible ring before she had to pick it up. Kameron had texted her to let her know he was home resting. In the text, he let her know Grossman wanted to thank them both as the kid he was chasing was his son. Alex understood; she would die to help her family because that is all that mattered.

* * *

Gron and Misluna had destroyed the conference room. There wasn't much left. The table was in pieces, and there were remnants of the chairs scattered all over the room. The two of them sat on the floor, bloodied, scratched, and their clothes scattered.

"That was fun," Misluna laughed as she kissed his chest.

Gron just stared. "What happened to the texts?"

"I burnt them," she casually replied.

Gron stood up and screamed as he threw Misluna into a chair.

"Round two?" She held her breath with excitement.

"You burnt them?!" His eyes glowed with fury; his fist lit– ready to kill.

Misluna just looked at him with lust. No fear present in her eyes. She was calm, as if she had all the answers. "Relax, it's all good." She tapped her finger on her head. "I've got it all up here."

Gron picked her up by the arm. "Why didn't you say so?" He felt her tongue lick his chin.

"I was busy." She smiled as she leaned closer to Gron's ear. "And I know how to get our Master back."

Gron smiled with the news. "What do we need?"

"First, we need to ensure the Sentry doesn't ruin it," Megan pointed out. "She could ruin everything."

"We've tried killing her, but she's become very powerful," Gron explained. "Plus, if we kill her, then the Lite will activate another."

Megan sat on what was left of the conference room table. "Then we don't need to kill her, yet. In fact, I think it would be more fun to watch her suffer."

"I can kill her boyfriend at any time." Gron put his pants on. "He's nothing."

"I'm talking about something more fun, but I need a few items." Misluna put on what was left of Gron's shirt.

"What's that?" Gron cracked his neck.

"I need the blood of pure Dark." Misluna matched him as he was watching her.

Gron didn't think anything of the request. "That's easy. We have Infiltrators for that, but not many."

Misluna nodded in agreement. "Secondly, maybe a little harder, I need the blood of the Lite Sentry."

"Does it have to be Alex's?" Gron checked the scratches he got from Misluna in the reflection of a F.O.R. picture.

Megan shook her head, "Just the blood of a Lite Sentry."

"Got that in my office," he answered. "Is that all?"

"No, the last one will be difficult to get. I need the blood of something pure Lite." Megan knew that request would be difficult. "Can you get that for me?"

"It won't be easy; the beast with Alex is far too powerful." Gron sat there for a moment. "What is the full plan to get our Master back?"

Megan walked over to Gron. As if afraid of letting anyone hear, she whispered her idea.

Gron smiled at the plan running through his head. "I need to call in a favor." The two of them walked out of the conference room, and the provisionaries fearfully looked out of their office doors. He turned to his secretary. "Fetch me, Shawn."

***

Alex was still waiting to be called back into the Cardinal's office. Komptin was laying on the ground next to her, using the bed Kameron had made for him following their first date together. The dog rolled over on his back, showing the scar he got from Sanah. He peeked an eye at Alex, almost knowing he was being watched. "What?" He just closed his eyes to go back to sleep.

The office door opened, and Anne stormed out, looking none too happy. "Alex," the Cardinal called for her.

"Anne?" Alex called to her, but she just turned to her to give her a fake smile. Alex wanted to chase after her, but the Cardinal called her name again. The tall, black man had gotten gray over the years, but he still had the sweet, caring smile he's always had. The memory of first meeting him when he was walking down the church steps always amused Alex because she thought he was God.

Alex sat down in the chair in front of his desk. The Cardinal threw Alex an Apollo drink, and she caught it. "Is she going to be okay?"

"She's a tough girl, but she's taking this personal," Cardinal Joe told her. "Keep an extra eye on her."

Alex nodded. "So, what's going on?"

"I'm sending Anne back home."

Alex immediately stood up. "You fire her; you fire me! I'm not Catholic. I'll go be the Methodist Sentry, or hell, once the LDS get inducted to the Council of Religions, I'll go work for them."

"They are strict on no swearing, no caffeine, or sex before marriage," Cardinal Joe alluded to her.

"No caffeine?" Alex stopped herself.

"Nope."

"No swearing?"

"No."

"No sex?"

Cardinal shook his head.

Alex gazed out the window. "Maybe the Contemporary Christian will take me?"

"Anne's not fired," Cardinal eased her mind. "Actually, I put her on a special assignment I need done. I thought she'd be happier than she let on."

"What did you assign her?" Alex was confused about everything going on.

The Cardinal made himself some black coffee. He savored the taste. "I'm sending her back home to Copper Top Mountain to fix up the old church. We finally got it back from the F.O.R."

"Wow, that's a small win for us," Alex was glad to hear some good news. She always felt like that church was a second home to her.

"Yes, well, what I remember is what you told me. The church is in need of some major work. I am sending Anne to survey it, get some estimates on how much it will cost to repair, oversee the construction, and most of all, relax," Cardinal Joe told her.

Alex got a worried look on her face.

"What's wrong?"

Alex knew Anne hadn't talked to Kale's mother since his funeral. She had tried to contact Anne a couple of times, but Anne had been dodging her. Almost as if she was afraid to talk to his mother. "Nothing Cardinal."

Father Richard finally spoke, "Also, we got word that we are going to be getting a potential Council Priest candidate. Once he gets here, he will not know what our job is until the Council grants him access, based on Cardinal Joe's recommendation."

Cardinal Joe spoke, "Which I will get from Father Richard."

Father Richard emphasized, "So you know, maintain a low profile when he gets here."

"That's easy." Alex got up. "If you excuse me, I need to go check up on Anne."

***

Gron sat at his desk looking over some of the financial records of the F.O.R. There was some drop in funds, but nothing came out that needed much attention. They just had to sell a couple of their buildings to make up for it. Misluna was sitting on the couch reading a gossip magazine. The office door opened to have Shawn come up to Gron.

"Roger," Shawn shook his hand. Gron winced at the sound of his human name. "Shawn, how've you been?"

"Not bad," the tall, blonde man said as he sat down.

Gron went to his chair as well. "Get you a drink? Scotch, with a touch of Sprite." He pointed to him.

"How'd you know?" Shawn asked him.

"Lucky guess." He turned to Misluna.

She got off the couch to go behind Shawn. She motioned to Gron that she would like to get with Shawn. Gron just shook his head. "Are you finally ready for absolute power?"

Shawn got excited. "It's about time; I've been waiting for a while for you to tell me your secret."

"True raw power is frightening," Gron told him while swirling his drink. "You think you are able to handle it?"

Shawn was a bit nervous as he took the drink from Misluna. She grazed her fingers down the side of Shawn's face. "How did you handle it?"

"With open arms," he replied. Gron got up from the desk. "Ready?"

Shawn nodded his head in a quick fashion. A dark mist seemed to appear from the walls and formed into a dark bear-like creature. It snapped along with a low, dark growl and its eyes glowing red. "What do I get if I do this?"

"High school wishes," Gron tantalized Shawn's interests.

Shawn looked confused, which was natural for him.

"A promise of power like you'll never know and the ability to fulfill something you always wanted to do," Gron looked over to Misluna and gave her a wink.

"I'm tired of being nobody. I want it; I don't care about the cost." Shawn dropped to his knees. "I want absolute power."

Gron nodded to the Infiltrator for permission. The Dark beast complied, as it jumped into Shawn's body that had his arms open. It now inhabited the body of Shawn.

"And now, who do we have?" Gron just loved watching primates become Hosts.

Shawn raised to his feet. "Call me Merik."

Gron smiled, and Misluna joined behind him, putting her arm around him. "Give him the good news."

Merik was still confused at what Gron wanted him to do. "Something I've wanted since high school?"

***

Anne sat in her office staring at random items on the wall. All those records gone. Father Raimondo's personal box of the perished Lite Sentry is now destroyed. She couldn't believe it. Now she has to go back to Copper Top Mountain, her and Kale's hometown. All those people coming up to her constantly reminding her that Kale is gone.

Even though the job of renovating the church was alluring, no work would be done today, so she decided to take the rest of the day off. Anne grabbed her white purse and started to head out, when she saw Alex with Komptin walking down the hallway.

"Hey," Alex said to her.

Anne smiled. "I suppose you heard."

Alex nodded. "How long do you think it will take?"

Anne shrugged. "I don't know, over a year, maybe two."

"Where are you going to stay?"

They continued to walk down the hallway together. "The Council offered me a furnished apartment, but I think I'm going to stay with my parents."

They both stopped at the door leading to the lobby of the church. "You know you are going to have to talk to her," Alex stated the obvious.

Anne fought back from being choked up. "I know. It's inevitable. I just don't know…"

Alex stood still; she, along with Komptin, looked in the same direction. "Damn it, that's another one." Alex regained her composure. "I'm going to have to go out tonight and find these guys." Alex seemed a bit worried. "I really was hoping we destroyed all these creatures when the F.O.R. was demolished."

"We didn't defeat the F.O.R. We just delivered a blow to them. They are still strong, influenced, and gaining support from the government and the public," Anne reminded her.

They walked up to the office where Kameron was with Grossman. They both had worried looks on their faces. "Alex," Grossman acknowledged. Kameron just smiled at her, but it seemed forced.

"What's wrong?" Alex asked the two of them.

"Just work stuff," Kameron told her.

Grossman's face was particularly worried. "I see your wounds have healed. Thank you for saving my life."

"I'm still in debt to you," Alex told him. "Just don't take too long to cash it in." Alex gave him a teasing smile.

"I'm ready to make us right," Grossman let Alex know.

Alex's interests peaked. She hopped on her desk with her feet dangling. "What do you have in mind?"

"My son got arrested for that riot and is getting bailed out tomorrow," Grossman informed her.

Alex was tight lipped. "Okay," she said with soft intensity.

"He's such an angry kid. He needs to be accountable for his choices," Grossman said as he tried to hold in his emotions. "I love my son."

"What do you want me to do?" Alex didn't know where he was going with this.

"He was such a sweet kid. Then all of sudden he just got angry. It's as if he's a different person. I need to know if he's possessed by one of those black bastards," he told her.

Anne's mouth dropped and Alex stopped her feet from swinging as she got serious. Cardinal Joe came out of the office. "What's going on?"

"You know what I'll have to do if he is," Alex informed him.

"If he is, then my son is already dead and you need to do what you need to do," Grossman gave her permission.

"Anne," Cardinal Joe said. "Can you please get Rabbi Freedman from the Jewish Council on the phone?"

Anne got out her phone to get the Rabbi's number. "I have it. I'll patch it through your office."

Cardinal Joe showed them into his office. "Come on, we need to talk about this. Anne, please call Father Richard to join us."

***

Alex was in her room in the basement of the rectory. She put her long, black weave in the back and made sure it was tied tight. The nightly ritual ended with her applying her black eyeliner to her eyes and a dark lip-gloss. For some reason this became her act before going for a hunt. However, this didn't seem like a hunt, it was more of a kill, or even a murder.

She hoped to God this teenager wasn't possessed by an Infiltrator. All she had was hope that he was just a confused kid. To fight someone's son who is a Demon right in front of the parent, wasn't something she was looking forward to. She put on a pine-green, long-sleeve shirt with a black, leather vest. The clock showed she had about twenty minutes before she was going to be picked up by Kameron.

Alex walked up to the congregation of the church. She noticed the church was particularly quiet this evening. Almost as if they knew– death was imminent. Alex sat in the back pew overlooking the church. The stained-glass window seemed to stare down at her.

"You are not looking forward to this night?" A voice appeared next to her.

Alex smiled, as she never knew how Celestial always came at the perfect time. Alex leaned her head on her godmother's shoulder. "This night isn't going to end well."

"Why do you say that?"

"Just a feeling," Alex told her. She peered over at her new guardians who were bowing their heads at the head of the church. "I miss Ariel."

"There were hard losses that night." Celestial comforted her. "But many were saved."

Komptin walked into the congregation in his gargoyle state. Celestial got up and formed something for him to eat from her hand. He gently ate out of her hand and then snuggled up to her. Kameron had texted Alex to let her know he was in the parking lot. She turned back to Celestial but she was gone. Komptin morphed into a German Shepard as they both went to Kameron's car.

It was dark when they finally reached the point in the forest. Kameron shut the car off and the two just sat there. "Nervous?"

"I don't want him to be a Demon, but if he is as angry Grossman says he is, and there was a lot of Dark at the riot, it's possible." Alex turned to her boyfriend. "I don't want you or Grossman to watch this." Alex was now staring out into the woods from her window. "I don't want you to look at me as the person who murdered your friend's son."

Kameron got out of the car and walked around to open her door. He held out his hand to show his support. She accepted it to get out of the car with Komptin following. With a gentle kiss, he made her feel at ease. "I know what you do and why you do it." He looked at his watch. "How much space do you need?"

"I will feel the Dark before he senses my Lite," Alex let him know. "But I need to see him up close to know if he's a Demon."

Komptin's eyes flashed blue which caught both Alex and Kameron's attention. They turned around to see Devine dropping from the sky with her Lite Bo Staff in her hand. "There is Dark approaching."

"Yes, I sensed it. That's not a good sign," Alex told Kameron. The woods around them seemed to become blacker. A faint chill of wind hit her neck.

Kameron grabbed his keys. "I'll go head Grossman off and have his son walk up the road."

"Komptin will scout the west, I will take the east," Devine informed them. The warrior angel confidently surveyed the situation.

"Why don't you watch from the sky?" Alex asked. It just so happens Osiah's purple star was above her.

"It will be easier to ambush any attempt of an attack from the ground," Devine told her. "If I am in the air, they will see me."

Alex turned to Kameron, "Be careful, Komptin will have your back until he starts walking towards me, then he will provide perimeter security."

Kameron nodded. He gave her a kiss and then got into the car to head Grossman off.

"You look nervous, Sentry," Devine commented.

"I don't want him to be a Demon," Alex informed her. They both looked around. "But the sense of the Dark is getting stronger." Alex tightened her mouth. "Shit."

Devine was looking at Alex's feet and then all around her. "I do not see any animal or human feces. Do you need a moment before this starts?"

Alex looked back at her with confusion. "What? No."

"It's quite alright; I have been studying humans quite extensively lately. The consumption, interactions, bowel movements," Devine told her. "The mating rituals you have are really-"

"Stop!" Alex put her hand up. "Have you watched...me...with Kameron?" Devine opened her mouth about to answer. "On second thought, I don't want to know. Just promise me you won't study me." Alex stopped in her tracks as a strong sense of the Dark was getting closer.

"I must go," Devine said. "Best of luck, little sister."

"Be careful yourself." Alex watched Devine go into the woods and then watched the road ahead of her. "This is going to suck." She could see the outline of a male walking in her direction. The time was coming.

***

Devine had found some high ground to cover herself in. This was the most logical place for the Dark to attack. Now for sure there was no doubt they were present. There was little doubt that the man's son was possessed by an Infiltrator. Then, he would have to be eliminated. She had complete confidence the Sentry's abilities would make her come out victorious.

Throughout time, Devine had seen the pain primates expressed when losing a child. She felt sorrow for the human. The angel had taken many lives and lost many colleagues. When she lost her sister to the Dark, she had never felt such pain. The sky now held Ariel's star as it shined bright. It deserved to be the brightest in the sky. The feeling of being incomplete since Ariel's noble death was hard for Devine. There was no one to look after or have her back. The feeling of not being able to protect the Conduit of Lite almost made her feel inferior.

She had found herself happy when the Lite Sentry asked her to help her with ensuring this mission goes by smoothly as possible. Devine would not fail in her duty. A sound in the distance caught the angel's attention. The Dark was nearing; she remained completely still. Something caught her attention. There was a sense of something she had never felt before. It was Dark, which was not in doubt anymore, but it was something she had not known.

***

"And who do we have here!?" Alex shouted out to the seventeen-year-old walking up the darkened road in her direction. The cocky kid walked up to her with confidence. Alex eyed him up and down, and then studied his face.

"Huh? Here I thought my pops was setting me up for some kind of intervention," he arrogantly studied Alex's body. "Nice to know he got me a hooker."

"Excuse me?" Alex was taken aback. "Did you just call me a hooker?"

"We going to do this here or head off somewhere?" His conceited attitude while scouting the area was truly revolting.

Alex walked up to him with disgust. "Let's just get this over with."

"Suit yourself." He went to zip down his pants.

"Look little boy, one, I have a boyfriend, two, you couldn't handle me." Alex got close to the kid to study his eyes.

"What are you doing?" He asked with agitation in his voice.

"Shut up." Alex did a final look. "Yeah, you're just a cocky, arrogant, piece of shit." She turned around. "And fortunately for you, that's a good thing."

"Who the hell do you think you are, saltine!?" he yelled at her. "You're just some little female, white bitch. You're just lucky I don't hit skanks."

"What the hell is wrong with you?" Alex turned to him. "Why are you so angry? You have a family that provides for you and loves you."

"My pops is an uncle tom sell out," he complained.

"Your dad is a good man who cares deeply for you. Me being here is proof of that." Alex just wanted to go home now. She wasn't cut out to deal with this kid. "What you need is a good ass kicking."

"You think you are going to do that?" He was confidently looking her up and down.

"I bet I could kick your ass without even hitting you." Alex stood her ground.

"Right, I swing at a little saltine like you and a whole bunch of white cops have a reason to kick my ass." Moses wrinkled his nose down at Alex.

"Chicken shit," she called him. "Sounds like you're afraid. I promise you, there are no cops. Just you and me, and the ass kicking you are about to receive." She got right up into his face. "What, you scared?"

"Get off me, ho." He tried to push her; she didn't even budge. He got a little bit more irritated. He went to push her a little harder, but Alex moved out of the way, and Moses stumbled forward, almost falling to the ground. Alex took an Apollo drink out of her backpack that she had on the ground. She opened it and took a sip as she motioned for him to attack her.

"You crazy bitch," he said, walking by her.

"Chicken shit," she re-emphasized.

Moses got more irritated and turned around to push her hard, but she moved out of the way still holding her drink. Moses fell to the ground; he clenched his fists with anger. He got up from the ground, panting with anger. "I'm going to knock some sense into you."

Alex's expression that he was nothing to her elevated his anger. He started to walk away, but then Alex made the sound of a chicken. That broke Moses's last nerve as he swung at Alex. She caught his fist with ease and then pushed him onto the ground. "Look, you are not as bad as you think you are. You really need to re-evaluate your life. You are heading down a path that is going to put you in danger, and you're not going to last long if little ol' me just kicked your ass without even taking a swing at you." Alex held out her hand with a caring look. "No one needs to know this happened, this will just stay between us."

Moses sat there for a moment before grabbing her hand.

"Don't feel bad, even I got my ass kicked once when I needed it." Alex was lifting when she got a very strong sense of the Dark. She let go of Moses' hand, causing him to fall back to the ground. Then

Alex stepped out in front of Moses as if protecting him when Komptin came running out of the woods. "What's wrong?"

***

Devine watched as the first sign of an Infiltrator started to make its presence known through the thicket of the forest. The fact there was just one confused her. It may have been a random scout just walking around hunting for a potential kill. This was a gamble. If she let it go, then she would put Alex in danger. She would have her hands full if that boy was infiltrated. Then again, it could be used just to draw her out to see if Alex was alone.

Devine decided to go with the likelihood that it was just a random Infiltrator looking for a kill. She attacked the black beast by knocking it into a tree with her Bo Staff. The Dark soldier screamed with hate and glowing red eyes. Devine was expressionless with concentration in her battle stance. The Infiltrator attacked Devine with a roar as it ran after her. She showed her proficiency with her staff before smacking it on top of its head, driving it into the earth. She quickly turned as another Infiltrator came to attack her. She swiftly kicked it into the air and swung her Bo, hitting the fiend on the way down. A third Infiltrator appeared out of nowhere, and she jumped over it, causing the third one to collide with the other Infiltrator trying to get up. Devine threw her Bo Staff into the weakened Infiltrator as it became stuck into the tree.

It howled in pain before disappearing into the ground. She surveyed the situation as a group of Infiltrators and multiple Demons surrounded her.

***

Alex's head moved in the direction where the sound of the Infiltrator being diminished. She turned to the woods and flashed her eyes, preparing for battle. Two Infiltrators viscously appeared out of the woods.

"Holy shit, bears!" Moses screamed as he hid behind Alex.

"Chivalry at its best." Alex rolled her eyes. "Komptin, get him out of here."

Komptin barked at Moses.

"Where do I go!?" He frantically cried out. It looked as if he was about to pass out from fear.

"Head back to your dad. Komptin will go with you." She just watched as the Dark beasts approached her position.

"Suit yourself." He turned and ran towards the car.

Alex turned to Komptin, rolling her eyes. "Do you mind?"

Komptin turned towards Moses, running to follow him to make sure he got to his dad safely.

Alex watched them disappear down the road before turning to the Infiltrators. "Just Infiltrators. Not going to lie, nice change of pace." She lit her fists and shot a Lite Beam at one of them, knocking it out of the game. She ran full force at the other to get up close and personal.

**

Gron watched the angel be thrown against the tree, causing it to break in half. "Ow, that must have hurt." The female angel was fighting back with all her might. He got word from one of his provisionaries that the purple-haired angel was seen with the Sentry. The young primate told a F.O.R. member about the meeting his dad had set up. Gron took a gamble it was the Sentry, and hopefully, the Lite being wouldn't be far behind.

This angel was putting up one hell of a fight, though. Gron was giving her some credit for that, but in the end, she was going to lose. He didn't know how she did it, but she did manage to kill one Demon.

Misluna and Merik were watching along with him. Merik stepped forward to help with the fight but Gron stopped him. "Why not?"

"Because, you idiot. I need you unharmed," Gron told him. "Just enjoy the show."

Misluna smiled as she watched the angel drop to one knee as the Demons continued to punch and kick her onto the ground. The angel was bleeding but not out of energy yet. The bruising definitely started to show. "Hey, hey, don't kill her; we may never get another chance at this."

"Why can't we kill her?" Merik asked out of confusion.

Gron smacked him in the back of the head. "Think about it. If she dies then everything about her disappears, including her blood, when she becomes a star."

"Oh, yeah," he said, still not getting it. The three of them saw it was now safe to approach the angel. She was down, beaten, and out of hope.

Gron used his foot and flipped her on her back. "Got the jar?" Gron was amazed that she was still struggling to try to break free. One of the Demons held a stick in her mouth, preventing her from screaming.

Misluna pulled out a glass container. "I need at least half of this full of her blood." She handed Merik the jar.

Merik took out a knife and got onto the ground with the being of Lite. Demons and Infiltrators were holding her arms and legs. He tore the suit of armor off her and ripped her clothing to show her stomach. He took the knife and slowly cut across her stomach going down to her side. She screamed in pain as the blue blood started to ooze. He caught the blood into the jar, filling it before covering it with the lid. He licked blue blood off his finger and gave her a wink before handing the jar to Misluna. Merik was standing up to stare down at the angel beaten before him. It was a shame that he couldn't kill her, but it was a necessity to bring back Vandor.

Gron and his mistress admired the jar. Misluna placed the jar in the safety of a chest. "One step closer." She smiled.

"Merik, make sure she doesn't die. By the time they find her, our job will be done." Gron reminded him.

CHAPTER FOUR

It was close to eight in the morning before Alex finally got back to the church. One Infiltrator managed to get a kick in that sent her flying into the air. When she landed, she felt a crack of glass and her phone bending; there was no doubt in her mind she had broken it. The walk home took longer than usual, as her body was hurting. She could have flagged down a car but she didn't want to draw attention to herself with her bloody lip and torn clothes. Those Infiltrators were particularly determined in their fight against Alex. Normally they fought because it's what they do, but these ones seemed to have passion behind it.

Each step going up to the entrance of the church hurt. A couple of elderly women watched her pass. "Isn't that the Cardinal's secretary?" Alex heard one of them say. Normally, she would have gone straight to her room to freshen up, but she needed to talk to Celestial. The church was the safest place for her. Alex sat down on the back pew waiting, and surprisingly, waited longer than usual. Alex put her hands on her head and prayed for the safety of her friends.

"My child." Celestial appeared next to her. Her blonde hair seemed to sparkle in the morning sun coming through the stained-glass windows. The smile she showed seemed to radiate the room with warmth. This morning, she had on a headband made of gold with a blue stone in the middle.

Alex took her head out of her hands with her makeup smeared. "I apologize for calling you, but it was a rough night."

"Yes," the Conduit of Lite agreed with the beaten down Lite Sentry.

"I know I don't normally ask for favors, but..." Alex started to say.

"Komptin is with Kameron at his place, the boy and his father are trying to heal their relationship." She let her know with a smile of pride at Alex.

"Thank God." Alex leaned back in the pew and put her hand on head. "And I'm assuming Devine is okay."

"I cannot see beings of pure Lite when they are here, but I can tell you, she is not in Heaven, and she is not represented as a star." Celestial undid Alex's small, black woven hair to let it flow. She combed it with her fingers to freshen it up.

"Well, that's good news." Alex was thinking of a hot shower.

"I have to go, my dear. You did well." Celestial sat up to kiss her on top of the forehead.

It felt comforting as Alex closed her eyes with her hands on top of her head. Her body was sore, she had a headache, and she really wanted an Apollo right now, but she was just hurting too badly to get up. "On the bright side, things could only look up," she thought to herself.

"Why am I not surprised to see you like this? Looking like you've been out all night and using

115

God to get you through whatever situation you've gotten yourself into?" a familiar ear-piercing voice asked her.

Alex opened one eye. "You wouldn't do this to me, would You?" Alex slowly turned her head to see Father Carl looking down at her. "Oh, you gotta be shitting me?" Alex just turned her head back to close her eyes, still leaning back on the pew.

"I can see some things haven't changed, still disrespectful as ever. I thought you'd learn maturity by now." He pushed her leg off the pew with his. "Get up, show at least some respect and decorum in His worship room."

Alex's body let her know she was in pain when she stood up. "Whatever, I'm already late for work." Alex went down to the rectory basement to get to her room. She stopped to admire the painting of Cara hanging outside her door. "Ever have the feeling you are going to have a bad day?"

After her shower, she got out to see Komptin fast asleep on her bed. "Hey, there you are, boy." He got off the bed and jumped up to lick her. "Glad to see you're safe." The two of them played around a bit. He started a playful growl when he was trying to grab her hands. "Thanks for getting my man home safe." Komptin flashed his eyes in acknowledgment. "Well, I guess I should get dressed."

She wasn't in the mood to be all dressed up, so she just clipped her hair up, then put on a sweatshirt and shorts. It wasn't the greatest outfit in the world, but she was comfortable. She headed upstairs to her office after she put on her socks and running shoes.

Megan was at her desk typing away when she looked up with a smirk. "Rough night?"

"Better than some," Alex acknowledged. She went to grab an Apollo from the refrigerator before heading to her computer, but it was empty. "This is not a good start to the day."

"You got a herpes." Megan pointed to her lip. "I hope you don't give that to Kameron."

That reminded Alex. "Hey, have you seen Kameron?"

"No, he just dropped off Komptin and left for work." She continued to type on her computer. "How do you forget your dog?"

Alex wasn't in the mood for Megan right now. "Have you seen Father Richard?" She was searching her desk to see if she had Kameron's phone number anywhere. She couldn't remember it. At lunch she needed to get a new phone. The council is going to ask about that one. It was the third phone this year. Alex was hoping Father Richard would back her up on this. It really wasn't her fault.

The door opened to the Cardinal's office. "Alex, can I see you for a second? I have a nice cold Apollo waiting for you," Cardinal Joe tempted her. "Megan, can you have Declan meet me up here in half an hour."

"Yes, Cardinal," Megan picked up the phone to start dialing.

"Alex, close the door when you come in." The Cardinal went back into his office.

Alex had her back to the Cardinal when she was shutting the door. "You'd never believe this but I lost my phone again. This damn Infil-"

"Alex," Cardinal Joe quickly interrupted. "This is, Father Carl."

She stopped in her tracks, closed her eyes and silently prayed she was dreaming. Since she never slept, this one prayer wasn't going to be answered.

"Ms. Johnson," Father Carl spoke with a sense of arrogance.

Alex put on a fake smile she made sure was obvious to everyone in the room. In the room was Father Carl, the Cardinal, Father Richard, and Anne. Alex looked for support from Anne who was motioning for Alex to calm down. "Father." She tried not to sound snarky, but didn't achieve it.

An empty chair was obviously for Alex to sit next to Father Carl. She sighed before grabbing the chair to move it next to Anne to sit down. "Well, nothing like mending bridges from the past." Cardinal Joe got up and gave Alex the Apollo he'd promised. "Drink it, Alex."

"What's going on?"

"Take a drink, sweetie," Anne whispered in her ear.

Alex took a drink of her sweet nectar when she heard, "Father Carl is going to be your new Administrative Priest." Alex spit her drink out all over Father Richard.

Father Richard took it with congeniality. He just calmly reached into his pocket to pull out a handkerchief to clean off his face.

"What?" Alex cleared her throat. "Where's Father Richard going?"

"He's going to be heading to the church back in Copper Top," the Cardinal told her. "And Father Carl is going to be the Administrative Priest there."

"I thought you said he was going to be my new administra-" Then Alex stopped herself. "I'm moving back to Copper Top?"

Cardinal Joe slowly nodded.

"Per the-" Alex stopped herself when Anne grabbed her leg and Cardinal nonchalantly nodded his head. That was Alex's clue not to mention the Council.

Alex found herself starting to tear up at the fact that she would have to leave Kameron behind. Would this end their relationship? Would he quit his job and live in her small hometown? Alex let it slip out, "Kameron-"

"If you don't like the orders, Ms. Johnson, you can find other employment. I do understand he may be an issue," Father Carl said to her. It seemed as if he was hoping she wouldn't go.

"I think it would be wise to let her soak this in," Father Richard stood up for Alex.

"Yes." Father Carl got up and shook everyone's hand, but Alex refused. Father Carl left the office being escorted to the door by Father Richard.

A split second after Father Richard shut the door to the office, Alex stood up. "Please, tell me that jackass was brought in here as some sort of practical joke?"

Cardinal Joe tried to calm her down, "Alex, he is a priest, he has military background, and he had Top Secret clearance while he was in. He's a good fit for the position. The Council needs good priests."

"He's a jackass!" Alex pointed to the door. She took a deep breath to ease her nerves. "Why am I getting sent back home?"

"The Council is finding evidence that the Dark is congregating back in that area. Perhaps Gron is kind of a homebody," Cardinal Joe stated.

Father Richard chimed in, "I'm going to be the head priest and Anne will work as the historian and admin."

"Why can't I be the admin?" Alex asked.

Cardinal Joe spoke up, "You will take over Osiah's old job." The Cardinal took a moment to remember his friend. "That way you will have less interaction with Father Carl. We know that you two don't exactly see eye to eye."

"This is bad," Alex shared her feelings. "How long do you think we can hide my true job?"

"He is being groomed for a council position based on Father Richard's recommendation," the Cardinal stated.

"This just keeps getting better." Alex sat back down in a state of shock. "When does this happen?"

"End of summer." Father Richard sat down next to her. "Anne will be going ahead to set the groundwork; the council wants you to...clean things up here."

Cardinal Joe stated, "Father Richard, it's all yours." Father Richard nodded as the three got up for the door. "Hey team," the Cardinal yelled to them. "God bless, you've got this."

Father Richard motioned to them to meet out in the hall away from Megan. "Alex, I know you are going to start your hunts tonight, but I would like to meet for dinner to discuss some plans."

"We can meet at my place," Anne offered.

They all agreed before Father Richard walked to his office. "Anne, can I borrow your phone?" She handed Alex her phone. Alex texted Kameron she was safe and broke her phone, but that was all she could muster to do.

"You okay, sweetie?" Anne took back her phone to put it in her pocket.

"Can I borrow your car? I need to clear my head. I'm going to go look for Devine to make sure she is okay." Alex wasn't too worried about her. It was mainly an excuse to leave the office. There was too much going on at work this morning.

***

Kameron finally got a text from Alex that she was back at the church. He always worries about her when he doesn't hear from her first thing in the morning. If he could, he would take that burden on himself for her.

Grossman took the day off to be with his son. They needed to work on the bonding time. He didn't say what happened, but Kameron thought those two must have had a good talk because he didn't say much on the way.

The operations plans for the FLOTUS visit were almost completed. There was just one more read-through before he submitted them for approval. The office was anxious when the new Director was being escorted by the Administrator showing him around. He seemed like a nice person, a little young-looking, but seemed legit. Kameron wished it would have gone to Grossman, but maybe this would be for the better.

The new boss said something to his secretary and then walked into the office. Ms. Margie came down the cubicles stating that there is an employee meeting in the conference room in fifteen minutes. That would give Kameron some time to finish the plan.

They all congregated in the conference room where Kameron sat in his normal seat far in the corner. The seasoned agents got the conference table while he sat by the wall. He didn't mind. He actually liked it. There was a lot of chit-chat about the new boss, but no one really knew who he was. They knew he was in charge of the POTUS detail and then worked with the CIA on liaison duty.

The crowd quieted when the new Director walked in. "Good morning. I'm Director Channel, pronounced and spelled like a radio channel. Obviously, you all know that I am your new

Director, if you didn't, you're not the agent I want in my outfit."

Kameron's first thought was "Friendly," in the most sarcastic tone in his head. The mood in the room went from relaxation to one of intensity.

"I would like you all to go around the room and introduce yourselves with name and how long you've served," he stated. They all went around the room with the request in a proficient manner. "Then, it looks as if the only one missing is Agent Grossman."

"Sir, he had to take emergency leave," Kameron interjected.

"I didn't ask you," he told Kameron. "Look, let's get this straight, here and now. You are a junior agent. The people sitting at the conference table are the ones who I will get my answers from. Your job is to sit back, observe, learn, and answer questions when directly asked."

Kameron swallowed his pride. "Yes, Sir."

Director Channel turned to one of the senior agents. "Emergency leave?"

"There was an issue with his son," he answered.

"What hospital is he in?" The Director was looking through some files.

"No hospital, just a family emergency," he added.

The Director didn't even look up from the file and said in a monotone voice. "And, his wife couldn't take care of that?"

No one in the room dared answer, as they were afraid to speak up. Kameron's nerves shot up. The rest of the meeting was laying the new groundwork for the office. New hours, mandatory team runs and workouts, and new drills on a random weekly basis. Normally, Kameron wouldn't mind the new change, but this was something different.

The meeting was dismissed, and Kameron made it back to his desk. A couple of the agents were talking about how they were glad they were already being transferred out. Kameron was logging into his computer, when he saw the reflection of the Director in his monitor. He turned to stand up. "Sir?"

"I didn't know that 'Hello Kitty' mouse pads were standard issue," he stated while studying Kameron's desk. Kameron noticed he took extra time looking at the picture of him and Alex.

"It was a joke gift from my girlfriend," he told him.

"It goes home with you tonight. Only standard issue," he told him, still looking at the photo. "This is your girlfriend? Looks young."

"She's only a year younger than me," he cautiously corrected.

"Yes, interesting hair. Come see me in my office in fifteen minutes." Director Channel left, going around to other cubicles telling them what items were not to be displayed.

Kameron knocked once on the door. "Sir, you wanted to see me."

"Agent Dutcher, come in, shut the door behind you, and sit down," he told him. Kameron sat down on the chair for what seemed like an eternity before the Director finally spoke. "I understand you were directly involved with Director Morkin in shooting him."

"Yes, Sir, he was-" Kameron saw the Director put his hand up as if he didn't want to hear it.

"You were cleared by Internal Investigations," he said. "That's all I need to know." He continued looking through his file. "You are being transferred to the San Diego division by the end of next month.

Kameron's eyes got huge. "Why?"

Director Channel turned to him, "Officially, because that's where they are sending you." He stood up and got some water. "Look, unofficially, you're lucky to be getting that. I wanted you out. I think you're a liability to any office you go to. You were directly involved in that F.O.R. mess, and then the headquarters for that organization burns down, killing agents in the process. All that, and you are dating a girl who happens to work for a church. Personally, I fought to kick you out but I was overruled."

Kameron sat there in shock. "What are my choices?"

"Go to San Diego or resign," Director Channel said. "Either or, you are not going to be in this office."

***

125

Alex and Komptin got to the woods where she had destroyed those two Infiltrators. "It's funny that no one has seen her." There was still a sense that the presence of the Dark was around. Alex continued to look around the area. Evidence of her broken phone was scattered on the ground, but other than that, there wasn't much to go on.

"Alexandria," Celestial's voice was behind her.

Alex did a quick bow. "You shouldn't be here." Alex looked around. "It is far from safe."

"The primate is correct," her guardian, Arome, told her.

"The Dark is near," Omiela, the second guardian, was on edge.

"We are going to find her," Celestial sternly told them.

Arome and Omiela were new to guarding the Conduit of Lite, but their very presence was enough to frighten anyone, including Alex. They too were direct twins, but unlike Ariel and Devine, who had different colored hair. These two were direct clones of each other. They had white, long, straight hair that was held together by a gold headband around their head. Alex never noticed it until now, but there was a small stone in each of the headbands. Arome had purple, while Omiela had green. Alex took it as a homage to Ariel and Devine's passed service to the Conduit.

A tall, built angel with light brown skin came from the sky, crushing the earth below him when he landed. Malkaroy walked over to them. "There is no sign of her from above. If she is here, she is hidden."

"But she's not..." Alex had to reconfirm with Celestial.

"She has not joined Ariel in the sky," she assured.

The Dark was getting stronger in the air. Malkaroy sniffed before he turned to Celestial, "You need to leave."

"Not without Devine," Celestial got firm with Malkaroy. It was the first time Alex saw Celestial get angry.

"Last night she went that way," Alex pointed in the direction. "Komptin can stay with you and the Guardians."

"The Sentry and I can look for Devine. We will find her, my lady," Malkaroy assured her.

Omiela interjected, "If the Dark shows."

"We will have to go," Arome finished.

"Find her, please," Celestial begged.

Alex and Malkaroy hurried off into the woods. They walked for a bit, but there was no sign of her. They both knew there would be evidence of a battle, broken trees, and scattered earth from where Devine was fighting.

Alex gave Malkaroy a plea for assurance, but he just shook his head. "There are a couple of broken trees ahead," Malkaroy stated. "I will go check that out."

"I'll check the surrounding area," Alex let him know.

The two of them went in their respective directions.

"There was a battle here," Malkaroy yelled to Alex. "A couple splatters of blood but not enough to be worried about."

Alex saw something that caught her eye. It was a faint glow of blue. She walked over to see the outline of a body. "Devine," she faintly said. "Devine!" Alex ran over to the body and uncovered her. She was covered head to toe in mud with blue blood, and severely bruised. "MALKAROY!" Alex yelled.

Alex was trembling as she was afraid to touch her with her shaking hands. There was a severe wound on her stomach. Without hesitation, Alex ripped the sleeve of her shirt for a bandage. Devine, out of pure survival instinct, grabbed Alex by the throat and threw her into a tree. She attempted to fly away but didn't have the strength and she crashed to the ground. Alex ran up to her. "Devine, it's okay, it's Alex." Devine passed out. "MALKAROY!"

Malkaroy broke trees to get to Alex and Devine. "Is she going to...?" Alex couldn't bring herself to say it.

"Not if I can help it." Malkaroy gently lifted her up. She winced in pain as blood dripped from her body.

Malkaroy carried her to Celestial as Alex took point to ensure no Dark would attack. They made it to Celestial where her Guardians and Komptin were in fighting stances ready to attack. "Devine!"

Celestial came running to her. Komptin and the Guardians maintained their guard. "We need to get her home." Celestial deep worry colored her voice.

Malkaroy carried Devine to the doorway. The Guardians turned to Celestial. "Madam, we need to go," they both said in unison.

"I'll be okay," Alex assured her. For the first time since Alex could remember, she had seen Celestial truly scared. Alex just wished there was something more she could do.

***

Misluna was in the middle of her mixture when she watched Gron walk into the room where her little chemistry experiment was. She was concentrating intensely to make sure she did this right. There was enough to do a backup batch in case something went wrong, but she was confident she wouldn't need it. "It's almost done; do you have the Lite Sentry blood?"

Gron picked up the ball he got from the Dark Priest in Brazil. "Who knew this was the reason we kept these?"

"Probably just a coincidence. My guess is the Dark just likes the memories of killing Lite Sentries, I know I would." Misluna looked up at Gron with hope. "Do you think I could kill one?"

Gron studied the mixtures. "Someday, perhaps. For now, I think you'll get your rocks off with this."

"It will be fun to watch," Misluna told him. "I'll try to record it for you." She continued to stir

129

and check the temperature. The odorless liquid was getting thinner as she was mixing the substance.

"So, what did you find out today?" Gron asked her, almost afraid to interrupt her.

"The Sentry is getting transferred back to your hometown," she told him.

Gron got annoyed. "Damn it, how do they always know where to send her? It will make Merik's little job a bit harder."

Misluna motioned she was ready for the Lite Sentry blood. "This will make it easier for him." He handed her the glass. She cracked it open like an egg into the bowl to make sure it was the right amount. Her facial expression showed that she was quite happy with the result. "Can I get some Dark blood?" An Infiltrator walked up to her and sliced his wrist with his own claw. The blood flowed into the bowl. Misluna grabbed the jar of neon blue blood made of the Lite. She studied it. "That was so fun to watch." She opened the jar and poured some into another bowl.

Gron watched her mix the liquid. "What are you doing?"

"It's all about offsetting the balance in favor of the Dark," Misluna commented. "First the blood of the Lite." She put a portion of the blood into a bowl. "Then the Sentry blood in the middle." She placed the amount needed in the bowl with the first ingredient. "And finally, a touch more, but not too much more, of the blood of the Dark to offset the balance. Mixed in with some other ingredients– and voila." Misluna was quite proud of her creation.

"It's pretty yellow," Gron commented. "How are you going to get her to ingest it?"

"That's easy." Misluna took out some food coloring. "Yellow and blue make green."

Gron smiled. "Nice, will it work with it?"

"As long as she doesn't go to the bathroom before leaving church ground, we'll be fine," Misluna held up the concoction for the Lite Sentry.

***

The smell of Anne's hometown brought a sudden rush of memories to her. There was always a different aroma in the air here. Maybe it was the mixture of pine trees and the multiple lakes with running rivers. People seemed to be taking their time heading down to the baggage carousel. Her parents were going to meet her down there to bring her home. There was a lot to do. She couldn't help but make sure she didn't run into Kale's mom, Kate. That was a stupid thought since she couldn't be past security. The moment she left her sanctuary would start her inevitable confrontation with Kate. Anne knew she was going to be on guard at all times.

"Anne," a familiar male voice came from behind her.

Anne turned around to see Shawn walking up to her. "Hello, Shawn." Anne put her briefcase in her other hand.

He politely shook her hand. "So nice to see you, what are you doing in town?" he asked as other passengers walked around them. Before she could answer, he gently escorted her out of the way to not interrupt the flow of traffic.

"Work, I'm in charge of getting the Catholic Church back up to code," Anne told him.

"Yes, so sad what happened to that building," Shawn said. "Can I escort you to baggage claim?" Anne nodded and the two of them walked down the hallway together. "I'm so sorry to hear what happened to Mole."

Anne got irritated to hear Kale being called by his nickname. Probably because she hadn't heard it for a while. Even after his death, his murder, Alex refused to call him anything but Kale. All Anne could do was nod.

"Well, I see your parents are there at baggage claim. Hopefully I get to see you later." Shawn gave her smile as he shook her hand again. "Take care, Anne."

"Thank you, Shawn. I'll probably see you around town," Anne forced a smile. She couldn't help but remember how awful he was to her and Kale while in high school. Although, that was a long time ago. There was something different about him. As if he were an entirely different person from high school. "Take care, Shawn."

"Hi, baby." Her mom came and hugged her. "How was your flight?"

"It was okay," she said, returning the hug. "Hi, Dad." She hugged him as well. It was so nice to feel their warmth. Anne had to fight back the tears that were forming. She didn't want to let go of her family.

Her dad grabbed her pink, flowered suitcases. "Come on. Let's go. Are you hungry?"

Anne was starting to people-watch, hoping Kate wasn't here. "I could eat, but not the supper club." She felt such shame telling her dad that. Anne was tired, hungry, and jet-lagged. She just wanted to eat before showering and take it easy the night before she started her project.

Her dad gave an understanding frown, but nodded. "I understand, but eventually you are going to run into her."

"I know, Dad. I just can't do it right now." Anne took her phone out to text Alex she'd made it back home. They decided to eat at Marty's, which actually made her feel a bit homier. Things hadn't changed much and the food tasted like it did back in high school. "How's work, Dad?"

"Five more years until I retire, but other than that, it's going well," he told her before biting into his chicken sandwich. "How are you holding up?"

"I'm fine," Anne was moving around pieces of her salad. Although, she knew her parents didn't believe her.

"Honey," her mom emphasized. "It's not good to hold things in."

Anne knew she was right. Although there wasn't anything she could tell her mom that came to mind. "I know." It was all that came out.

"We ran into Kate the other day. She always asks about you," her mom, Willow, told her.

Her dad chimed in, "When was the last time you talked to her?"

"Kale's funeral," Anne shamefully admitted. "She sends me boxes with stuff, like Kale's Iron Man picture during the race and other things."

"She told us she's tried calling you but you won't return her messages." Willow's voice almost had a tone of disappointment to it.

"I just...I can't face her." Anne instinctively made sure she wasn't around. "Not right now."

Her dad spoke in his tone which meant he had to say something that needed to be heard. "You're going to have to at some point; we are in a small town."

"Dad, if there is anything I'm positive of, it's that." Anne knew he was right. There was no doubt she would have to face her. The thought of it just made Anne put her fork down.

To Anne's surprise, after she took a shower, she got a sudden burst of energy. After she was settled into her old room her mom let her borrow the car. Alex had Anne's car and was going to drive it home after she cleaned up as much as she could in DC. Anne drove to the church where it was beaten up pretty bad. There was graffiti on the doors and walls, windows smashed, and weeds growing in between the cracks of the steps and sidewalk. Anne sure wished she had Alex here or Komptin to keep her company. However, if Alex ever said anything repeatedly to her, it was to go to any church ground to protect herself from the Dark.

Anne took out the keys and opened the door. The sound of the church door opening echoed throughout the hallway. She went directly into the main congregation to see pews knocked over. Up on the wall was an upside-down cross that seemed to point to an altar. As she approached it, she felt a cold shiver down her spine as she noticed blood was on the top of it. There was animal fur with teeth mixed in a pile on the floor. The realtor had told her she had an analysis done to make sure it wasn't human.

Anne felt a small animal brush against her leg. "Jesus," she said as she lifted her leg.

"Do you think he is still here?" A voice from behind her asked.

Anne turned around to see a man in his thirties. He was a light brown-skinned man with a shaved baldhead. He was wearing a dark blue suit coat with maroon tie. He carried a bag with him that looked old. "I would like to hope so."

"It's still a house of God, regardless of what was done to it," the man said as he looked around the massive room.

"Yes, I suppose so. Can I help you?" Anne cautiously asked.

"No, I just saw the car out front and was hoping it wasn't a bad thing." He bent over and picked up a pew to put it in its normal position. He sat down on it. Anne wasn't sure, but he seemed to give a small prayer. That made her feel a little bit safer.

"I would hate to kick someone out of a church, but I don't know the extent of the damage," Anne told him. "I'm here for a site survey."

The man nodded, "I understand." He got up. "It truly looks like it was a beautiful building during it's time."

The man had a peaceful nature to him with a face of kindness. Anne thought the man was innocent enough. He had a wedding ring on, so he was a family man of some sort. If he was a Demon, he couldn't hurt her here. "If you would like to see the rest of the church, I wouldn't mind an escort to make sure there is no one in here."

"I am armed," he informed Anne unexpectedly.

Anne's nerves shot up. His hand moved slowly into his inner pocket to show Anne a badge with government credentials. Anne slowly walked up to him, emphasizing that she didn't trust him. She studied the man before going peeking at the identification. "You're CIA? INT Weston Mallory, is it?"

"You can call me, Weston, I'm not a full out agent, but Intelligence Division," he said putting his creds back in his pocket.

"What are you doing here?"

"I'm looking into all past dealings with the F.O.R. This building was theirs before the Catholic Church repurchased it." Weston did another look around the building. It was almost as if he was disappointed in what had happened to it.

"No offense, Weston, but isn't that a job for the FBI? CIA is for foreign matters." Anne sat down on the pew in front of him.

Weston was a bit shocked, "Yes, you are correct. I'm on loan to a task force office since the F.O.R. has locations all over the world."

"I didn't know they were that big." Anne wasn't surprised at that though. Considering the source of influence and money the F.O.R. had, it was no surprise how far spread they were around the world.

"And appeared out of nowhere, but it seems as if they were always there," he told her. "How'd you know about the roles of the agencies?"

"My sister-in-law's boyfriend is in Homeland Security," she let him know.

"Ah, that makes sense." He got up to stretch out his back. "Well, would you like me to walk ahead of you in case there is someone here?"

Anne nodded. "I would, thank you."

***

Alex was snuggled up to Kameron in bed lying underneath the covers. His arm gently held her as he played with her black, woven hair. Alex couldn't help but think on what they were going to do once she got transferred, transferred back home, ugh, with Father Carl. Nevertheless, Alex wasn't the only one with something on their mind. Kameron seemed like he was staring off into space a lot.

"Something on your mind?" he asked her as he just stared into the wall.

"I was about to ask you the same thing," she smiled up at him.

He looked over at the clock. "It's getting late." He kissed her. "Can we have lunch tomorrow?"

"Where?"

"Your choice," he told her.

"Pick me up around noon?" she smiled. "I should get going."

Kameron nodded with a smile. "Where are you headed?"

Alex knew it always felt like Kameron needed to know in case something happened to her. Almost a safety net of some sorts for her. She always hid from him that if she died using her powers, she would go to the stars. It was something she could never tell him for some reason. That was her way of protecting him she guessed.

"The docks." As she got out of bed, she turned around to see him sitting up. His body twitched from his stitches from the stabbing he took. She wished she could just sleep in his arms, being held tight in his embrace. There was no way she could; she had a job to do. The Dark was out there and, as a Lite Sentry, it was up to her to stop them. "I drove by there the other day and sensed a stronger presence, so naturally…" She moved her head side to side.

Kameron was always amazed by the strength she showed. She never let fear overtake her perception of life. No matter what, she was Alex. Kameron smiled at his girlfriend as he watched her get dressed. His girlfriend? She was much more to him than that. He watched her put on her black pants and dark blue long-sleeved shirt. The leather vest she wore was evident of being worn down from her battles with the Dark. A genuine smile that he could not hide emerged as she put on her dark makeup on her pale face.

Alex turned to him once she had her hair tied back. "How do I look?" Alex asked him with her soft face glowing in the moonlight. "What?" she asked shyly with Kameron staring.

"Nothing, I just had a problem, and the answer was right in front of me." He got out of bed and put his bathrobe on. "I'll walk you to the door." Komptin came up to them and he petted him, roughing him up a bit. "Be safe, come home alive." He kissed her goodbye.

"I'll see you at lunch." She caught herself smiling in return.

***

"You piece of shit, seriously?" The Infiltrator ran from Alex towards the docks. Alex lost sight of it in the shadows of the buildings. Komptin was sniffing the air hoping to find a trail. "Can Infiltrators swim?" It would seem Komptin didn't know the answer to that one either. "A lot of help you are," she teased him.

The two of them walked towards the docks where she saw the outline of a man in a jean jacket and a knit cap. He turned to the soldiers of the Lite and flashed his red eyes powered by the Dark.

"Damn it." Alex lit her fist as she took off running. "Go after the beast, I'll take care of Popeye."

Komptin ran after the Infiltrator as the Demon charged Alex. It hissed just before the two collided by shoulder-tackling Alex into a fishing shack. She fell into a web of ropes with the Demon on top of her. He continued to punch her in the face with happy fury. Alex managed to get her feet onto his chest to push him off her. The glass broke as he flew out the window, which gave Alex the time needed to get herself out of the tangle of ropes.

She formed a knife with Lite and cut free of the ropes before jumping out the window after the Demon. It managed to make it to one of the fishing boats docked on the pier. He turned around to see she entrapped him on the boat. The two of them stared at each other before he calmly walked out. They approached each other as the two of them both flashed their eyes before starting to exchange punches.

The Demon kicked Alex in the side and dropped her to the ground. Alex felt it grab her hair to throw her into the captain's cabin window. "Did that hurt!?" The Demon called out to her. "Because that looked like it hurt." Alex came out of the cabin with her fists lit and charged the Demon. She found an opening to punch the Demon under his chin causing him to stagger backward. An advantage came from the situation which allowed her to pick him up to throw him onto the ground. Alex jumped off the banister of the boat while forming a knife in hopes to stab into the Demon.

The Demon moved out of the way, and she fell through the boat into the deck below. She landed in a massive pile of small bait. It was as if she was bathing in the slimy fish. "Ugh!" She stood up to walk out of the bait room. Alex lost her footing and fell back into the pile of fish. Multiple baitfish managed to get down her shirt. The cold slime of the fish made Alex shiver.

To make sure she didn't fall again, she started to crawl on her hands and knees out of the bait room. Once she got out of the bait room, she stood up to assess the situation. Alex made it to the deck of the boat where Komptin joined her. He had a bit of blood coming from a scratch on his shoulder but other than that, he seemed fine. Komptin came up to her but stopped in his tracks to smell the air and made a face at Alex before turning away. "Not a word from you," she told him.

Alex made it back to the church as everyone started to get in for the day. Father Richard and Megan were talking in the parking lot with coffee in their hands when they both saw Alex approach. The smell coming off Alex was obviously protruding in their direction.

"What the hell happened to you?" Megan pinched her nose. "You are covered in...something." Megan took out some perfume out of her purse and sprayed it in Alex's direction.

Father Richard was trying not to laugh. "How was your night, Alex?" The smell was foul enough to make them sick to their stomach.

"I'm never going to get this out, am I?" Alex still had fish slime on her clothes.

Father Richard shook his head. "Nope. Look on the bright side, you get to get a new outfit. I'll see you inside." He found amusement in it as she walked away.

"I hope you shower before you come to work," Megan said with a face of disgust.

Alex stopped in her tracks to turn to Megan. "What a great idea, I would have never thought of that. Thanks, Megan." Alex wrapped her arms around Megan for a big hug. A smile generated on Alex's face as she left to take a shower.

Alex couldn't shower long enough to get *that* stink out. The smell mixed with the steam of the shower seemed to amplify the odor. It was as if someone was boiling fish in the bathroom. Alex got dressed after putting her hunting clothes in a plastic bag to throw away. She sprayed a couple of extra pumps of body spray on before heading off to work. It didn't seem to help.

Days like this she wished Anne were still here so she could vent about her night. She made it upstairs and grabbed an Apollo from the fridge. The chair next to her desk moved before she sat down, causing her to crash to the floor. The next thing Alex knew, she was on the ground. She crawled from the floor to the top of her desk for her Apollo. It was a little taste of happiness, she desperately needed. This day was not going well. Kameron sent a laughing image after texting him about falling off her chair at work.

Father Richard came from his office down the hall. He opened the door to see Alex rubbing her head. "Alex, you wanna talk about it?"

Alex knew that meant about her hunt. She nodded and locked her computer to join Father Richard. "I just have to use the bathroom and I will be right there." She carefully got out of her chair to go to the bathroom.

Misluna couldn't believe it. Alex left her open can of Apollo sitting on the desk. There was no better opportunity to do this than now. She knew the Cardinal was out and Father Richard was with Alex. It was as if it was meant to be. Misluna reached into her pocket and grabbed the vile. The glowing, green liquid caused an evil smile to blossom. "This is going to be so much fun to watch."

She walked over to the door to make sure no one was coming. Misluna carefully walked up to the Sentry's desk. She had to take a moment to calm her excitement before putting the mixture into the Apollo drink. The liquid started to fizz a little when the mixture was added. Now, all she had to do was wait for the show. The anticipation was something she could hardly contain.

It seemed like an eternity before Alex came back from talking to Father Richard. She sat back down at her desk. The first thing Alex did was drink the rest of her Apollo. "Oh, that's good." Alex studied the can. She turned to Megan. "It's the little things, you know? It really was a rough night." Megan tried everything not to laugh.

Alex's face showed that something was wrong. She looked around before grabbing her hair to bring it to her nose. "Kameron is picking me up to go to lunch. I think I better take another shower."

"Whatever gets that smell out of here," Megan told her as her nerves shot up. There was a possibility she would use the bathroom before leaving church grounds. It was a gamble that now presented itself. She did have that back up, just in case this didn't work.

Alex finished her second shower to find Kameron coming into the church. "Hey how was your night?" He asked her as he came into the building.

"Don't ask, damn thing got away," she told him, as she nonchalantly smelled her hair again before coming over to kiss him.

Kameron, in a supportive calming voice, said, "You'll get it next time."

"You look happy." Alex noticed his body language had changed from this morning. He almost looked as if he had life all figured out. "What's going on?"

"I'll tell you at lunch." He kissed her. "Don't worry, it's something good. What are you in the mood for?"

"You pick."

"How about fish?" Kameron innocently suggested.

If Alex didn't know better, she thought he did that on purpose. "No fish, red meat."

"I'm good with that." He grabbed her hand with a smile of affection. "Come on. Let's walk 'til we find a place."

Alex peaked her head into the lobby office. "Megan, I'm going to lunch."

Megan smiled. "Have fun."

Kameron and Alex walked out of the church building from on top of the stairs. "How's Anne doing?"

Alex laughed as Kameron seemed to have an extra skip in his step. "Fine, she met a CIA officer, Weston, something, I think," Alex told him. "Know him?"

"Name sounds familiar. I rarely work with the CIA unless FLOTUS is going overseas," Kameron explained. "Ready to go?" He seemed to swing his arms like a little kid.

"You're happy." She smiled in return. They both walked down the steps of the church on this very clear, sunny day in the city. They got onto the sidewalk when Kameron felt Alex let go of his hand. He turned around to see what was keeping Alex.

"You okay?" Kameron was a bit concerned.

"I think so. I just got an upset stomach all of sudden." Alex put her hand on her stomach. "I'm probably just hungry." Alex took another couple of steps before stopping again. She held her stomach tighter. "Kameron, something's wrong."

Kameron turned around to have Alex vomit all over him. She dropped to the ground screaming in pain as she crouched into the fetal position. Father

Richard came running out of the church with Megan trailing behind him. Father Richard ran to Kameron. "What happened?" He gently put his hands on Alex.

"I don't know." Kameron's fear was evident at first but then became calm and stoic. "She said she had an upset stomach and then started screaming."

Alex flung her head back as she arched her back screaming in pain. Then immediately went into the fetal position grabbing her stomach. "Alex." Father Richard grabbed his cell phone to call the doctor.

Kameron took his jacket off to cover Alex as onlookers were starting to gather around. He tried with all his might to keep her from convulsing. Alex continued to scream in pain as she was moving about. Tears now were dropping from the pain. "Make it stop," she pleaded to him. "Just make it stop." Alex's body twisted more as she screamed in pain. Alex grabbed onto Kameron's suit coat to pull him closer to her. "Kameron," she begged. "Listen to me. Shoot me, you hear me? Shoot me," she quickly said as she quivered. Her body started to fling again as she screamed in pain. Alex went for Kameron's gun but he pushed her hand away as she screamed again.

"Alex." Kameron pulled her into his chest, holding her tightly. She tensed her body up as if it was a last-ditch effort. Her grip was tight as she just started to mumble slowly to herself. Her eyes remained forcefully shut as her body remained tense. Alex held onto Kameron's shirt, forcing her

146

face into his chest with Kameron's hand on the back of her head for support. "Father, look at this." A mixture of black, red, and Lite blue fluid moved underneath her skin before the black overtook it. Alex just continued to painfully cry into Kameron's chest.

CHAPTER FIVE

Lights and sirens were blaring from Kameron's BMW as he weaved through traffic trying to get Alex to the hospital as fast as possible. Kameron was never so focused. They got her admitted quickly and sent her up to a room supported by the Council of the Religions. Doctor Smithon was reading her medical file as her vitals were being checked by the nurse. "What's her blood pressure?" He was trying to hide the fact he was confused but failing.

"Eighty-nine over sixty-five," she said. "Pulse rate is fifty-eight."

The doctor, who was also a priest, rubbed his face. "What did she eat this morning?"

Father Richard spoke up, "As far as I know she skipped breakfast and had one of her energy drinks. She may have picked something up on her way back home, but other than that, I don't know."

"That doesn't explain her vitals, if anything, her pulse should be going up." Dr. Smithon felt the side of her face and then forehead. "What's her temperature?"

"101.4," the nurse replied.

The doctor put his hand on her hand. "She's cold to the touch." He opened up her hospital gown to view the stab wound from Sanah. "Any issues with her wound?"

Kameron contributed, "She hasn't complained about it, but you know Alex."

"Yes," he said as he just studied Alex for any reaction. When he touched her stomach, she winced in pain but still kept her eyes shut.

Father Richard was worried when he asked, "When was the last time she slept?"

Doctor Smithon reviewed her chart. "When she got put into surgery to seal her wound from her attack while in college. We put her under and then Conduit of Lite put her to sleep for a night."

"Well why can't we do that now? She's in obvious pain." Kameron was getting a little irritated.

"We don't even know what's wrong," Doctor Smithon explained. "You put a Lite Sentry under, it is a huge risk. I was amazed she even came out of the first surgery."

"The Conduit of Lite put her under the second time, can't she do it again?" Father Richard was now getting irritated at his helplessness as well.

"I don't know if that's wise. We know nothing about what is happening to her," the doctor explained. "There's nothing I can medically find wrong with her. I'm afraid she's got to be awake to battle whatever it is that is happening to her." He called the nurse over. "Let's see if we can ease the pain a little bit." He gave her some prescription orders.

Kameron walked over to her bed in his vomit-soaked shirt. "Alex, you are the strongest person I know, you can beat this." He sat down next to her as her face was twitched from pain and tears dropped down her cheek. Kameron gently grabbed her hand and kissed it.

The doctor motioned for Father Richard to join him out in the hallway. The only ones that stayed in the room were Komptin and Kameron. The German shepherd had a look of worry on his face mixed with anger on what was happening to her. Kameron got up and sat next to Alex in a chair. He's been trying to get ahold of Anne by calling and texting her, but there was no answer.

"Kameron," a groggy Alex mustered out.

He immediately turned his attention to her. "I'm right here."

"What happened?" She started to wake out of her daze.

"We don't know, you just started screaming in pain and we brought you here," Kameron told her. "Do you remember anything?"

"Everything." She wiped her eyes from crying. "I feel weird."

"I'll go get the doctor." Alex sat up feeling a little stronger but not too much. In service against the Dark she'd been hit, kicked, and stabbed, but this pain was something she had never felt before. It covered her body entirely.

The doctor came rushing back in to check on Alex as her vitals were improving. "This is good. I wish I could say it was my doing."

"I'm feeling better." Alex scanned the hospital room with confusion before staring out the window. "Am I in a church or something?"

"No." Father Richard got out his phone to call the Cardinal. "You're in a hospital downtown."

"Okay." She intently stared out the window. Alex turned to Komptin as if studying him, then around the room, and finally back out the window.

"What's wrong Alex? Is it the Dark?" Father Richard asked.

Alex shook her head and then winced as if there was more pain. There was a knock on the door and Kameron went to answer it. To his surprise, it was Celestial. She had golden tears dropping from her face. "Where is Alexandria? I cannot sense her. She is not in the stars."

"She's right here. We were scared for a bit but she seems to be getting out of it," Kameron showed her where Alex was laying down.

"Kameron, who is it?" Alex tried to move her head to see who it was.

Celestial's face turned to a mother's concern. "She is in this room? Excuse me, everyone please."

Everyone bowed as they all left the room. She grabbed Kameron's hand. "You need to stay." She calmly walked up to Alex. "Alexandria."

Alex was shocked to see Celestial. She stared at her in confusion, and then turned her attention back to outside. Lastly, she looked to Komptin before turning back to Celestial. Alex broke down crying.

Kameron stepped forward but the Guardians of the Conduit stopped him. "What's wrong, Alex?"

Alex turned to Celestial with silent tears streaming down. "I can't feel you. I can't sense the stale of the Dark." Now her crying was uncontrollable. "I can't feel the warmth of the Lite. I can't feel anything."

***

Anne decided to call it an early weekend. The church renovation had taken a lot out of her. The office in the house was welcomingly quiet; enough to get some work done. The biggest problem was trying to find a legit contractor. One accomplishment she achieved was getting the nerve to contact the Council.

Father Partinello tried to ease her mind regarding the loss of the records and the Dark texts. She appreciated the sentiment but in the back of her mind, she knew it was her fault. It was a beautiful afternoon, so Anne decided to take advantage of it. She got on her shoes to go for a walk down to a creek down the street from her house.

It was a nice this time of year. It hadn't been too hot yet, the birds were active, and it just seemed peaceful. The creek was a little high but nothing to be concerned about. It only flooded once that she could remember. She sat down on the road watching the water move under the bridge. To her surprise, there was a mother deer and her fawn getting a drink of water upriver. It was a peaceful sight, and Anne wanted to take a picture of them, but she soon realized that she'd forgotten her phone. The two deer bolted, alerted to a truck stopping down the road.

"Anne?" A big man came out of the truck.

"Dan?" Anne got up and gave him a big hug. "It's so good to see you."

"You too," Dan said, smiling after letting go of her. The passenger side of the truck opened to see Jessica, who was obviously pregnant.

"Hello, Anne." Jessica was waddling towards her. The two of them started to date in college when she woke up one night from partying a little too hard next to Dan.

"Oh my, Jessica." Anne hugged her. "So nice to see you again. May I?" Anne showed Jessica her hand.

"I'm a house. You can, he's kicking up a storm in there." Jessica laughed as she led Anne's hand onto her stomach. "I need Dan to grease the side of the doors just to get through them."

"No, you're beautiful." Anne took her hand off Jessica when she felt the baby move. "Congratulations to you both."

"Thank you." Dan was glowing with a smile. "How have you been doing?"

Anne knew where he was going with this. "I'm fine."

"Kate would be so glad to see you," Dan told her. "She talks about you and Kale quite a bit."

Anne got a little tense. "Yes, I haven't seen her yet."

"Dan sees her more than he sees me," Jessica joked.

"You do?" Anne was shocked.

"I thought she told you. I've been managing the supper club for a bit now, and then I'm going to buy it at the end of next year. It was all her idea," Dan explained.

Anne felt awkward asking, "How is she doing?"

Dan's tone in his voice dropped a bit. "She was rough for a bit, but she's getting a lot better. It would be good for her to see you."

"Hey, Dan, we need to get going, baby checkup in twenty minutes." Jessica showed him the time. "I'm sorry Anne, but we have to go. Can you have dinner tonight?"

"I can," Anne eagerly said. "I guess we can meet at the club."

Dan nodded his head. "I'm working tonight, but I think that would be a good idea."

Anne agreed but with reservations. "I'll see you tonight." Anne watched them take off so she decided to walk a little more to ease her mind. A group of bicyclists were coming her way so she moved on to the shoulder of the road. One of them stopped to remove his helmet.

"Hi, Anne." Shawn grabbed a water bottle from his bike. "What are you doing out here?" He unbuckled his helmet to wipe off the sweat.

"Just going for a walk. I didn't know you liked bicycling." Anne was admiring his bike. "Nice bike."

"Thanks. It's a good workout, I've been doing this for a while now," Shawn told her. "I couldn't pass up this beautiful day."

"It really is a nice day." Anne gazed up at the sky. "I really should get going. It was nice seeing you again."

"A couple of us are going out for drinks, if you would like to go?" Shawn asked as he put on his helmet. "It would be great to catch up with you."

Anne couldn't help but think of Kale from the sound of Shawn clipping his bike shoes into the pedals. "Thanks, but I'm having dinner with Dan and Jessica tonight," Anne told him. "Maybe some other time."

"I'll make sure to keep my calendar clear. Take care, Anne." He gave her a kind smile before taking off on his bike. "I doubt they are going to wait for me. Hope to see you soon."

Anne thought that he seemed to have matured some. There was genuineness in his actions. The rest of the walk was nice. It was the perfect temperature and calming atmosphere. She didn't know how long she was gone before making it back to the house. She went straight to the kitchen for a drink of water. Out the kitchen window was a pair of mourning doves eating seed from the feeder she'd filled earlier.

"Hey honey." Willow came in to rub her shoulder. "How was your walk?"

"Nice. Ran into a couple of people from high school." She was trying to hide the fact she was feeling down. For some reason her mind was thinking of the night Kale crossed the finish line in his Iron Man race. She was afraid the memory of that feeling of the two of them together would fade away.

Her mom recognized her daughter's state and just put her arm around her. Anne placed her head on her shoulder allowing a single tear to drop. Bless her mom's heart, she didn't say anything at all. Anne just stayed in her mother's embrace for a minute or two. "Anne honey, your phone has been ringing quite a bit."

Anne looked around for it, "I forgot to take it with me."

"It's in the living room on the end table," her mom said. "You want a snack?"

"Yogurt would be great." Anne went on to get the phone where she had multiple messages from Kameron and Father Richard.

***

"This is the best part." Misluna was over Gron's shoulder showing him the security feed from the front of the church. The video was showing Alex arching her back in pain from the poison. "Here, this is where she begged Kameron to shoot her. I tried everything to keep from laughing."

Gron couldn't help but smile. "I wish I could have been there."

Misluna got in between Gron and his desk. She kissed and started biting his neck. "It was so awesome watching her suffer. Made me kind of…" Gron picked her up and slammed her on top of the desk with force.

"She won't have any idea on our plan to bring our Master back. She won't see it coming." Gron bit so hard into Misluna's neck that it drew blood.

***

Alex couldn't help but just stare out the window overlooking the city. It seemed so empty, not cold, not warm, but just…nothing. It was such a hollowness not being able to feel anything. The only thing she could compare it to was purgatory. Maybe she was dead. Death would be better than what she was going through now.

It was as if a part of her had died. She tried shaking off the comparison of feeling handicapped. Others had it worse than her, but she just couldn't bother to care. People have the choice to push the warmth of the Lite away. She had it ripped from her, the connection severed. Her hand ignited the neon blue mist. The ability of her strength and Lite were still available, but she couldn't sense a thing. Right now, Alex would settle for the ability to just sense the Dark.

Komptin was still in the room even though she couldn't feel him at all. His sad eyes stared at her. The severed connection Alex received from the Lite probably made him sad as well since he couldn't feel her. She felt like an abomination. Thinking back, she didn't know how this could happen. There was nothing out of the ordinary about her days. Maybe God was punishing her for not being a better Sentry; perhaps she just kept on disappointing Him.

She got word that Anne couldn't get a flight until tomorrow, but by then she would be back home in the church. Maybe she could feel the Lite once she was inside. Then it hit her. She was in a hospital, so there must be a chapel in the building. The nurse came in to check up on her.

"Feeling better I see." She came in to check on Alex.

Alex forced a smile, but it was obviously fake. "Excuse me, but where is the chapel?"

"Down the hall, to the right," she said. "I'll make sure your bedding is switched out while you go."

"Thanks." It would make sense for her to be close to the chapel. Alex moved toward the door, her stomach and muscles aching with every step. Komptin was beside her, staying closer than usual. Alex walked out of the room, and it felt as if all eyes were on her. Her pulse quickened; her throat became dry. She didn't know if there was a Demon here. How could she? There was no way to tell if the Dark was nearby.

She grabbed the entryway to the door as if trying to maintain her balance. "Are you okay?" The nurse touched her on the back. Alex screamed and turned around with a glowing fist in the air ready to punch her. The nurse hid her face and Alex quickly diminished her Lite before anyone saw. The only redeeming feature she had was the nurse was cleared by the council. "I'm sorry," Alex told her. "I'm so sorry."

"It's okay." The nurse regained her composure. "Go for your walk."

Alex's heart began to race as she ventured out to the hallway. As she passed people, it was as if everyone was a potential Demon staring at her. Komptin stayed by her side, almost guiding her to the chapel. She made it to the small room with only five pews. Up ahead was the cross. Alex felt as if it was staring down at her in judgement. She shut the door behind her before sitting down in the front pew.

Since she became a Lite Sentry, any house of worship always had a sense of warmth. It almost felt as if it was a protective blanket over her, but now she felt nothing. She closed her eyes and prayed, if He even could hear her silent plea. Alex heard the door open to the congregation to see Devine in civilian clothes standing there.

"Are you okay?" Devine asked coldly.

Alex didn't understand why Devine seemed so distant. Perhaps because she was leery because she couldn't feel Alex's Lite anymore. "I didn't know you were there. How are you?"

Devine stayed at the entryway. "I..." She stopped herself. "I wanted to, I just…"

"You're welcome." Alex forced a smile.

Devine just concurred with her head. The purple-haired angel turned around to leave.

"Hey Devine," Alex called out to her.

"Yes," the angel of the Lite turned to the Sentry.

"Did God send you? Did He answer me?"

"I was right behind you, following you in the hallway," she told her.

It was a gut punch. This answer wasn't what Alex wanted. "Can you feel me?"

Devine stared at her and without expression, "No."

The next morning Alex sat in the back seat with Kameron. Declan was driving with Father Richard in the passenger seat. Komptin left in the middle of the night probably to go on a hunt. Alex just stared out the window at all the people on the sidewalk. There was no way for her to know if the Dark was among them.

They pulled into the back parking lot. The Cardinal was there with Anne. The bags underneath her eyes showed she had traveled all night. Alex was still a bit sore when she got out of the car. Anne cautiously walked up to her and gave her a gentle hug.

"I'm fine." Alex put one arm around Anne. She turned to Kameron. "Can I call you tonight? I just want to go to my room."

Kameron was disappointed she didn't want his support, but he also knew she was feeling vulnerable. "I understand. I'll call you tonight."

Alex didn't really give an acknowledgment; she just stared at the church. She closed her eyes hoping she would feel the Lite. The warmth should have been felt once they walked through the gate to get onto the property. When she got inside, she took a moment to feel the warmth of the Lite. There was no feeling. She couldn't feel anything. "Father." she turned around.

Father Richard came to her. "Take your time. Don't rush anything."

"Alex, do you need anything?" Anne asked her with a worried look on her face.

Alex just stared at the painting of Cara fighting Infiltrators. She concentrated on Osiah, wishing he were here. "No. I'm going to rest." She started to close the door but stopped. "Thanks." Then shut the door behind her.

Anne walked with Father Richard down the hall. "Do you think she'll be okay?'

"I don't know," he responded. "She not only lost the ability to sense the Dark but lost the comfort of connecting to the Lite. It acted as a balance for her and gave her comfort. Now, it was suddenly taken away. I don't know where to go from here."

***

"Kameron, the Director wants to see you as soon as you come in," the secretary said, rolling her eyes. "He's not happy."

"Is he ever?" Kameron took a deep breath before he knocked on the door, "Sir, you wanted to see me?"

"Shut the door behind you," he coldly demanded. Kameron shut the door. "I'm denying

161

your emergency leave and docking you two days' pay."

"What? Why? I put it under an emergency doctor's visit," Kameron explained.

Director Channel sat back in his chair with irritation. "Your girlfriend was the one in the hospital, right?"

Kameron responded, "Yes, sir."

"She's not family, so you can't use family leave. You were not the one that went to the doctor, so you can't use sick leave. You didn't give a 48-hour notice so you can't use annual leave. You made a very poor decision, and it will cost you by having a letter of reprimand in your file." Director Channel handed him the memorandum. "You are just lucky it didn't affect an operation."

"Yes, Sir." Kameron could normally tell how he portrayed himself. Even in stressful situations, he knew he kept a calm demeanor, but he knew he wasn't hiding his emotions in this position.

"Look, Kameron, you have the potential of being a good agent," the director said from behind his desk. "But you have to realize we are protecting the wife of the most powerful man in the world. That comes before anything."

"I thought I was being transferred," Kameron asked in hopes he was staying.

"You're not gone yet," he sternly told him. "I need you to accept your assignment by the end of the month. If you don't, the Secret Service will no longer require your services. You can leave now to think it over."

Kameron didn't know how to respond, the only thing he knew was that he was worried about Alex. He stepped out of the office to see the secretary on a government job website. "Are you looking for a new job, Pam?"

"I'm not putting up with him for the next five years. The Director of White House Operations told me his secretary is leaving. It's a lateral move, but I don't have to put up with him." She pointed her pen to the closed office door.

That was the final sign Kameron needed. It was so much clearer now where he was needed.

***

Alex was just playing with her French fries by dunking them in and out of the ketchup, but not eating them. Her burger only had a couple of bites in it. Kameron had finished his boneless chicken with mixed vegetables. He studied his girlfriend's actions, knowing she wasn't herself. The worst part was there was nothing he could do to make her feel any better. It tore him up to see her in such misery. "Not hungry?"

"Not really," she softly replied.

"There's a first. Do you want me to get you something else?" He asked her as he went to grab her food container to put it in the garbage. "I'll take this out on my way home."

"I can do it," she sharply snapped at him.

"It's no big deal, my car is right next to the dumpster," he let her know.

"Whatever. If it's an issue for you if you don't do it, then knock yourself out." She handed him the box. She crawled to her bed and turned the television on to some reality show.

"Do you want me to get you anything, water, Apollo?" Kameron sat back on the bed next to her.

"No," she said sharply as she stared at the television.

Kameron could obviously tell she was in a difficult place. This was not a good time, but he was on a time crunch to get an answer from his director. "Hey, there's something I need to talk to you about?"

Alex just moved her eyes at him. "Yeah."

Kameron got up from the bed. "Are you sure I can't get you anything?"

"Will you just man up and tell me what's on your mind?" Alex was starting to get annoyed.

Kameron was now getting a little agitated with Alex, but he reminded himself that she was going through a lot right now. He needed to tell her he was going to quit the Secret Service for her. Maybe he should just do it, and not put that on her. "Never mind, it's my issue."

"Stop doing that, you don't need to protect me. Just tell me what's on your mind." Alex was determined to get out what Kameron was thinking.

Kameron calmed himself down before saying, "I just got transferred to San Diego."

Alex's anger suddenly burst out. "Really, you just dropped this on me, now?"

"You pushed it," he snapped back. "I haven't…"

Alex didn't hear anything he was saying. "When do you leave?"

"What do you mean?"

"Well, you're obviously going to go," Alex barked at him.

Kameron put up his hands. "I haven't decided that yet." That statement came out a little harsher than he wanted it to. He closed his eyes for a quick second and pushed down his angst before going forth with the conversation.

"What's there to decide?" She just turned her head to avoid eye contact with him. "Why wouldn't you go?"

Kameron was shocked at her question. "Well, for starters, you."

Alex jumped out of bed and pointed to him. "Don't you dare put that on me." On the counter was her medicine. She took the prescribed amount with some water.

With a calm voice, Kameron replied, "I'm not putting that on you, I'm just saying I got transfer orders to San Diego."

Alex slammed her glass of water on the vanity dresser. "So, what are you telling me?"

"I don't want to break up. I lo…" he started to say before she interrupted him.

"It happens, Kameron. People break up all the time because of work. And besides, what were you thinking was going to happen with us?" Alex turned to him with her hands on her waist. "Seriously, you never thought about it?"

"What?" Kameron did not like where this conversation was going. It wasn't often he was shocked to the point of not being able to think clearly. His mind went blank trying to think of a way out of this situation on a positive note. The feeling of falling down a deep, dark, cavern entered his mind. That is what this conversation felt like.

"I can never be your perfect wife. I can't give you children; I will not be in the same bed with you when you wake up. Most of the time you won't know I'm alive come morning," Alex preached to him. "You're not capable of handling that."

"I've managed so far." His face lost all expression with his voice remaining calm and collective. "I'm stronger than you think. I'm not a child. You don't have to protect me from your life." It felt as if Kameron was in a murky swamp sinking.

"You're not that strong." Alex coldly stared at him. "I was never long-term. I'm not the type of girl who goes long-term. Ask anybody from my high school."

Kameron, for the first time, didn't know what to say. He just remained calm. "So, this is it? That is what you're saying?"

"It was inevitable," she told him. "It's better we just part ways now before you get too attached. Clean break and carefree when you go to San Diego. You're more of a blonde girl type anyways."

"You're breaking up with me?" Kameron asked in a calm voice, as he wanted to hear flat out that is what she wanted.

"It's better that you just leave." She laid back on the bed to watch television. "Just go," she said softly.

It seemed like an eternity for Kameron. He stood there dumbfounded. "If that's what you want." Kameron calmly grabbed his coat. Komptin walked up to Kameron with sadness. He petted him goodbye and knelt down to him, "Take care of her." He flashed eyes affirming. "Take care of yourself, Alex. Be careful." He made no expression as he went out to his car.

She turned to the door when he quietly shut it, as a tear fell down her cheek.

***

Alex's body was feeling better, but she was cold, empty, and alone. She was in pajama bottoms and a long t-shirt that had the Secret Service on the back of it. The feeling of the church building seemed so frigid and vacant. The blanket around her was wrapped as tightly as possible when she walked into the congregation hall. She just stood in the middle of the aisle, trying to hold back the tears streaming down her face.

"Just because you cannot feel the Lite, does not mean it is not there," Celestial said behind her.

She turned her head to Celestial. "Does He even know I'm here?" Alex sat down next to the Conduit of Lite.

"Of course He does, Alexandria," Celestial had a teardrop from seeing her Sentry in so much pain.

"Can He sense me?" Alex pleaded.

Celestial didn't know how to answer her question. "Alexandria." She wrapped her arms around her.

"What's the point anymore?" Alex put her head on her shoulder.

Celestial was taken aback a bit. "What do you mean?"

"Lite Sentries. What is the point? What's the point of any of it?" Alex quietly said as she wiped tears from her face.

"Alexandria, tell me what happened." Celestial tried to comfort her.

"You don't know?" She tried to solicit an answer from her Godmother. "Can't you sense anything in me?"

"Just because I cannot sense you, does not mean I do not know you are in pain." Celestial failed in trying to comfort her. "I am still the Conduit of Lite. Alexandria, tell me, what is wrong?"

Alex just shook her head, crying. "Not this time. No one can help me."

CHAPTER SIX

"You broke up with him!" Anne yelled. The news of this break-up caused her to stop packing her suitcase to head back home. "When?"

Alex was acting as if she didn't care much about it by reading her phone. "Last week." Alex opened a can of Apollo to take a drink as she was petting Komptin on the hotel bed.

"And I had to find out from Kameron?" Anne scolded out of disappointment.

Alex tried to steer the conversation away from Kameron. "What time is your flight?"

"Alex, come on, what happened?" Anne insisted. She moved over to sit next to Alex on the bed.

"He got transferred to San Diego, that's it," Alex told her. "Long distance relationships don't work, so we broke it off. Why did he call you?"

"I was checking up to see how you were doing. He sounded upset. It took a good hour before he finally broke and told me what happened," Anne informed her. "He said he had a problem but it fixed itself. I pressured him into telling me what happened." Anne watched her friend scroll through her phone full out knowing she wasn't reading anything. "Wanna talk about it?"

"Nope," Alex quickly told her. "Come on, I'll take you to the airport"

After Alex dropped Anne at the airport, she went into work for the first time since her incident. Megan was sitting at her desk doing whatever it was she did to kill a day. Komptin followed her there and curled up on his dog bed that Kameron made him after their first date. Alex stared at it for a bit. "Do you want me to get rid of it?" Komptin lifted his head up and gave her a scowl. "Okay, okay."

"That must have been some stomach bug." Megan sat back in her chair with her feet up as if she was ready to enjoy this conversation. "I hope it wasn't contagious. Is Kameron feeling okay?"

A text message came in from Kameron on Alex's phone. It stated, "I don't know where we stand, friends...strangers, but I wanted to let you know I'm leaving tonight."

Alex didn't even log onto her computer before she got up. "We broke up, so you can dig your claws into him now." She got up and left with Komptin following her.

"That would be a bonus." Misluna smirked as she went back to her work.

Alex made it to the back of the church to get away from anyone who would happen to see her. She hopped on the outside banister to stare out into the city. Declan was escorting the Cardinal from their meeting with the Washington DC Police Chaplain about the shooting of Darius King. "Alex," Declan said as he waited for the Cardinal.

"Declan," Alex stared down at the sidewalk.

"Go on in, Declan," Cardinal Joe told him. Declan left as the Cardinal joined her on the

170

balcony banister. Both their feet were dangling over the edge. "That was a lot harder than I thought it was going to be."

"I don't want to talk about it," Alex sharply stated.

"Talk about what?" Cardinal Joe asked her.

"Nothing." Alex just continued to stare. They sat there for a while, neither of them saying a word. Alex finally spoke, "Do they teach you how to use silence in Cardinal school or something?"

"I don't know what you are talking about?" the Cardinal just stared out at the city.

"Nothing, just a memory about Cardinal Frank." Alex realized she came out here with nothing to drink.

Cardinal Joe handed her his coffee. "He surely is missed. He was a good man."

"Yeah," Alex softly said. "Lost a lot during that time." The sky was still daylight, but that didn't stop Alex from looking to Heaven. The two of them just sat there, not saying a word.

***

Anne spent the entire flight thinking of Alex. Guilt overpowered her over leaving her behind. She knew Alex was hurting but wouldn't open up about it. Anne came down the corridor of the airport not paying attention as her thoughts were still on Alex. The sheer shock that she and Kameron broke up was something Anne couldn't believe. The sound of Anne's name being called when she was walking to baggage claim grabbed her attention.

Shawn came down the hallway in a red safety vest carrying a radio. "Hey Anne, I thought that was you."

"Hello, Shawn," Anne replied to him. "How are you?"

"Oh, you know, some problems down on the tarmac with Scarlet Roberts coming into town," he told her as he walked with her to baggage claim. "I didn't know you left town again."

"There was an emergency back in DC I had to attend to." Anne told him.

"I hope everything is okay." Shawn stopped by a coffee stand. "Want anything?"

"Actually, I could go for a coffee," Anne took him up on the offer. "Thank you."

"Order anything you want," Shawn offered. "Charlie, just add it to my business account."

"Will do, Mr. Haywood." They both gave them their orders. Shawn had to answer his phone while the coffees were being made. He hung up the phone once the coffees were handed to them.

"Mr. Haywood?" Anne teased him.

"Well, it's amazing what one can do when shown focus." Shawn got a call over the radio that he was needed. "Always work. You look good, Anne." He gave her a smile.

"You do too, Shawn." Anne watched him go. Once she got to her car, she decided to go back to the church. There wasn't anything that needed to be done right away, but she wanted to see her project.

In addition, she thought she just needed to think about some stuff.

She pulled into the parking lot, where it looked as if it wasn't disturbed. The contracting service she hired for boarding up the windows was already done. It was nice that it was now secured. She walked around the building before undoing the padlock to get in. The main worship hall had someone standing in front of the stained-glass window. To Anne's surprise, it was Devine.

Anne never really saw the angel without Alex being nearby. "What are you doing here?"

"Is the Sentry okay?" she quickly asked.

"Physically, yes," Anne answered.

"Good," Devine said, heading out of the church. "That is all."

Anne thought Devine was a little bit more distant than usual. She tried to follow the angel, but she disappeared before Anne could catch up to her. Anne made it down to what would be her office. She felt a little selfish, but since she was here alone to deal with this, she was going to clean up her office first. An old desk had an upside down four carved into it. There were some papers scattered on the ground. Nothing seemed important, just some bills and invoices. There was a piece of paper with Father Tom's name on it that caught her attention.

"The priest is eliminated, Pure of Heart obtained," was written on the notepad. Anne thought back to the memory of how tragic those two nights were. Anne decided to keep that piece of paper, so she put it in her purse.

It was getting late when Anne was notified by her mom that dinner was going to be in an hour. She locked up the church and turned around to see, Weston Mallory, taking pictures of the church. "What are you doing?"

"Oh, I'm sorry, but I was just taking some pictures of the church for my report," he said. "Is that okay?"

"Doesn't bother me." Anne tugged on the padlock to make sure it was secure.

"Are you going to model?" He started teasing.

"No," Anne quickly replied.

"Then," he motioned for Anne to get out of the way.

"Oh, sorry." She stepped downstairs to stand next to him. The two of them both stared up at the church. "It really was a beautiful church. Are you religious?"

"I believe, but they are my own beliefs," he told her. "My father served Him ever since I can remember."

"Ah, preacher's kid," Anne concluded.

Weston gave a small laugh. "I guess you could say that."

"Hey, would you like to join me and some friends for dinner tomorrow night? Strictly platonic," Anne asked him.

"That sounds nice," He took out his phone. "What's your number?"

Anne gave him her number before joining her parents for dinner.

***

Alex was sitting in her room drinking an Apollo in the dark. The only light was a small crack in the curtains letting some sunshine in. She took a sip of her drink. The only sound in the room was the ice hitting against the glass. A knock came on the door; she just moved her eyes in fear it was Kameron.

"Alex," Father Richard called out to her.

"Just a minute." The light from opening the door made Alex block it out from her eyes. "Yah?"

"Are you okay?" Father Richard looked as if he was heading out for the night.

"I'm fine." She turned to sit back in her recliner. "I'm going to go on a hunt tonight."

"I don't think that is a good idea," the father told her.

Alex sighed out of frustration, "Father, I'll be fine."

"Let's just wait until next week, okay?" he offered.

"No, I think…" Alex started to say.

"Alex!" He raised his voice, which he was not happy about doing.

Alex succumbed to her defeat, but she didn't like it, and she made sure to show it. "Well, you stopped by for a reason."

Father Richard saw that her room was a bit messier than usual. Alex wasn't always the most organized person, but there seemed to be a system to it. This was her place to live so Father Richard felt like he couldn't really say anything. "I just wanted to check in. I understand you snapped at Megan today?" Father Richard moved some laundry from the bed to sit down.

Alex rolled her eyes. "All I did was tell her news that she was waiting to hear."

"I know that you have a hard time working with people you don't like," Father Richard said. "But you need to work on it, preferably sooner than later."

"Why?" She knew something bad was coming.

"Father Carl will be shadowing me until we all move to the remodeled church," he told her. "He starts tomorrow."

"And he still isn't cleared by the Council?" Alex took a sip of her drink.

"No," he said. "That means we need to be a little stricter on your cover."

Alex got up to grab the television remote. "How long before he is cleared?"

Father Richard shrugged his shoulders. "Look, Alex, I'm not stupid."

"Never said you were," Alex defended.

"Please, let me say this," Father Richard solicited. "Alex, I know I'm not Father Tom, I am a priest, but I wasn't always." He started to pet Komptin who was sleeping on the bed. "You know

176

I was almost engaged to be married before I joined the priesthood?"

Alex looked at him. "I just always thought priests never had relationships."

"I was still a young man. Trying to figure out what I wanted to do with my life," he told her. "I loved her, but when we graduated from college, we had a choice to make. Get married or go our separate ways for our careers."

"Do you regret your decision?" Alex engaged in the conversation.

"That's between me and God," he said to her. "That's not the point. My point is, when we made our decision, and went our separate ways, we made sure to say goodbye. Because if we didn't, we'd have no closure. It will eat at you forever."

Alex sat there and thought about it. "I don't want to see him." She tried to convince him, or was it herself?

Father Richard just nodded. "No hunting tonight." he got up.

"Father." Alex sat on her bed.

"Yes."

"Whatever happened to her?"

"She became mayor of a small town in Missouri," he told her.

"Ever see her?" It was almost as if Alex was seeking permission for something.

"I performed the marriage ceremony for her and her husband. We keep in touch every now and then," he told her. "I will always cherish our friendship. Good night, Alex. God bless." He gave her an assuring smile before retiring for the night.

Alex had the television on but wasn't really watching it. She didn't even know it was on the news channel. They had a news report covering the president and first lady who were making an appearance at a local restaurant. Alex couldn't help but look around in the background to catch a glimpse of Kameron. She knew he wouldn't be there, but she had a small bit of hope.

It must have been a couple of hours before Alex finally got out of bed. She felt trapped at the church and wanted to go out. She got dressed in black stretch jeans along with a purple t-shirt with a butterfly skeleton on the front. She put on her black hiking shoes before heading out to the hallway. She was about to call for Komptin but she didn't need a constant reminder of her lack of ability to sense the Lite. She couldn't feel the Lite and he more than likely couldn't feel her at all.

Alex stepped out of the church and found herself at a mall where a local movie theater was playing a mindless zombie movie. She got one ticket and sat in the back of the movie theater. She was drinking an Apollo she snuck in while eating some chocolate from the snack bar. The movie theater was about three quarters full. There were many types of people in there, but Alex couldn't help but feel as if they all were just sneaking peeks at her.

The movie was over, and Alex felt as though her brain cells were actually more depleted after watching it. Although, it did provide a service, it kept her mind off everything going on. Many loving couples were leaving the theater. Alex found them annoying. Outside the mall, the church was to the left of her, but she didn't feel like going back there.

She decided to go for a walk, where she found herself in the depths of a suburban housing development. The lots looked as if they were going to be nice for families. They all had a decent backyard. Right now it was just dirt, but they all had potential. Alex strolled down the streets imagining all the happy families that were going to live there.

A sudden tackle from the side knocked Alex from her reverie into a rolling ball as she was battling an Infiltrator. Alex got the advantage; she was able to swing the beast into a realtor sign in the front of a random yard. Another Infiltrator tackled her from the back where her face scraped across the pavement. The second Infiltrator dropped its knee into Alex's side where Sanah had stabbed her. She screamed, as her eyes began glowing neon blue. Her hands pulsated the blue mist. She was able to elbow the one directly on top of her in the mouth as it went to take a chunk out of her neck. It was enough for Alex to roll away on the ground, but she was met with a boot to the face.

A second stomp was coming, but she grabbed the ankle and broke it. There was luck as it was a provisionary, which meant he was human earning his right to become a Demon. The man screamed in pain as he held his leg, "You, bitch!" he screamed.

Alex got up quickly and grabbed the man by the ankle to throw him into an Infiltrator running towards her. The two collided into a tangled pile on the road. Alex ran towards a house close to being completed. She shot a Lite Beam to force the door open but as she entered the house, she was met with a fist straight into the nose.

Alex fell to the ground knowing that it was a punch from a Demon. This night just got more difficult. She bounced back up to be met by an Infiltrator that threw her back into the street. Her arm was caught in between the road and her wounded side. She crawled for a bit before being lifted by an Infiltrator. She hit back with all her might, wounding it. Limping into the nearest yard was not productive. There were two infiltrators and a Demon waiting. She lit her fist and shot a Lite Beam at the Demon, knocking him over, but both Infiltrators got the best of her. They both tackled her into a framed building. Pieces of wood broke as Alex's body smashed through them.

She managed to pick up a piece of wood and jab it into an Infiltrator as it came running towards her, its momentum doing most of the work for her. It howled in agony as she formed a knife with her fists and jammed it into the neck of the beast. It disappeared into the ground, showing her the next attacker.

The Demon followed through with a kick to her side sending her back into another room. By this point, Alex just wanted to die. This needed to end.

One way or the other, Alex was going to get out of this. "I know that look," the Demon told her.

Alex spit on the ground, a mixture of blood and saliva. "Will you just finish it?"

"Gron told me you were tough." He confidently stood over her body. "I don't see it."

Alex tried to stand, but he kicked her in the stomach, sending her back through the wall leading outside. The blood was starting to get into her eyes. Alex lifted her head to blurred visions of Infiltrators approaching. Alex now accepted her fate when a familiar, yet unusually loud, roar arrived.. Komptin came in tackling the soldier of the Dark. The Demon screamed while in the mouth of the big gargoyle dog. The other Infiltrators attacked Komptin but he held his own. The Demon body was torn to pieces while still living. He managed to limp away while the Infiltrators continued to attack Komptin.

Alex got up to help but she was too injured. She fell back to the ground wanting to die. Komptin finished killing the last two Infiltrators. The sound of their destruction was a mixture of happiness and regret. The battle was over. Komptin surveyed the battlefield before walking over to Alex who was now on her feet. The massive gargoyle stared at Alex as he stepped up to her with a stern, hard gaze. The two stared at each other before Komptin gave an echoing roar close to Alex's face. She could actually feel her hair move from the force of the agitation. He remained panting exhibiting pure anger at the reckless endangerment Alex put herself in.

***

Anne was not looking forward to this. She walked into the supper club; it looked a little bit busier than usual. The hostess came up to Anne. "Can I help you?"

"I'm just meeting some friends, thank you." Anne saw Jessica sitting down at a corner booth while talking to Dan, who was obviously working. The two of them saw Anne and waved her over.

"I will send over your waitress for your drink." The hostess went to find the server.

"Just a glass of wine, waitress choice," Anne surveyed the restaurant.

Anne started walking over to the table. The walk seemed long because she was on the lookout for Kate. "Hey, sorry I had to leave last time. I had a work emergency in DC."

"I get it," Dan said, giving Anne a big hug.

"How are you feeling, Jessica?" Anne couldn't help but to gaze down at her stomach.

"Oh, he's going to be a linebacker." Jessica leaned back trying to get comfortable.

"For anyone but Green Bay," Dan chimed in. "I'm hoping for a ten pounder." He rubbed his hands together, giving a teasing laugh.

"Are you going to give birth to him?" Jessica laughed. "Oooo." Jessica twitched a little and held

182

her stomach. "Maybe a kicker the way he's moving around in there. Do you want to feel him, Anne?"

Anne smiled as she felt Jessica's stomach. "You two are truly blessed." Anne felt a little envy towards the happy couple. She couldn't help but think that it could have been her and Kale sitting in his mom's restaurant preparing for a family.

"Thank you," Dan said politely. "I need to go check on the kitchen." He kissed Jessica before greeting some other guests as he walked by them.

Anne couldn't help but watch Jessica admire him as he went to do his job. "He seems natural here."

"He loves it, and I would never tell him this, but he's really good at it," Jessica teased as she continued to rub her stomach. She grabbed her glass of soda and lime and took a sip.

The waitress brought Anne a glass of wine. "Thank you."

"Will there be anything else?" She asked Anne.

"No, thank you," Anne let her know. She turned her attention back to Jessica. "Kale would be happy Dan is taking over the place."

Jessica gave her a sympathetic smile. "How are you doing with everything?"

Anne took another sip of wine. "I'm fine. A couple ups and downs."

"I wish there was something I could say that could help you," she offered.

Anne smiled. "It will just take time." Anne saw Kate from the corner of her eye. The two of them locked eyes and Anne's stomach turned in knots. It was as if Kate hesitated before making a decision to come talk to her. Anne took a deep breath and a sip of wine.

"I heard you were in town and then your parents said you had to leave," she cautiously said.

Anne could tell she wanted to hug Anne, but Anne remained seated. "Yes, there was an emergency at work."

Kate opened her mouth but stopped. "You're fixing up the old Catholic church."

"Yes," Anne said. "How..." She took a moment. "How've you been?"

"I would love to have dinner and talk?"

"Okay, I promise." Anne instantly regretted agreeing to meet Kate for dinner.

Kate wiped a tear. "I would like that."

Anne nodded and watched her walk away wiping a tear from her face. She just sat there watching. There was a strong urge to go talk to her, just to hug her, but she couldn't. Anne felt ashamed.

"You okay?" Jessica asked.

Anne nodded. "Just haven't talked to her since the funeral."

"I thought you were close," Jessica asked.

"We were, but it's complicated," Anne said, taking another sip of her wine. Anne saw Shawn come into the restaurant with a couple of his friends. He saw her and gave a small wave. Anne smiled while returning the gesture.

Shawn took that as an invitation for him to sit down next to Anne. "Hey, how are things going?"

"I'm fine, Shawn," Anne moved over. "Shawn, do you know, Jessica?"

"Yes, not officially though." Shawn extended his hand. "Shawn."

"Jessica." She shook his hand and then twitched hard. "Ow, that was a big kick there, buddy." She rubbed her stomach some more.

***

Kameron thought he was just wasting his time. On some level, he was hoping Alex would show up to see him off, to clear the air. That was probably the reason he was going to leave at night. That and he didn't want to deal with traffic. He figured he would get a hotel once he was out of the city. His household goods had already been shipped out and the only thing he was taking with him was a couple of suitcases.

He already arranged to send his apartment key to the manager by parcel service. The last suitcase was in the trunk of the car. When he shut the door, he looked around the city. This is where he had his first assignment as a Secret Service agent, where he was shot, and he truly fell in love.

A strong feeling came over him as if he was making a mistake. Almost as if he should go straight to the church and tell Alex the hell with it. That they should be together. He knew though, she didn't feel that way. Otherwise, he would be

185

looking for a new job in the city. The decision was made. Now he just needed to follow through with it. There was one final scan of the area, with a glimmer of hope before getting into his car, but no sign.

However, Kameron didn't know that Alex was nearby. She stood on the rooftop of a nearby building overlooking the apartment complex. Her face was bruised, her lip and nose bloodied. She held onto her side hoping the pain would alleviate. That was nothing compared to the agony she was experiencing watching Kameron drive off in his car.

Alex turned to Komptin sitting down, not taking his eyes off her. Alex walked by Komptin with a sense of hostility in her voice. "I know what I'm doing."

CHAPTER SEVEN

Kameron wasn't fooling himself on how much time he took to get to San Diego. Normally, he wouldn't have taken the full seven days to get there, but he stopped a lot to figure out what he was doing. A couple of times he had to pull over to fight the urge to go back. Despite all his setbacks, he made it to the federal building and his new office. The parking lot seemed different here. It was almost as if it was pushing him out of it. Once he finally got the strength to make it to the front door, he showed his identification to the security guards to get in. They allowed him to pass as he waited by the elevator.

"Kameron?" a female voice said behind him.

He turned around to see a blonde woman with her hair pulled tight into a bun. "Midnight?"

"I thought that was you." The two of them gave each other a big hug. "How've you been?"

"Not bad, how are things with you? How's Logan?" It was so nice to see a familiar face here in San Diego.

"Oh, I'm sure he's great. He is with his new wife, the TV weather girl," Midnight's voice was a bit acerbic. "I'm sure they are living great in Los Angeles."

"I'm sorry to hear that; I always liked him," Kameron comforted her.

Midnight laughed, "No you didn't. You hated him."

"Well, I liked him for your benefit," he assured her. "How long have you been here?"

Midnight scanned her card for the elevator. "Just about a year now. I was on the embassy detail for foreign travels down in Florida and suddenly got transferred here."

"Without notice?"

"Yep, came into work one day and got the orders for here. It's not so bad." Midnight tried to ease his anxiety. "The weather is nicer, the job is routine and not stressful." The doors opened to the elevator, and they stepped inside. "We are on the fourth floor."

Kameron hit the button for their office floor. The two of them walked to the office where there was a man in a turquoise shirt with a salmon-colored scarf around his neck. "Good morning, Midnight," he said. "Is this the new agent?"

"Kameron," he extended his hand. "Nice to meet you."

He gave Kameron a feminine handshake. "I'm Lane, the morning meeting starts in fifteen. We had to move it up due to the Resident Director having a meeting with the FBI at nine-thirty," Lane let them both know.

"Thanks." Midnight showed Kameron into the office. "Come on, Kam, I'll show you where you're going to sit."

Kameron followed Midnight to his new desk. He was led to a cubicle with just a computer on the desk. It was empty– just as Kameron was feeling. There was a window, which was actually a nice surprise. He could actually see a view of the vastness of the ocean. "What do we do here?"

A male voice came from behind him. "We are the first line of defense to ensure the safety of American diplomats' safe passage to maintain relations with foreign dignitaries." A young-looking man came up to them. "In other words, we're a liaison office. All we do is push paperwork."

Midnight gave a small giggle. "He's not wrong, but there is more than that. We do get to knock down doors. Kameron, this is Scotty. He's our Homeland Security liaison, Scotty, this is Kameron. We were in the same class while at the academy."

"Nice to meet you," he shook his hand. "I guess we should get to that meeting. They are so dreadful." They all went into the conference room. "As long as you don't sit at the head of the table, you can sit anywhere."

"What's the Resident Director like?" Kameron asked as he scouted the room.

"I'm not that bad," a small woman with blonde hair and freckles came up behind them. "I'm Paige. Let's all have a seat. We are going to keep this short because my meeting got moved up again." She shook her head out of disgust. Everyone sat down at the table with one empty seat. "Okay, everyone this is Kameron. He came in from DC, the FLOTUS detail."

"FLOTUS? Hey, wasn't that detail involved in that F.O.R. thing?" One of the people in the meeting asked.

Kameron was hoping his uncomfortableness wasn't evident. "Yes."

"That matter has been cleared," Paige told him. She gave off the impression not to press the issue.

"Right," the man went back to his phone. "I'm Jared, FBI."

The rest of introductions had representatives from San Diego Police Department, California State Patrol, Homeland Security, and a representative from the CIA who was out traveling to look into a case.

"Okay, so Kameron, you'll shadow Midnight with a follow-up on the threat to POTUS. Apparently, he's screaming about government conspiracies and so on. He crossed the line when he stated." The director started to read from the email, "'I don't want to, but I will kill all government employees, including the president, to stop the takeover of innocent American lives. Why must I be the only one who chooses to protect us?'" Once she was done reading the email, she addressed the group. "Pleasant, isn't it?"

"Sounds like a nut ball," Scotty said while looking on his phone. "But it is in the ghetto part of town, so that's a bonus. Hey, on the bright side, it's near a great sushi restaurant."

"Yes, he probably is in need of some help, but we must take all threats against the president

190

seriously," Paige lectured. "What's going on with the Jose Lanisio case?"

The Border Patrol liaison, Jim, spoke up, "He's claiming he's selling coke to some congressman up in LA. I was going to have Harry lead it. I think the LAPD would rather have the State Patrol be the lead interview over a federal boy." Harry nodded at Jim with agreement.

"Sounds good," Paige continued to review her notes. "Lane, could you do the travel authorization for that?"

"Will do," he said, while sipping on his tea.

Paige read her notes for a second and then lifted her head up. "Scotty, any news on that pro who was caught with Senator Rashmere?"

"She's going to come in tomorrow; I just need someone in there as a witness, during the interview." He looked around the room but everyone put their finger on their nose. "Come on, guys."

"She's just trying to get out of trouble," Jim said. "I'm surprised she didn't go to the press."

"I'll do it," Kameron offered his services. "I'd like to get my feet wet in something."

"Sounds good. Remember people; be safe so you can go home to your families. Damn it, I have to go." Paige gathered her stuff to go to her meeting. "Kameron, I would like to see you this afternoon around three."

"Yes, ma'am." He couldn't help but wonder whether this meeting was going to be the same as the one with the last Director.

***

Komptin wouldn't leave Alex's side all week. He made sure she was always in constant eye contact. It was getting a bit annoying to Alex. Her faithful friend was irritated with her for the first couple of days before he finally started warming up to her.

Alex didn't know if he was irked with her because she took off without him knowing, or the fact that she let Kameron go without saying anything. Maybe that was just her imagination. Alex got up from her desk to go to the bathroom with Komptin getting up to follow her. "You wanna wipe for me too?" she snapped at him. That didn't change Komptin's stance on making sure she was safe.

Megan did everything to keep from laughing at how miserable Alex was.

Komptin followed Alex regardless of how annoyed she was with him. Alex walked out the door to see Father Carl and Father Richard talking in the hallway. Seeing Father Carl was just what Alex, didn't want, this morning. "Father." She nodded to Father Richard as she walked by them. "Jackass." That was directly towards Father Carl.

The two of them watched Alex go into the bathroom. "What happened between you two?" Father Richard asked. He couldn't help but think he was going to have to play referee between the two of them. That, and how was Father Carl going to react when he finds out about Alex's true role here.

Father Carl spoke, staring at the bathroom, "She was a student at St. Mary's when I was the Dean of the school." Father Carl remembered back. "We had a talk."

"Must have been some talk." Father Richard got an update on his phone from Anne about the contractor listing for the renovation.

"She was nonconforming and extremely disrespectful. I see she hasn't changed," Father Carl told him. "Why did you give her the position of groundskeeper at the church?" The two of them walked into Father Richard's office. "And then you are taking the Historian with us?"

"Alex may have her quirks about her, but she's great at cleaning things up. Anne has gone through a lot this year; she needs family. If I can provide that to her, I will." Father Richard told him. He took off his black suit coat. "How many bibles and hymnals do you think we'll need to start?"

***

Midnight knocked on the door of the suspect who threatened the life of the president. "I wonder if he's home." She knocked again. The door had every religious symbol carved into it. There was a bunch of crosses, Muslim symbols, Jewish stars, and rosary's all over nailed to the doorframe.

A couple of minutes passed by. Scotty looked down the stairs to cover them in case anybody was coming. He peaked out the window and then nodded to them it was all clear.

Kameron moved to the other side of the door. "Maybe he's not home."

Midnight hit the door harder, "Mr. Petarowlski." Midnight put her head closer to the door. "I think there is someone there." She knocked on the door again. "Mr. Petarowlski."

"Who's there?" a scared voice came from the other end of the door.

"Can you open the door, please? I'm Agent Soliss," she told him.

"Tell me who you serve," the man demanded.

Scotty rolled his eyes. "Great, a religious nut. Of course."

Midnight motioned for him to be quiet. "We just want to talk."

"So talk," the man said. "I can hear you just fine."

Kameron snickered, "Want me to try?"

Midnight showed him the door.

"Mr. Petarowlski, I'm Kameron, how's it going?" He spoke to him through the door.

"How do I know you are you?"

"We have IDs," Midnight told him.

Kameron looked over the door. "Mr. Petarowlski, can I call you Brian?"

"Sure, what's your name?"

"I told you, I'm Kameron," he answered.

"Is that your real name?"

"I assure you, it's Kameron," he confirmed. "We just want to talk, and really I'd like to get this

194

over with because I'm new in town and I need to find a nice church to attend."

The sound of the door chain was on the other side just before the door opened. A young man opened the door. He was wearing a black tank top with a pair of shorts. He had homemade tattoos of random religious symbols and bible verses. "You believe in God?"

"Of course I do." Kameron showed him a crucifix on his necklace.

The man nodded before giving them permission to enter his domicile. Inside his apartment were framed bible pages, crucifixes, Star of David, and even some Muslim symbols. Scotty was the last to come in and looked uncomfortable when he did. "Nice place, you got here. Looks like you got them all covered," Scotty observed. "I'll be in the hallway."

Midnight nodded, as it was standard protocol to ensure they were covered during the interview. "May I call you, Brian?"

Brian threw a bible at Midnight. She caught and flipped through the pages. "Am I looking for something in particular?"

"No, I'm good," he let them know. "Please have a seat."

Kameron and Midnight sat down. Brian seemed to be a little more at peace as he sat down. Midnight motioned for Kameron to initiate the conversation since it was Kameron who broke the ice. "Brian, can I talk to you about that email you sent?"

195

"I send lots of emails," Brian admitted. "Which one?"

Midnight spoke up, "The one where you threatened the President of the United States."

The man seemed to be a bit shocked. "I don't know what you are talking about." He was a bit agitated.

"Brian, you know it is a federal offense to threaten the life of the president," Midnight told him.

"Don't you know what is going on out there?" He started to get up.

Kameron kind of spoke up. "Brian, it would be wise for you to calm down and not make any sudden movements." Brian closed his eyes and took a deep breath. "Thank you. Do you fear the fight of good versus evil?"

Midnight was shocked over that question but was more shocked at the answer from the suspect. "Yes, you know about the fight."

Kameron nodded, "What do you know about it?"

The man stood up and lifted his shirt. It was a tattoo of an upside down four. "More than you could ever imagine."

***

Anne was walking with the electrician discussing the power issues with the church. "It's going to cost how much?" she asked out of pure shock.

196

The electrician reiterated, "Look, they did some real damage to this building. We are going to have to run all new wiring; even the outlets are damaged. It's as if they took a hammer to each one and smashed it. The breaker box is completely destroyed. They even dug up the wiring from underground. It was as if it was pure focused intent to ruin it. Why would anyone do that?"

Anne put her hand on her head. "Ugh, I'm sorry; I know it isn't your fault."

"Look, I know you are going to get more quotes, but I guarantee you they are all going to say the same thing. Let me know what you think." He tore off the quote. Anne thanked him and walked him out where Shawn was coming up the stairs with bags in his hands. "Shawn, what are you doing here?"

"You seemed a little stressed last time I saw you. I just wanted to give a little hope," Shawn replied. "Hey Pete, I hope you are treating her well."

Pete smiled, "Of course, I'll see you Thursday."

"I'll be there." He watched as Pete left. Shawn handed the bag to Anne. "It's just a salad from Marty's."

"Thank you." Anne looked in the bag. "How do you know him?"

Shawn was caught off guard. "Oh, we bowl together."

Anne was surprised that Shawn even got her favorite salad dressing. "Thank you for this." She lifted up the bag. "Ever been here before?"

"I think it was at Sara's funeral," he told her. "So tragic."

"Yes," Anne took a second to remember that time. "She was a good person. You wanna tour?"

Shawn took a deep breath before walking into the church. "I'd love one."

Anne began with the main worship hall. "This is the congregation hall; obviously this is what everyone mainly sees."

"It looks empty," he observed. "No one's home."

"Well, hopefully when we get this place up and running that will change." They continued the tour as they made it to the top floor. "This will be Alex's office."

"Alex?" Shawn said with amazement. "She will be back as well?"

"Yes," Anne smiled. "She has some stuff to take care of back in DC but she will be here by the end of summer."

"What is she going to do here?" Shawn asked.

"She is going to be in charge of the grounds," Anne let him know.

Shawn looked out the window. "She's going to have a lot to do; do you think she can handle it?"

Anne joined him at the window and stared out over the town. "Of course. She is tougher than she looks." Plenty of memories came flashing back to her. Maybe it was a mistake to come home. The memory of Anne holding Kale in her arms, hoping they would survive the attack from Gron. Then the other memory of Gron shoving his fist through his back and out his chest. Without even realizing, she started to cry.

"Are you okay?" Shawn asked her.

Anne turned to him and just nodded, but her tears were more than evident. Shawn turned her around to give her a big hug. There was comfort from being held by him. He pulled her away a bit as the two of them locked eyes. They remained staring at each other when they both started to lean into each other before a car pulled up. They both looked when they drew apart.

Anne looked out the window to see Weston outside of the church, walking up the steps. Anne put her hand over her mouth. "Excuse me, Shawn. I need to talk to him."

"Of course." He watched her walk away. Things were going his way and soon Merik would be with the Pure of Heart.

"What are you doing here?" Anne turned to see if Shawn was following her out.

"I just wanted to apologize for missing dinner with your friends that night," Weston told her. "Something came up."

"I understand." Anne eased his worries.

"Well, I'm off back to the office. I was just informed of some new leads that I need to look into," he told her. "I'm sure we'll cross paths again."

"I look forward to it," Anne told him. "Take care."

He left before Shawn came down the stairs. Anne turned shamefully to him. "I need to get to work. Thanks for lunch."

Shawn smiled. "No problem. I'll see you again."

***

Alex was blaring her music loud enough for her mirror to vibrate as she was putting her makeup on. She was going to go hunt and she didn't care what Father Richard, the Cardinal, or even the Council said. She was going to go find some action tonight.

Komptin was lying on the bed with his ears covered from the noise. Alex put on red lipstick and darkened her eyes. Even though her skin was pale, she applied more make up to make it paler. She tied her hair up as tight as she could. The tank top that she was wearing showed the bottom part of her stomach. Her black spandex underneath her black miniskirt with a skull belt emphasized her petite figure.

"Come on, let's go," she opened the door to see Father Carl outside her door. "What?"

"Your music was ridiculously loud, vulgar, and inappropriate for a House of God," Father Carl told her.

"And? This is where I live." Alex wasn't backing down. "Now, if you will excuse me." Alex whistled for Komptin as loud as she could. "Come on."

Alex walked into the heart of downtown. People were all around shopping with their friends and families. Alex couldn't tell if there were Demons in the mixture or not. She couldn't feel anything. The Dark could pounce at any moment and, frankly, she didn't care. There was a small synagogue she walked by. She stepped in hoping she could feel the warmth of the Lite, but still there was nothing. She didn't understand why she tortured herself by still trying. She angrily left the synagogue with the questioning feeling of why she kept on torturing herself.

"Alex, hi." Michal Grossman and his family were walking together.

"Hey, what's up," she said looking around, not knowing what to do.

"I was just out with my family going to dinner and a movie," he told her. "This is my wife, Talia, and you remember my son."

"Yep," Alex veered away. "If you will excuse me."

Grossman had a confused facial expression, "Have you heard from Kameron?"

She snapped her head around. "No. Why would I? He left. We're done." She strutted off to disappear among the people.

"She's pleasant," Talia said as she watched her leave. "Sounds like she's hurting."

Grossman just watched her leave. "Come on, let's go to dinner."

Alex walked by a dance club where the music was loud. It was dark, it was foggy, and the people inside seemed like they were having a good time. She walked into the entrance and turned to Komptin. "You can't come in here." She didn't even wait for Komptin's reaction. She just wanted in. The music was loud and thumping as some people turned their attention to the pale-skinned girl with black weaves.

One guy approached her with a drink in his hand, "Hey, are you here with anyone?"

Alex took his drink and chugged it down. "Are you?"

He shook his head. "Nope."

Alex grabbed his shirt. "You wanna get something to eat and have it at your place? We can skip the food."

He quickly agreed. "My place is just around the corner."

The two of them walked out of the bar with Komptin staring at her as she marched by him. "I'll be back in a bit," she told him.

***

Gron got off the phone with Merik. It would seem that the Sentry isn't reporting to their hometown until the end of summer. That would make the timing close. He scanned his calendar on his desk.

Misluna was sitting on the couch playing with her hair. "Has he finished his task yet?"

"No, but he said he's working on it," Gron let her know. "I'm not too worried about that."

The buzzer on the intercom flashed. "Vernick is here to see you."

Gron gave Misluna a confused look. "Really?"

She just shrugged her shoulders. "I thought he was dead."

Gron flashed his eyes. "Send him in."

Vernick came in with a chunk of his side missing, but it looked as if it was healed over. "My leader," he bowed. "We had her cornered; we were going to kill the Sentry."

"And, why didn't you?" Gron just stared at him behind his desk with his feet up.

"The dog creature. It came out of nowhere." Vernick was still in pain.

Gron looked at him with calmness. "And why are you telling me this now?"

"I was healing my wounds." Vernick showed him the missing chunk out of his body.

"I see," Gron got up from behind his desk. "Are you okay now?"

"Yes, my leader."

"I'm glad. You glad, Misluna?" Gron asked his mistress.

"Oh yeah, ecstatic," she rolled her eyes.

Gron put his arm around Vernick's neck, bent him backwards, and lit his fist with the raw power of the Dark. He formed a knife, jabbing it into the Vernick's chest. His body dropped to the ground and then disappeared.

Gron wiped the remnants of the Demon off his clothes. "You said she's falling apart at work?"

"Yes, she's playing her music loud and being disrespectful. I'm actually starting to like her," Misluna smiled.

"She was like that in high school as well," Gron thought back. "We need to separate her from that mutt. Then I think we will have a chance to kill her."

CHAPTER EIGHT

Initially, Alex's plan was just to catch a movie, but that all changed when she met this guy in the lobby of the theater. They talked for a bit when she said she didn't really want to see the movie, so she offered an alternate plan. No doubt, he accepted.

The door creaked to get out of his bedroom. Alex carried her clothes to change in the bathroom. Her scarred body reflected back to her. There were so many wounds, but for some reason, she seemed different. It was almost as if she was a dismal shell. The lights reflected off the necklace Kameron had given her at Christmas. It actually felt like a small dose of serenity as she held the sapphire angel in her fingers. Tears were forming but she held them back. She was so tired of crying. After getting dressed, she came out of the bathroom to see the guy who she had been with.

"Leaving so soon?" he asked. "Want anything to eat or something?"

"Yes, I'm leaving; and no, I don't need anything." Alex checked her watch after she put on her jacket.

"Can I see you…" he started to say before Alex stopped him.

Alex put up her hand. "Look, this just isn't going to go anywhere. So, just stop." She left the apartment to find Komptin outside. She scratched his ears as she tramped past him. The massive

German shepherd tailed her to a park where she sat on a park bench. She had no expression on her face. The Lite Sentry's body just sat straight up, staring at nothing. Komptin just watched his hunting partner motionless, not knowing what to do. Alex just continued to sit on the park bench, facing forward with a blank stare. Komptin slowly started sauntering up to her with his head down. His eyes casted up with sadness as he cautiously approached. The gentle giant very carefully and gently placed his head on her lap. A single tear dropped from his master's cheek as she stroked his head.

***

Kameron brought up his box from the car that held all his personal items for his new desk. He placed it on his chair to start setting it up. Midnight came up to him to peek in the box. "Hey Kam, did you eat?"

"I ate after my morning run." A picture of Michelle and Alex laughing together, cheek to cheek was in his box. It was one of his favorite pictures. The inclination of throwing it away was being thwarted with a voice telling him to keep it.

"Still doing those runs, huh?" She reached into his box to pull out a Hello Kitty mouse pad from his box. "This is cute."

Kameron took it from her hands. He stared at it for a bit with a bunch of happy memories coming back to him. The main one was when he brought Alex to Christmas with his parents. That was such a

perfect time; he thought for sure she was…
Kameron stopped that line of thought. "It's trash."
He tossed it in the garbage can underneath his desk.

Midnight tightened her lips and her eyes
widened. "Okay."

Scotty came in and sat down at his cubicle
directly across from Kameron. He had some bags
underneath his eyes and yawned. His coffee must
have been hotter than he expected based on his
facial expression when he took a sip.

"Late night?" Kameron asked him.

"You have no idea. I met up with this luscious
redhead at the bar down the street from my
apartment." He turned around to make sure no one
was listening. "She's a spokeswoman for Apollo
energy drink."

Kameron's attention turned to what he was
about to say next.

"She had the energy, trust me," he laughed. "A
credit to her company."

Midnight just shook her head. "You're a
walking disease." She handed him a pair of latex
gloves for evidence gathering. "Here, for your next
date."

Scotty didn't take offense as he put them in his
pocket. "Good idea. Hey Kameron, are you still
good to witness at two o'clock for my hooker
interview?"

"I'll be there." He continued to set up his desk.

"You wanna know what I like about high
politician hookers? They are usually drop dead
gorgeous," Scotty laughed. "They're not going to

risk all this trouble for some dog. Look at this picture of her." He pulled up her file on his computer.

"You couldn't afford her. There is a reason they only stick to the high-end clientele." Midnight sat down at her desk. "Hey, can you sign that report from yesterday if you aren't too busy with your body parts falling off?"

"Yah, yah." Scotty went back to the picture of the alleged prostitute. "Definitely makes a case more interesting. Do you think she prefers Democrats or Republicans?"

"Speaking of interesting cases." Midnight sat back with a cup of coffee. "What do you think of our former F.O.R. member yesterday?"

"No doubt, he was scared." Kameron continued to put his desk together. "Do you think he sent those emails or was hacked to frame him like he said?"

Scotty grabbed a power bar from his desk. "I don't know," he said with a mouthful of food. "If he was a member of the F.O.R. Concealment Measures Department like he said, it may be possible."

Paige walked up to the group. "Your interview yesterday, Brian Petrolowski, said he was a member of F.O.R.?"

"Former member," Midnight clarified. "He was pretty scared."

"I just got word he's dead," Paige gave the news.

Scotty immediately chimed in. "I guess all those symbols didn't work. Shocker. Case closed on our end."

"What happened?" Kameron continued to unpack his box.

"Completely butchered in his apartment," Paige told them. "There were drugs in the apartment." Paige showed them the police photos. "Probably drug related."

Kameron peaked over. "Drugs almost looked planted."

Scotty popped out of his chair to see the picture. "Why do you say that?"

"The drugs. They are just out there. You think if it was a drug deal or drug user, they wouldn't have taken them."

"There's no blood scattered on them either," Midnight pointed to the drugs in the picture. "That close to the body and there's no blood splatter on it."

"Well, the FBI has it now in coordination with SDPD," Paige let them know. "Kameron, can I see you in my office for a second?"

"Yes," he followed her into the office.

"Go ahead, shut the door. Don't worry it's not a bitch out session," she sat down at her desk. "You all settled in? I know you left DC rather quickly when you decided to take this assignment." Paige took a sip of water from a bottle. She offered him a bottle of water. "Sorry, I had to push back our initial meeting. Unexpected tasking came up."

"I get it. Yes, plans didn't go through as I wished," Kameron sat down in front of her desk. "I wanted to get out of there as quickly as I could."

Paige tapped her water bottle. "Yes, I know Director Channel. He's not the most pleasant person to be around. Did you find a place to live?"

"Yes ma'am, but I still have to unpack," he told her.

"Good. Maybe you can take off early all this week to get that done." Paige picked up her notepad. "About Director Channel, he gave me a call yesterday. Seems like he's not your biggest fan. He gave me a heads up about your involvement with the F.O.R."

"I wasn't going to say anything because the investigation was closed and my supervisor at the time told me the file was locked," Kameron let her know.

"Well, just don't shoot me, okay?" she joked.

"Don't kidnap and torture me and we have a deal," Kameron returned the humor.

"Deal, but I wanted to let you know that, as far as I'm concerned, the file will remain locked. You have a fresh start here, so make the best of it," Paige told him.

"Thank you," Kameron said.

"I'm all about fresh starts, Kameron," she told him. "Everyone deserves them."

***

Alex finished her shower before barely making it into work. Cardinal Joe and Father Richard called Alex into their office. Alex was feeling worn out; she just wanted to crawl into her bed to watch mindless television. The Cardinal's office had the two of them sitting on the couch with a spot for her in the middle. "Am I in trouble?"

"No," Cardinal Joe patted the open spot next to him. "But we do have some news for you."

Alex sat down in between the two of them. "Yes?"

Cardinal Joe took a deep breath before getting started. "Alex, we just got word from the Catholic Council."

"About?" Alex was leery that it was going to be some sort of intervention or something.

"The other Councils had reported the activation of four new Sentries," Cardinal Joe told her.

Alex was shocked, "Four?"

Father Richard nodded, "Yes."

"Which council has them? What sanctions?" Alex's interests were intrigued.

"We don't know," Cardinal Joe stated. "The United Council has agreed not to tell the new Sentries about each other."

"Why the hell not?" Alex started getting agitated. "I'm not going to train them?"

Cardinal Joe softly answered his already upset Sentry. "No."

"They don't trust me," Alex concluded instantly.

"Alex, don't think like that," Father Richard tried to comfort her.

She just sat there feeling betrayed by the Council. "When am I able to leave and join Anne?"

"Soon," Cardinal Joe told her.

"I can't believe this." Alex got up and faced the two. "Do you trust me?"

"Of course, Alex." Cardinal Joe got up to comfort Alex but she backed off. "With my life and the lives of the world."

"Do you?" She turned to Father Richard.

"Yes, Alex. Without a doubt," Father Richard included.

"I'm glad someone does." She didn't even say goodbye as she left the Cardinal's office.

The two members of the Catholic Council watched her leave. Cardinal Joe got up and went to his desk. Father Richard grabbed a soda from the bar. "You think she'll snap out of it?"

"She's hurting and she won't talk to us." Cardinal Joe sat back in his chair. "You will get to know Alex; you can't force her to open up. For such a tough exterior, her feelings run really deep."

"So, what do we do? She's falling." Father Richard had genuine fear in his voice. "We can't lose her to the Dark."

"There was a situation while she was in college that caused her to lose her track, but this... this is something different." Cardinal Joe took a sip of some black coffee. "She's not ignoring her duties. She's feeling betrayed by them."

"What do we do?" Father Richard tapped the can of his soda.

"Have faith," Cardinal Joe told him.

***

Kameron was staring out the window at the girl who was allegedly prostituting herself to the Senator up in San Francisco. Her hair was tied into a ponytail, and she was dressed rather nicely. There wasn't much worry in her demeanor— the kind of confidence where she knew she wasn't in trouble.

"Cute, isn't she?" Scotty came up to him. The both of them looked into the two-sided mirror.

"Hard to believe she's a pro?" Kameron couldn't help but think she reminded him of someone.

"A very good one, apparently." Scotty put a mint into his mouth. "She's got over three hundred K in the bank." He looked through her file, "I give her credit though; she's paid all her taxes."

They walked into the interrogation room. "I'm Agent Pardon. This is Agent Dutcher."

"I'm Genavene," the young woman said, staring at Kameron.

"It says here, your name is Lana Mahlaner. A professional therapist," Scotty looked up at her. "What field?"

"Sex therapy," Lana said to Scotty and then stared back at Kameron.

"Hey, hey," Scotty was snapping his fingers. "Sex therapist. You must be very good."

She smiled, "You can't afford one of my sessions. What am I in here for?"

"Prostitution, like you were charged," Kameron told her.

"No, I was acquitted. The senator's wife was mad I was sleeping with her husband, so she said I was a hooker. Next thing I know, I'm getting arrested," Lana let them know.

"Of course, here it is, wow, didn't see that," he said in a sarcastic tone. "Since we're here, anything you want to talk about?"

"Nope," she said and went back to Kameron. "You look familiar."

Kameron laughed, "Of course, I do."

"You've never been to a therapy session of mine, but you do look familiar." She studied him. "Do I know your wife?"

"Nice try," Kameron could tell she was trying to get any bit of personal information.

"Gentlemen, if I'm not being charged, then I'm going to go. If you need me, here's the number for my lawyer," she pulled out a card. "Oh, if you can't get a hold of him, then you can just use this." She drew a middle finger on the back of the card. "There you go."

The two of them watched her leave. "Does it make it weird that I want her even more now?" Scotty watched her walk away.

"She did look familiar," Kameron let him know.

Kameron decided to go for a walk to get a snack from a local vendor selling some fruit at a

214

stand. A group of girls dressed in black and pale skin walked by going into a tattoo parlor. Kameron couldn't help but think of Alex. For some reason he had a sudden urge to go back to DC, but he knew he couldn't, or shouldn't. Alex wanted nothing to do with him. They hadn't talked to each other since the breakup.

"Glad to see you made it out alive," Lana said as she bought a piece of fruit. "Gotta keep the moneymaker looking good." She showed Kameron the apple she bought.

"Where do I know you from?" he asked Lana.

"We off the record, no bullshit?"

Kameron nodded, "Yes."

"I was there at the church when Father Tom was murdered," she reminded him.

"Now I remember. You were on the plane with him." Kameron put the pieces together.

"I'm assuming you got that girl out of there?" Lana asked him.

Kameron replied, "Yes, but at a cost."

"Is your girlfriend here?" Lana was surveying the area for any sign of her.

Kameron shook his head. It seemed to him that she had a disappointed face when she saw Alex wasn't around. "We broke up when I got transferred here."

"Too bad. You guys were cute together. Total opposites that complemented each other," she told him. "Look, I don't have much time. I knew you were here. That's why I came in. I was hoping the Sentry came with you."

"Why?"

"Someone is going around killing ex F.O.R. members." She put on her sunglasses and fancy hat. "Not the ones who just leave, but the ones that 'found religion'," she air-quoted. "Or the ones that saw some shit they shouldn't have."

"How'd you stay alive?" Kameron was making sure the area was safe. "I know you saw some interesting events."

"I found my way into bed with some very powerful people. If I go, then some bad shit is sent to the press. Pictures, videos, tape recordings of classified material," Lana told him. "I even have some pretty messed up stuff about shifty election manipulations."

"That would be bad if it got out," Kameron understood how she stayed alive all this time.

"Really bad, but the only way that it gets out is if I die," she let him know. "Take care of yourself. This battle you're in is far from over."

"You too." Kameron took out his phone with a sudden urge to call Alex. He found her number and was about to hit send, but instead he deleted her contact information.

***

Anne decided to meet Kate in a neutral location where they could talk. They met at the kid's park on the edge of town. Anne wanted to be in the fresh air as she was talking to her. She sat in her car staring at Kate who was sitting at the picnic table waiting for her with a box next to her. She opened up the car door, the last place of haven, before deciding to get this over with. The bench on the other end of the table was rough sitting, but she wanted the table to separate them.

"Anne," Kate smiled. "I'm glad you came."

"Ms. Moler," Anne started to say, but that hurt Kate.

"You used to call me Mom." She started to cry.

Anne held in her tears. "I'm sorry, I just...I didn't..."

"Anne, when Kale died-" she started to stay.

"He was murdered," Anne corrected. "He was taken away from me by a monster."

"I lost him as well." Kate took out a tissue. "But when he was taken, it seemed like I lost you as well."

"I've tried to call you, to answer your calls," Anne started to say. "It's just...it's just too hard."

Kate wiped the tears from her face before bringing up a box that was next to her. She pulled out a small pair of bronzed shoes. "I was saving these to give to your children when you had them."

Anne swallowed hard. "This is Kale's first pair of little shoes. I bronzed these when he grew out of them."

"I can't take those," Anne was in pure torture. If there were any way to get out of this, she would take it in full force.

"That night...that night when we were all together, meeting Alex's boyfriend, he pulled me to the side for advice," Kate started to tell her.

217

Anne turned around to some children screaming while playing tag. "About what?"

"He wanted to know if he was too young to start having a family. The only other time I saw him that nervous was when he was going to ask you to marry him," Kate told her. "He had such a glow talking about being a father to your children."

"Ms. Moler, Kate, ma…" Anne got up. "I can't do this." Anne urgently got into her car and drove away hoping she wouldn't cause an accident from her crying.

***

Alex's room was a disaster. It had always been disorganized, but this was just a mess. She started to put things away when she noticed the picture from Christmas time at Kameron's parents' house. That week was pure happiness. Komptin was sleeping on her bed. She knew he was there but could not feel the Lite he generated. Her room felt cold, as if she was alone.

Alex grabbed a picture of Kameron, her, Anne and Kale. "How much more can I lose?" Alex pleaded. The sound of broken glass woke Komptin up when Alex threw the picture frame against the wall.

She went to leave her room but stopped to place her head against the door. The sound of her banging it slightly was barely heard as she was tightly closing her eyes. She tried to feel the Lite but still there was nothing. Maybe there was small hope she could feel the Dark. It was night when she went outside of the church. The air was humid with a hint of chill to it. Alex still couldn't sense anything. The star-lit sky was starting to become consumed with storm clouds.

A man in his twenties was walking by with a bottle of alcohol in his hand across the street. She walked over to him and took the bottle from his hand. Alex showed no remorse as she chugged some of the whiskey from the bottle.

"What you doing, you crazy…" before he could finish Alex kissed him. She started unbuttoning his shirt with her hands. He returned the kiss and moved hands up her shirt but stopped after he felt her scars. "Gross! What is that? That's nasty." The man took his hands off Alex to look at them. "What the hell is wrong with your skin?" he asked as he walked away shaking his hands in disgust. "Yuck."

Alex didn't know she could feel any lower but that guy walking away achieved it. A man standing across the street was staring at her. Father Carl had his arms across his chest in sheer disappointment. She buried her feelings deep as she headed back into the church.

"Is that what you do? You disgrace Him with your actions! You will not be staying in the new church. If I had my say, you would not be working for this church." Father Carl followed her down the hallway to her bedroom. "Hey, you stop when I'm talking to you."

Alex turned around with her finger in Father Carl's face, "No, you listen, you asshole. You are damn lucky we are on church grounds you son of a bitch! Now get the hell out of my way!" Komptin was barking, trying to calm Alex down or asking others for help. She stopped to go back to her room, but she didn't want to stay. With a determination in her mind, she walked by Father Carl to leave.

"Who do you think you are talking to me like that?" Father Carl turned yelling at her with force.

Alex snapped around, "I'm a Lite Sentry." She looked up to the ceiling screaming, "YOU HEAR ME? I'M STILL A LITE SENTRY!" The pure emotion of her voice echoed throughout the hallway of the rectory.

"ALEX!" Father Richard came down the hall in an almost run.

Alex tensed, trying to control her emotions before running out the door. Komptin flashed his eyes before going in a full out sprint after her.

"What is with her?" Father Carl was in complete shock.

"Father, she needs us. We have to get her before she leaves church grounds," Father Richard ran by him fast.

Both the priests went running out the door. Father Carl looked down the streets. "Where is she? How did she disappear so fast?"

Father Richard got on the phone to call the Cardinal about what transpired. "We have a situation. Can you please come down here? Roger that. We'll meet you in your office." He hung up and called Megan. "Can you come into the office? It's an emergency." Father Richard rubbed his head.

"What is going on? Is she mentally ill or something? Delusional?" Father Carl asked him. The sky was being consumed by dark thunderous clouds.

"Delusional, no. What we have is a heartbroken little girl who feels abandoned by all that she held important."

***

The lake was glistening with clear skies with the reflection of the moon acting as though it was the background of a painting. Anne found herself staring into the horizon. There was a stomach full of guilt for leaving Kate crying at that picnic table. The sight of his bronzed shoes when he was a child particularly marked in her memory. He wanted to have children; he wanted a family.

Anne started fantasizing how their family would have been. The perfect scenario. The two of them would have grabbed their two kids in the car. A seven-year-old boy and a five-year old girl. They would pack the car with food and swim clothes, then drive to their Aunt Alex and Uncle Kameron's house out in the country for a summer barbeque.

Upon arrival, the kids didn't even wait until the car was shut off. They would go play in the field with Komptin as he protected them from any danger. Their relationship would be as close as a

221

family could be. When the kids were sleeping, the four of them would be sitting on the porch, talking and laughing as families do.

Then the fantasy morphed into an image of Komptin lifting his head with eyes glowing with a low growl. Alex's attention was to the fields as a bunch of red eyes appeared. Alex ran off the porch with her eyes glowing and fists lit ready to defend her family. Komptin morphs into his gargoyle form giving a thunderous roar. Kale, Anne, and Kameron go to protect the children, but they are getting overwhelmed by the black monsters. The children are surrounded by Infiltrators.

Anne quickly shook off that line of thought as she heard the sound of someone coming up behind her. She turned around to see Shawn. "What are you doing here?" She started to get a bit scared.

Shawn gave his charming smile. "Don't worry, I'm not stalking you. I was driving by on my way home when I saw your car in the parking lot."

Anne nodded. "Okay." She turned her attention back to the lake. She saw some dark clouds starting to form in the distance.

"I can see you want to be alone." Shawn turned around.

"No, wait," Anne pleaded. "Please, you don't have to go."

"Is everything all right?" Shawn sat down next to Anne.

"I met with Kale's mom today," Anne admitted to him.

Shawn gave a sympathetic smile. "How'd that go?"

"I couldn't look at her. I couldn't give her what she wanted," Anne started to open up.

"What was that?" Shawn asked her.

"She started talking about how Kale wanted to start a family. He asked her if it was time," Anne was having a hard time letting it out. "He wanted to give me children." Anne started to wipe tears from her eyes. "Now, I can't do that."

"Anne, I'm pretty sure you are still going to have children," he said to her. "There is still time." He started to rub her back in comfort. "Kale would want you to live your life."

Anne turned her attention up to heaven. "You wanna know something I never told anyone?"

"Of course," Shawn told her.

"I'm the reason he's dead," Anne started to cry.

"What do you mean?"

"I was the one who was supposed to die. I made a deal with the Demon himself," she started to break down in a full outcry. "I lived and he took my Kale as punishment." She broke down in Shawn's arms.

"Anne, it's okay," he lifted her chin up. He gently put his hands on her cheeks and kissed her forehead. They locked eyes and Shawn leaned for a kiss. Anne returned the kiss as she pulled Shawn on top of her. The sounds of dark low thunder carried them into the night.

CHAPTER NINE

Father Richard wiped his baldhead with his handkerchief. It wasn't sweaty and he wasn't hot. It was purely a nervous habit. The two priests sat quietly with the Cardinal in his office, no one saying a word. There was nothing but silence as the sound of hard rain hit the windows. Thunder roared with lightning flashing across the sky. The three of them just sat, not knowing what to do or say. The only reason the eerie quietness broke was when Megan came into the office with her hair wet.

"I like this storm." She wiped the water off her jacket as she checked in. The mood of the room was quite somber. "What's going on?"

"Alex has gone missing." The Cardinal got up to see his reflection in the window. It would seem this night was adding a grayer blend to his head.

"I just saw her today; maybe she is spending the night at some guy's place. She's been doing that a lot lately," Megan gave them an option on where she could have been.

Father Carl joined in, "I did see her in the back alley trying to engage with some stranger off the street."

"Alex has always had a temper and a bit of a free spirit," Cardinal Joe told the group. "What's been going on is beyond us. We need to find her before she gets herself killed."

"We can't call the police; they won't even consider her missing. Plus, there is no way we are going to find her if she doesn't want to be found," Father Richard pointed out.

"Megan, Alex didn't take her phone with her. We found it in her room. Can you just stay by the phone in case she calls?" Cardinal Joe rubbed his face with his hands.

"Of course, Cardinal," Megan was drying off her red-streaked hair.

"We could go at least try to look for her," Father Carl offered. "I've been with patrol groups in the Middle East that found missing soldiers against all odds."

Father Richard spoke, "It's better than just sitting here. We should make sure to wear our collars. People tend to help more when they see them."

"Agreed," Father Carl got up to go to his office.

"Good luck and God Bless," Cardinal Joe told them. "I will call some of the other churches. Perhaps she will find sanctuary in them."

The two fathers got their coats on but made sure to show their collars. They both stood out in the lobby looking at the storm. "We need to walk to find her. Driving is going to be no good," Father Carl stated the obvious.

"Yes," Father Richard turned to the priest. "Carl, Alex is very important to us. She may not be the perfect Catholic, for that matter she's not even Catholic, but she does wonders for the church." They both put on their black round clergy hats.

"Why did she call herself a Sentry?" Father Carl asked.

"Probably because she stays in the church at night and protects it," Father Richard said as if it was common knowledge. He snuck a peek to make sure Father Carl bought it. "Let's go find our girl."

***

Anne was sick to her stomach. What did she just do? She looked over at Shawn who was putting his pants back on. The clouds now covered the sky, making sure no light from the moon or stars were present. Anne put on her clothes as she was cold, empty, and felt ill.

Shawn zipped his pants on and turned to Anne, who was still on the ground. "Thanks, Anne. I needed to do that." He put his shirt on. "I'll see you around." He grabbed his phone and texted someone before taking off as the rain started.

Anne lifted her knees to her chest and wrapped her arms around them to bring them in closer. She couldn't get warm. She just shivered as the rain came smashing down on her.

***

Gron got a text from Merik of his recent conquest. The Dark Sentry couldn't help but think of how wonderful it was delivering another blow to Mole. The thought of his love, the Pure of Heart, sitting there in the rain alone. Her shivering from shame was just the icing on the cake. Things were falling into place rather easily. Another message came in from Misluna. It would appear that the Sentry has taken off lost and hopeless. She felt she was abandoned by her so-called loving God. That was just the sprinkles.

He hit the intercom, "Bring me, Rollmak."

"Yes, my leader," the secretary affirmed over the speaker.

Gron got up from his chair and stared out the window at the storm. "You will not see it coming." Lightning flashed and the sound of a knock on the door echoed in the room. "Come."

"Rollmak is here, my leader," his secretary smiled at Gron before leaving. The door shut with the slender Demon awaiting his instruction.

"Yes, my leader." His British accent was something Gron found soothing for some reason.

"Gather a team of three Demons and three Infiltrators. You'll have to subdue the dog. Go now, a fourth Demon will not be that far behind," Gron commanded.

"Has there been any sign of her?" He stood so properly polite. A sophisticated arrogance protruded off him.

"A Provisionary caught her full out running out of town to the west," Gron let him know. "Find the Sentry and kill her."

"To your command," Rollmak bowed.

He watched his murderous Demon leave the room. He whistled for the secretary to appear. "Yes, my leader."

"Do you have a replacement in mind?" He was getting tired of her and needed some new blood up in the front office.

Her smile was one of accomplishment. "Yes, my leader. She will serve you well."

"Are you ready for absolute power?" he asked as an Infiltrator came from out behind the desk, sniffing the secretary to see if she was ready.

"Absolute power," she told him.

He whistled to get the Infiltrator's attention. "Wait outside, this won't take long."

The secretary looked confused about his actions. "I thought I was about to…"

Gron put up his hand. "One last time."

The secretary grinned as she started unbuttoning her blouse. Gron knew what was about to happen tonight. The Sentry would be killed while the key to bring Vandor back was growing.

* * *

Alex ran hard with the rain hitting her in the face. She ran fast, so fast the droplets of water were starting to sting against her skin. Komptin had a hard time keeping up with her. Alex ran and ran until she didn't recognize where she was.

She started panting, not out of a lack of energy but out of emotion. Around her were a set of train tracks and a small building. She stood in the middle of an empty parking lot where people put their cars and took the train into town. There was a light above her, shining down on her. Alex put her fists out to her side and her eyes glowed. Alex, with a determined stance, stood in the middle of the lot. She didn't know the Dark was there. She had no idea where they were. With all her emotion, she screamed, "I'M HERE!" She looked around for any signs. "I'M HERE, YOU DARK BASTARDS!"

Komptin finally caught up to her. There was nothing in the situation he found was tantalizing. He growled and let out a bark that seemed to echo into the night.

"Come on, what are you afraid of?" Alex surveyed the surrounding area before spitting on the ground. "Chicken shits." Alex turned to Komptin, whose eyes were a steady glow. All around them, red eyes appeared in the depths of the hard rain. Komptin morphed into his hunting state. He gave a threatening roar to the Infiltrators and Demons running towards them.

Alex gave a scowl and then shot a Lite Beam at the closest Infiltrator, knocking it into two other Demons. The biggest of the Demons came running after her as he knocked an Infiltrator to the side to clear the way. "Die, you Lite Harlot!" The Demon smacked her to the ground. Alex returned the punch and the Demon spun around with Komptin jumping on his back, biting into his shoulder.

The other two Demons both jumped on Komptin's back bringing him down in a crashing thud onto the pavement. Alex jumped in the air and landed on the big Demon's chest. She punched him multiple times before being tackled off by an Infiltrator. The big Demon broke free from

Komptin's bite as he was trying to fend off the two Demons on his back.

Only one Demon faced Alex. The two of them circled each other before Alex got annoyed and shot a Lite Beam at the Demon knocking over a bench bolted down to the cemented sidewalk. Alex followed behind the beam and started to fight the Demon. Alex's fist stung as she punched the Demon across the face. Her hands grabbed the Demon's clothes to pull its body into her knee. Full of anger, she challenged the next being of the Dark after she threw him onto the ground.

Alex turned to see how Komptin was doing. There were three Infiltrators in a horseshoe facing Komptin. Two Demons were behind them, slowly walking towards him. Komptin was waiting for the attack. Alex saw an armored vehicle start to back up. "Komptin!" Alex yelled. She went to help, but she was grabbed by another Demon. The caramelized skinned demon dug her nails into her arm as she flung Alex into the train scheduling board.

The armored truck quickly backed up with the doors open. Then the five Dark soldiers rushed Komptin at the same time, pushing him into the armored truck. A group of prospectors locked the door as the big demon took a piece of crowbar. He bent the bar to lock Komptin in the armored vehicle. "GO!" he commanded. "Take him far away from her! Bury it, drown it, get it away from the Sentry."

"Komptin!" Alex screamed. The Dark now turned to Alex and rushed her. She shot a Lite

Beam at the nearest one as she tried to get to Komptin. A monstrous sized Demon swung his arm across Alex's chest. It spun her around sending her crashing to the ground. She lifted her face out of a puddle of rainwater and mud. The massive Demon pulled her up by the hair to come face to face with her. Alex lit her fist pushing her thumb into the Demon's eyes. He screamed in pain, as he was frantically moving about, knocking into his fellow Dark companions. This gave Alex room to get out of the way.

"He's useless, kill him and get her," the slender Demon commanded.

The Infiltrators all jumped the injured Demon to tear him apart. There were pieces of Demon showering the ground. The Infiltrators with blood of the Demon dripping from their mouths turned to Alex.

Alex flashed her eyes, ready for the attack. The female Demon jumped on Alex's back, choking her. The Demon gave a shrill scream when Alex took a hold of her hair and flipped her onto her back. Alex instinctively dropped her knee on top of the forehead of the Demon. All present heard the crack of the skull. Alex could only guess that the Demon was weak enough to destroy since she could not sense the vile creature. The Lite within her formed a knife to stab into the Demon's chest. The Demon howled in pain as it disappeared into the ground forever.

The Lite Sentry had little time to celebrate when she was clawed by one of the Infiltrators behind her. Alex screamed before being blindsided from a punch by the big Demon, knocking Alex backward onto the train tracks. The train approached close enough to kiss before Alex rolled out of the way onto the other side. This caused her to be separated from the Demons.

"Jump on the train! Make sure she isn't on it," the slender Demon commanded. "We'll stay behind and finish her off when the train ends."

The big Demon acknowledged with a nod as he jumped inside of an open boxcar. They waited for a while before the train ended. The Infiltrators ran to the other side– to find no trace of the Sentry. Rollmak got irritated. He got on his radio to the driver of the armored vehicle. "Get him far away from here, quickly."

***

Kameron was in his new apartment putting things away. Most of the boxes were broken down except for one that wasn't opened. He placed it on the table. There were a pair of blue eyes he drew on it when he packed it back in DC. It was as if they were staring at him. Inside the box were all the things Alex related. The box cutter in his hand seemed like a weight too heavy for him to pick up.

The dancing can of Apollo that Alex got him when he took her to the Apollo manufacturing plant made him smile. She was like a kid in a candy factory. She drank so much of that stuff, he thought she was going to pee neon green for a week. There was a picture of the two of them at Christmas. This emotional scene was when he gave her that necklace. He thought he had loved before, but he now knows whom he had really loved. A knock on the door got him out of his trance. The box was placed inside the coat closet before he answered the door to Midnight and Scotty on the other side. "What's going on?"

Midnight looked frustrated. "There was an explosion downtown."

"Okay," Kameron was confused. "What does that have to do with us?"

Scotty answered Kameron, "Apparently, when Lana went to talk to her lawyer, the whole building blew up."

"What?" Kameron didn't get flabbergasted often, but this one took him by surprise.

"She's dead," Scotty said. "You know the paperwork that is going to be tied to this one?"

Kameron grabbed his keys. "Let's go."

The three of them arrived on the scene of the fire. As fires were concerned, it was a massive specimen, but it seemed to be contained. It was a single building completely engulfed. The heat could be felt from where they were standing.

"It's still going?" Kameron was shocked.

Scotty was entranced by the flames. "Either that, or they got one hell of a bond fire here."

Midnight studied the firefighters ensuring the fire didn't spread. "Lana was inside."

Kameron didn't believe in coincidences, especially when it came to the F.O.R. "This is too big to be natural."

"It's almost as if they wanted to make sure nothing in the building survived." Scotty was now joining Midnight in watching the firefighter, making sure the fire didn't break containment. "Everything would be gone; including what is in the safes."

"Well, this sucks," Midnight pointed out. "I say we go out and get drunk, because this investigation is now dead in the water."

"Sounds good to me." Scotty turned to go to the car. "Come on, Kameron. I know a great place with the best service in town."

"We are not going to Harry Palms Gentleman's Club, Scotty," Midnight told him.

"Why not?" Scotty argued. "I'm a gold member, no cover charge."

"How about we just go to the pub near the office?" Midnight jumped in the passenger seat of the car.

Kameron agreed, "That way we can leave our cars in the garage."

"Harry's got a great driver program where the dancer's drive…" Scotty started to say.

"No," Midnight and Kameron both said.

"I'm just talking facts here," Scotty pleaded.

They got to the pub where Kameron ordered the first round. They all ordered whiskey and cola. "Here you go." Kameron gave everyone a drink.

"Thanks," Midnight grabbed her drink. She smacked the leg of Scotty who wasn't paying attention.

"Huh, oh, yeah, thanks," he was scouting the room. "Just viewing the next victim to my desire."

Midnight laughed, "You're such a pig." She turned to Kameron. "So, whatever happened to that girl you were dating in college?"

"Oh, you mean the one that video-taped herself with some dude in the backseat of my car?" Kameron gave her some insight on what happened.

"Wait, what?" Scotty turned to the conversation and laughed. "Are you serious?"

Kameron nodded. "Last I saw her, she was a stripper at some club. She was trying to ruin the life of a friend of mine, but luckily I got him out of there."

"Wait, you prevented some dude from getting some from a willing stripper? I thought you were his friend," Scotty couldn't believe it. "Please don't ever do that for me."

Midnight ignored Scotty. "What happened to him?"

Kameron wanted to give Kale the honor he deserved by saying he got the life he should have had. "He ended up with the girl he was always meant to be with."

"That's sweet," Midnight chimed in.

"Aren't you the romantic," Scotty made a kissing face towards Midnight. "Would have never thought that."

"And now I'm a lesbian," Midnight pushed Scotty's face away from her.

"You think the F.O.R. could be behind all this?" Kameron asked the two of them when he put his drink down.

"Could be, it's a radical organization." Midnight took another sip of her drink.

"Why?" Scotty asked. "They may be behind it or maybe not. But any organization that supports getting rid of religion has got to have something, right?"

"So, I take it you're not religious." Kameron was tapped on the leg by Midnight as she shook her head.

"Religion is stupid. There's not some powerful entity looking over us, because if he is, he's doing a piss poor job. There is so much death, scum, and disgusting filth out there. So, the only reasoning is that there is no God." Scotty started to get irritated. "That is why, me, myself, and I, am going to make the best out of the time I have here on Earth." Scotty caught sight of a girl smiling at him. "Starting with her."

"You need Jesus," Midnight told him.

Scotty chugged down his drink before. "Just another historical radical that upset a corrupt government. Now, look how many people died because they think he's the son of a made-up God?"

"You really have issues," Midnight leaned back in her chair.

"Yep, and she's going to help solve them for me." Scotty got up to talk to the girl. He motioned to the bartender for another round for the two of them.

"He may be a chauvinistic, sexual deviant, but he's a good agent," Midnight told Kameron. The two of them watched him work his magic on the girl with obvious success.

Scotty went by their table with the girl as Midnight lifted up her hand giving him a high-five. "You have to hand it to him, he is good." She turned to face Kameron who was studying his phone. "So, was there anyone else after the stripper?"

Kameron paused for a second before answering. "No," he said quietly. "No one."

***

Alex painfully crawled to the end of the boxcar so she could rest her head on the back of the wall. She took a couple of breaths to try to figure out what was going on with life. Now, on top of everything, she lost Komptin. The lack of a phone in her pocket was just another form of bad news on this horrible night. Father Richard was going to be mad that another phone was lost. She rubbed her forehead with her hand. There was blood on her hand that seemed to glisten from the flashes of lightning. A small cut made itself known on the back of her neck that stung when she touched it. It wasn't bad, but just enough for her to feel it. She put her hand back there and her heart stopped. The necklace Kameron had given her was missing. She frantically started searching for it, hoping that it was down her shirt or something. It was gone. She slammed the back of her head against the wall of the boxcar. How did she get here? What caused all this? There has to be a reason why her connection to the Lite was taken away. She would cry but she had no more tears to shed.

"You look like shit," a man with no teeth appeared out from underneath a blanket.

"Thanks," Alex acknowledged. "It's been a rough couple of months." She closed her eyes, and then opened them right away to look at the old man. "Don't try anything— it won't end well for you."

"I'm a political government refugee, not a rapist." The man pulled out a can from inside his pants. "Sardine?"

"I'm good," Alex put up her hand. "Thanks."

"Whatch ya runnin' from?" he asked as he sucked down a fish.

"Darkness, lack of Lite, pain, and heartache." She could not help but hope Komptin was okay, but she had no way to know where he was. "You?"

"Taxes." The man ate another sardine. "These might have gone bad." He ate another one after a belch.

Alex made a face of disgust. "I'll take your word for it." There was no way to know how long she was on the train, but it was well past midnight. The sound of the man getting up had Alex open one eye to see what he was doing. He farted as he scratched his butt.

"This is my favorite part of the trip, once we go over the bridge, you'll see..." his sentence was stopped when the Demon grabbed his chest with his clawed hand. He squeezed the chest as Alex could hear the bones break. The massive monster threw the old man out the door, crashing into the ground.

Alex shot a Lite Beam at the Demon hoping to push him out the door but he dodged out of the way. He caught up to her and punched her across the face, hitting her in the scar. It stung enough to daze her. The Demon smashed her head against the wall of the boxcar. Blood dripped from her head, the throbbing pain pulsated; for a split second, Alex thought she was dead as she felt her body start to rise. The Demon had lifted her above his head. She fell with force as her chest was met with the Demon's knee. The sounds of her bones cracking in her chest coincided with sharp pain. There was no energy left for her. The Demon had picked her up with his massive hands around her head. When she tried prying his hands off, the Demon countered with a massive punch to her face.

She spun to the ground, crashing on the boxcar floor. She turned to the Demon with blood dripping from her mouth. "You hit like my grandmother, you fungus licking, piece of…" Alex didn't get to finish her sentence as she was kicked in the side where her charred scar was. It sent her flying out of the boxcar. They were over a bridge with a rapid river below them. All the Demon saw was the faint color of neon blue disappearing into the river's rapid water below.

239

CHAPTER TEN

Kameron woke in the middle of the night trying to catch his breath. The bed was soaked as if he had taken a shower but didn't bother drying off. A moment had passed where he had to take a moment to calm down. Outside the window, he thought he heard a girl screaming on the ground. There was nobody outside of the window. "Man." Kameron wiped his face with his hand.

He got his breathing under control before going into the kitchen to get a glass of water. The glass slipped out of his hands. Luckily, it landed on his foot, preventing it from breaking, but water spilled on the kitchen floor. "Damn it," he muttered. The paper towels were in the closet. Inside the closet was a box with blue eyes that seemed to glow at him. Kameron grabbed the paper towel roll to clean up his mess.

After he cleaned up his mess, he decided to try to go back to bed. He turned over to see the empty space. It was such a big bed for just one person. It was so difficult to try to get back to sleep. His mind was racing, and he was thinking of everything. For some reason, Kale was on his mind. He picked up his phone since he couldn't sleep and noticed he had a message from an unknown number. It was from Father Richard asking if he'd heard from Alex and to give him a call. He replied that he would. He went to bed hoping that he would wake up to Alex laying in the bed next to him.

***

Alex crawled up onto the shoreline, coughing up water. She turned her head to lay down on the shore. She wanted to get up and try to walk, but she had no energy. The water was rushing by her feet as she just laid on the embankment. When she opened one eye, she came to see two boys staring at her with lanterns.

"You think she's a witch, Samuel?" The young boy with a black hat poked her with a stick.

"She looks like a witch, Eli." The other one was studying Alex. "Her skin is so white."

"Look at her hair, I have never seen anything like it. She's no doubt a witch." Samuel went to touch her hair.

Eli cautioned, "Careful Samuel, she may cast a spell on you."

Alex now opened both eyes. "Can I help you?"

The boys stepped back. "Don't eat us," Eli begged.

"I'm in no condition to eat anything." She tried to get up but fell back down.

"Father!" Samuel yelled. "We have found a witch."

"Father, father!" The boys went running away.

Alex tried to get up but all she could do was stumble, falling on the ground. A man holding another lantern came up to her with a beard and no mustache. The light was close enough for Alex to feel the heat. Alex squinted from the light as she put up her hand to shield her eyes. "I don't think she's a witch, boys, but she does have some interesting hair and clothing." He poked her with his finger. "Miss, are you all right?"

"Can you get the light out of my face?" She asked.

"My apologies." He pulled the lantern away. "Do you need help?"

"No, I can get up." Alex stood up but crashed to the ground again. "Maybe not."

"Eli, Samuel, help me get her into the cart," he told them.

The three of them got Alex into the cart. The horse buggy wasn't the most comfortable ride as Alex pretty much felt every stone in the road. It was much appreciated though. The boys' father stopped the cart. "Dorothy, come please, give me a hand."

A woman in a white bonnet and a long dress appeared. "What is it, Jeremiah?"

"We found a witch, mother," Samuel was bragging a bit.

"There is no such thing as…" Dorothy stopped herself with the moonlight that lit Alex's face. "Oh my, Jeremiah, where did you find her?"

"She is injured, lying on the road." He tried helping Alex out of the buggy. "Come, help me."

Dorothy came running to help carry Alex into a bedroom. Eli and Samuel peeked into the room where their mother was tending to Alex. "Boys, fetch me some hot water and rags." She turned to Jeremiah, "Your eyes are not meant to see this." Dorothy grabbed a hold of the door to shut it.

"Yes, of course," Jeremiah concurred. "Come boys, I will get the water, you get the rags."

"Yes, Father." Eli did as he was told. "Come, Samuel." The two boys went with their father to fetch what their mother required of them.

The door closed and Alex was being undressed by Dorothy. "Tell me your name."

"Alex," she told her as she tried to remove some of her clothing.

"Alex, you say. That sounds like a boy's name." Dorothy was going over the situation in front of her. "Don't overdo it. I will help you." Dorothy took off Alex's leather jacket. The rips from claws on her jacket were evident when Dorothy hung it up to dry. "Tell me, and I would like the truth. I invite you into my home, the same one as my family. Tell me, are you a witch?"

"No," Alex snickered. "Even though I've been called a lot worse."

Dorothy in a protective tone asked, "Then, you will not hurt my family?"

"I swear to God, on the Bible," Alex assured her. "I will cause no harm to your family."

Dorothy nodded in acceptance. "So, you are a woman of God. I believe you and we will help you." She folded Alex's leather coat with the claw marks showing. "You townspeople have some interesting ways about you." She took off Alex's shirt. "You have many scars."

"Yes." Alex helped as much as she could to get undressed.

"Take it slow, Alex. You are safe here. I will remove the rest of your clothing, okay? I need to clean your wounds." After Alex agreed, Dorothy helped Alex remove her clothing. Dorothy was a natural nurse as she helped Alex to get her wounds cleaned. "Your wounds are deep. I should get you to a hospital."

"No, I'll be fine. I just need to rest," Alex told her. "I beg of you."

"We cannot harbor someone who is unlawful, Alex," Dorothy told her. "I must think of my children."

"I'm not in trouble with the authorities, I promise you that." Alex cringed in pain as Dorothy started to pull some of the bigger chunks of debris out of Alex's body.

Dorothy nodded. "Okay." There was a knock on the bedroom door. "Yes."

Jeremiah pushed in the hot water with rags without coming in. "Here is what you wish. I shall put the children to bed."

"Thank you, Jeremiah." Dorothy returned with the rags. "This may be a bit hot."

Alex finished bathing and getting her wounds cleaned. Dorothy suggested she get some sleep. To amuse her, Alex went into the bed. The bed was warm, soft, and comforting. Alex wished she could fall asleep to enjoy such a haven.

"You rest, I will check on you throughout the night," Dorothy smiled at her. "May God protect you." She closed the door behind her.

Alex just laid there in bed, staring out the window at Osiah's star. "If He knew where I was."

***

"We searched all night but didn't find anything," Father Richard came into the Cardinal's office with Father Carl behind him. "But if she took off, there is no way we are going to find her."

Cardinal Joe ran his fingers through his gray hair, "Do you think she would go back home with Anne?"

"Maybe she went after Kameron." Father Richard stated.

Father Carl chimed in. "I don't think so. Anne was letting Alex use her car until we transferred back to her hometown. It's still in the parking lot."

"The Council checked her credit card and there was no activity on it," Cardinal Joe stated. "Any news on Komptin?"

"The dog?" Father Carl asked. "Wouldn't he be with her?"

"If he were, it would be easier to find out where she was through him." The Cardinal was no doubt starting to get tired.

Father Carl thought about it, "Is he GPS tracked?"

"In a way," Father Richard confirmed.

"Then all we have left is to pray." Cardinal Joe got up to the window. "For such a beautiful morning, it sure seems dark out."

***

Alex didn't know what time it was but there was a knock on the door. "Come in."

Dorothy approached Alex with a pile of clothes. "How did you sleep, Alex?"

"As expected." Alex knew Dorothy came in to check on her three times last night. Every time Alex heard her about to come in, she had to pretend she was sleeping. "Thank you for all your help."

"Well, it wouldn't be godly of us to have you laying in the river to die now," she said observing the status of her wounds. Dorothy's face was a bit relieved as she examined Alex's body. "Maybe they weren't as bad as I thought. Your wounds are healing nicely."

"I appreciate your help." Alex got out of bed and stretched.

"Of course," Dorothy studied Alex's body scars. "What is your plan, Alex?"

"I haven't thought that far ahead," Alex admitted. "I should really go into town and try to find a phone."

"The nearest phone is a six-hour carriage ride," Dorothy told her.

"Well, that sucks. I guess I better get walking." Alex got up but winced from the pain.

"You are not going anywhere until you are healed." Dorothy got a little stern. "Come, I have food ready for you." Dorothy handed her a pile of clothes. "I am washing and mending your clothes, so you will have to wear these."

"Thank you." She got dressed when Dorothy left the room. Her long braids hung over the back as she tried to get them into the bonnet. They kept on falling out. It took time trying to get them up there so she just stuffed her hair inside the back of her dress. She stepped out to the kitchen where there was food waiting for her.

Jeremiah, with his two kids, were going over some scripture. "Good morning, Alex," he said. "I hope you slept well."

"Good morning, Alex." Samuel was holding a toy wooden horse. "Would you like to read some scripture?"

"What are you reading?" Alex looked over the shoulder of the boys.

"The devil's temptation of the Lord while in the desert," Eli told her. "He's so evil."

"I like that one, the best part is when the Dark one gets put into his place," she smiled.

Dorothy spoke, "Alex, you must eat."

Jeremiah added in, "Would you like some coffee?"

"Yes, yes, oh please yes," Alex grabbed the coffee and she didn't care how hot it was. She chugged it down. "Second cup, please."

"Yes, of course." Dorothy poured her another cup of coffee.

Alex sat down to have some biscuits and eggs. "This is really good, thank you."

Jeremiah spoke, "So where did you come from?"

"DC." Alex told them. The biscuits were moist with real butter sliding down her throat. Alex welcomed this breakfast as a moment of bliss.

"That is quite far away." Jeremiah closed his Bible. "Samuel, will you please put this in the common room."

Samuel grabbed the Bible. "Yes, Father."

"I wouldn't know. I don't know where I am," Alex admitted. "Is there a way I can get to a phone?"

"We will leave the day after the tourists. It is a long way, but a very beautiful route," Jeremiah told her. "We all can go."

The kids got excited at the sound of the trip.

Alex saw something out the window. "There is someone coming."

Jeremiah smiled. "That would be my grandfather."

The door opened to an old man walking stiffly into the house. "That walk is getting longer and longer as my time on Earth is getting shorter and shorter. What the Lord giveth, he taketh away."

"Papa, you should not be walking that yourself." Dorothy handed him a cup of coffee.

"Yes, well." He was about to speak until he saw Alex. "Forgive me, I didn't know you had company."

"I'm, Alex." She stood up, going over to the old man.

"I'm, Uri," he said, studying Alex. "You are not from here, are you?"

"She is a townswoman. We found her by the river injured." Jeremiah stole another biscuit from a bowl Dorothy was carrying over to Uri.

Uri laughed, "She is not a wounded animal. She is a soul. Tell me Alex, what brings you out this way?"

"I fell in the river and the current caught me," Alex told him.

Jeremiah looked out the window, "Papa, did you know town elders were following you here?"

"Ah yes, I forgot to tell you. There is a meeting about the renovation of the town church," he told him. He took a biscuit and a cup of coffee.

Alex immediately thought of Anne, hoping that she was doing okay.

***

Anne took her third shower within a few hours. Nothing she could do was giving her the sense of being clean. The only thing that felt right was wearing clothes that covered her body. She put on a baseball cap with her hair coming out the back before heading into the kitchen. Nothing seemed good to eat, as her stomach was getting tighter and more nauseous.

"Are you okay, honey?" her mom asked. "You don't look good."

"I'm fine, Mom," Anne told her. "Just a late night."

"Okay." Willow handed her a cup of coffee. "Kate called. She wanted to make sure you were all right. She said you were quite upset."

"Mom, I can't do this right now, okay?" Anne took a sip of her coffee. "I just need time to sort some things out."

Her mom nodded. "Will you be home for dinner?"

"I should be." Anne grabbed a travel mug from the cabinet to pour her coffee. Her mom grabbed the other cup to be washed. "Thank you. I need to get going."

Anne didn't get to the church until well after two o'clock. Her stomach was so upset that she had to vomit on the side of the road. She was hoping that would make her feel better but it didn't. Anne got a call from Father Richard. "Yes, Father?" She listened to what had happened last night. "If I see her, I will let you know. Yes, of course. Bye."

Anne couldn't believe Alex had gone missing. There was no way to know where she was. Anne wanted to go pray in the church with everything that was going on. She removed her hat before walking into the congregation where Devine was again staring at the stained-glass window. "Devine?"

Devine turned around. "Pure of Heart," she acknowledged.

"Don't know how pure it is anymore," Anne said as she sat down on a pew.

"Your hair changed color," Devine made a face of disapproval at the jet-black hair.

"You noticed that?" Anne said, fluffing it.

"I do not like the color on you. You do not look pure with dark black hair," Devine observed. "You look different. You look shaded."

"Let me know when you lose your better half, and see how you feel," Anne snapped at her.

"I have," Devine calmly reminded.

Anne turned her head in shame, "Of course, I'm sorry. I shouldn't have snapped." Anne got up and joined Devine at the altar. "I haven't been myself since last night."

"May I ask why?" Devine studied the Pure of Heart.

"It's shameful, and not worth repeating," Anne quickly said. "It shouldn't be talked about."

"I see," Devine turned to look down the aisle of the congregation. "It changed who you are and you do not like it. You feel like you are no longer pure."

"Devine, I said I don't want to talk about it," she told her.

"Alexandria. She is your friend. You will talk to her." Devine started to walk away.

"She's missing," Anne let her know. "They don't know where she is."

Devine stopped. "The Sentry cannot be found?"

Anne shook her head.

"Komptin?"

"No sign of him as well." Anne held her stomach as if she was going to vomit again.

"Devine, perhaps…" Anne looked around but she was nowhere to be found.

***

Jonkur and Platonx were driving the armored transport as the Provisionaries behind them drove in a backup car. It was a nice sunny day as they were driving to trap this gargoyle dog in the depths of the ocean. They had been driving for hours and had another day of driving ahead of them, plus the boat ride out to the depths.

The trail car was too quiet for Charles. "Should we play some music?"

"No, let me get a couple hours of sleep and then I'll take over driving," Leo said in return. "We've been provisionaries for a while. Perhaps once we complete this mission we can become Hosts. To his command."

"That would make this trip worth it. It's clear the F.O.R. is the correct path for absolute power. To his command." He drove for a couple more hours when he thought he heard thunder, but it was still clear blue skies. He slapped his partner on the leg to wake him up.

"What? Is it my turn already?" He rubbed the sleep out of his eyes.

"I thought I heard thunder," Charles was looking up to the sky. "I'm telling you, I heard thunder."

There were no thunderstorms evident in the sky. "There isn't a cloud in the sky." Then the thunder got louder with a flash of lightning in an all of sudden thunderstorm. Devine came crashing down on the hood of the car. She was in full body armor with her Lite Bo activated. She stabbed through the windshield killing the driver. The car spun out of control, causing Devine to fly above the car as it smashed into the median rail. Devine ripped off the passenger door. She grabbed Leo by the shirt. "Where is the Sentry?" she demanded.

"Dead if all went well." He grabbed Devine's arm. She quickly threw the primate to the ground. The armored car had started speeding up. Devine walked by the human, killing him with ease before she started running to take to the skies.

Devine landed on the roof of the armored car. The Demons knew they were in trouble. They slammed on the breaks, stopping the truck instantly. It launched Devine off the armored truck but she just flew in the air to the back of the vehicle. She ripped the bar off the door and grabbed the Demon as he rounded the corner to stop her. She threw him like a rag doll as the other Demon came around the other corner, causing Devine to show skill with her Lite Bo as she swung her bo on the side of its head. The Demon slammed into the truck and Devine followed with a kick, dropping Jonkur to the ground. He got up but Devine jumped in the air and landed on his back, sticking her pointed end bo into the back of the Dark minion. The shell of the Demon disappeared into the ground.

Platonx got up as he was met by Komptin when he broke out of his cell to tackle the Demon. He clawed into his chest and then held it down as he tore the head off with his mouth. The body disappeared and Komptin gave an angry roar of disgust. He took a sniff in the air to make sure no one was around before he joined Devine.

"Are you injured?" she asked the Protector. Devine dissipated her misty wings and halo. "Do you know where the Sentry is?"

Komptin's face turned to sorrow as he couldn't help Devine.

"I do not know either. Come, we will go get help," the Lite Angel morphed her battle armor into a primate running out. Komptin transformed into a German shepherd and the two went running down the road.

***

Alex helped Dorothy collect some apples from the orchard. When she reached up to grab an apple, it caused her to twinge a little from the pain. She didn't want to show pain, but it hurt.

"Who are you trying to be strong for, me or yourself?" Dorothy was studying the apple.

"It's just second nature, sometimes I don't even realize I'm doing it," Alex admitted to her. There was a barrel full of apples down at the end row. Alex went to pick them up to carry them to the house.

"What are you doing?" Dorothy stopped her. "You will not be able to pick that up. Jeremiah will come by with the buggy for those."

Alex stopped herself. "Yes, of course. I meant to pick up the basket."

"You are a strange one, Alex." Dorothy gathered the basket of apples.

The two of them walked into the kitchen with the apples. In the common area were a group of five older men and one middle-aged man with Jeremiah. They all stopped their conversation to look at Alex. Her pale skin and hair that obviously tucked inside her clothes caught their attention. She smiled and waved at them. They all returned the wave and then turned to Jeremiah in question.

"We found her injured by the river. Her name is Alex, that's all I know," Jeremiah told the group.

The youngest of the group leaned in, "Bringing a stranger who looks like that into your home with your children is dangerous."

"She needed help, Leroy," Jeremiah stated. "I could not leave her out there."

Uri chimed in, "We must start renovations soon if we are to beat the winter weather."

"We have time, Uri," the older man said. "The young men can help just before the harvest."

"They have families they must take care of, Reuben," Uri reminded.

"God will provide, but we must have a place for worship," Reuben said.

"Why does this conversation always lead in the same direction, but nothing gets done?" Leroy was getting agitated.

The elders all leaned back and sighed.

Uri looked to Alex who was trying to figure out how to use the apple peeler. "What do you think, Alex?"

"About what?" she replied, tearing her apple apart.

"I know you have been listening." The old man winked at her with a smile.

"Go," Dorothy grabbed the peeler. "This apple has suffered enough." She grabbed the apple from Alex's hand.

Alex walked into the common area with all eyes on her. "I think it doesn't matter where you go," she told him.

"See, I've always said townspeople are godless people," Leroy waved his hand over at Alex.

Alex squinted her eyes at Leroy. "How about you let me finish?" Uri snickered while the other elders were somewhat offended by the manner Alex spoke to Leroy. "As I was saying, it doesn't matter where you worship, as long as you thank Him for all He does. That's all He really wants."

"Are you speaking for God?" Reuben was offended by Alex's words.

"I would never; it's just, I don't think God would be so egotistical to want such a thing. He just wants us to have a good life and appreciate what He has done for us," she told him.

The elders just nodded but Leroy didn't like her answer. "Sounds like blasphemy to me."

"To each their own is what I say. Do what is good for you." Alex went back into the kitchen. "Which apple is going to be my next victim?"

Leroy got up, "You all are invited over tonight for dinner. My wife is making a wonderful apple pie."

"Yes, we all should be there," Jeremiah let him know. "Please set us up for five plus papa."

"Five?" Leroy asked.

"We cannot leave Alex alone." Jeremiah escorted the gentlemen out of the house.

"Yes, of course," Leroy said, leaving the house staring at Alex.

***

Kameron was typing up his report about the interview from yesterday. He debated on keeping his word to Lana about being off the record, but she was already dead, so no harm done if he put it in there. It was late into the afternoon when he finally got the report done.

"You're quiet today," Midnight said, approaching his desk drinking a bottle of water.

"Didn't sleep well," Kameron told her. He went into his desk and pulled out some dehydrated apple slices. "Want some?"

"I'm good," Midnight put her hand up.

Scotty leaned over in his chair as he was sitting at his desk. "Kameron, get that report done? I need to close this case."

"I just saved it. You can view it now." Kameron closed the report program.

Scotty started to read it. "Hey, when is Weston coming back?"

"Tomorrow, he said he's taking a personal day," Midnight told him. "Weston is the CIA liaison. He sits behind Scotty. Nice guy. Writes a lot though. His reports are so detailed."

"Hey, what's this?" Scotty re-read the report.

Kameron told him, "My report."

"Why didn't you tell me you talked to Lana after we did?" He was irritated and rightfully so.

"She talked to me off the record. She was scared that she had a target on her head," Kameron told him. "There was no witness, so anything I would have written would have been dismissed."

"I can't use this," Scotty lectured Kameron. "It will keep this case open with no way to close it."

"But it's what happened," Kameron argued.

"Yes, off the record, remember." He deleted that portion of the report. "There, sign it please so we can now close the case. Enough of this F.O.R. crap."

"It's your case," Midnight let him know. "Do what you want." Midnight leaned back in her chair going over some case notes. "What happened to your conquest last night?" Midnight took a sip of her water.

"It was all good, but this morning she was like, 'I would like to see you again'," Scotty started to tell the story. "You meet a guy at a bar, hook up with him that night, and you think it's going to go long term? Don't they teach girls the code for 'one night stand'?"

Midnight just stared at him. "When was the last time you were checked for an STD?"

"Last week," he came back calmly. "I get them on a monthly basis." Kameron and Midnight both looked at him but didn't know if he was serious or not. Scotty suddenly glanced out the window and then he looked at his watch. "I have an appointment with the AUSA, I gotta go."

"Later." Kameron sat at his desk staring at his notes, debating in his mind about shredding them.

"You think that portion of the report should go in the file?" she asked.

"I do," Kameron told her. "Why is he so anxious to close this case?"

"He hated this case." Midnight took a sip of her water. "Right from the start he said it was going to go nowhere."

Midnight could tell Kameron was in deep thought. "What's on your mind?"

"Just a racing mind, that's all," Kameron admitted.

"I've got a meeting with SDPD about some whack-o they arrested talking about the typical anti-government mumbo jumbo. I think this is a case with Brian Petrolowksi's name in it. Wanna come?"

"Yeah, I'll join you." Kameron grabbed his jacket to start heading downstairs.

Lane came up to the two of them. "Kameron, I just got notified by security downstairs that a girl with a German shepherd is here to see you."

Kameron stopped in his tracks with all the blood rushing out of his face. "Tell them I'll be right down." He took a moment; it seemed like time just stood still.

"Want a breath mint?" Midnight broke his trance.

He turned to her. "Do you have one?" She handed him a piece of gum. "Thanks."

On the way down, Midnight noticed that Kameron really didn't say a thing. They walked down to the lobby. Kameron didn't see Alex, but almost gave up until a dog barked and he turned around to see Komptin running up. Kameron knelt down, "Come here, boy." He roughed him up while playing with him.

"Friend of yours, Kam?" Midnight asked him to back up from the dog.

"He's the dog of..." he started to say.

"Kameron," an athletic girl with bright neon purple hair came up to him.

Kameron stood up with a confused look on his face. "Devine, I...I wasn't...what are you doing here?"

Midnight could see something was going on. "Kam, do you want me to go get the car?"

"Sorry, do you mind?" Kameron asked her while still studying Devine. The angel had always been an expert at hiding emotions, but even now, he could see something was wrong.

"I'll take my time." Midnight smiled as she went away.

"Come with me," Devine said as she went outside.

The two of them were outside the federal building. Devine hasn't always been the most emotional individual Kameron knew, but this time it was something different. "Is Alex…"

Devine cut him off. "She is missing."

A moment of relief came over Kameron, as he'd feared the worst.

"Have you seen Alexandria?" She flat out asked.

Kameron shook his head. "No, I haven't."

"We do not know where she is. Would you be able to find her?" Devine asked.

"I'm going to ask the obvious question; you still can't sense her?" Kameron stood by a water fountain.

"If I could, I would not need your help," Devine sharply told him.

"Ask a stupid question," Kameron put his hands up.

Devine agreed, "Yes, it was a stupid question."

"Have you talked to, Anne?" Kameron asked her.

"There is something wrong with her," Devine told him. "She is not herself."

"What's wrong with her?" Kameron became concerned for his friend.

"She had an upset stomach and her hair is now black," Devine told him. "There is something new going on that the Lite has no knowledge of."

"Could explain Alex's condition," Kameron commented.

"To prevent her from sensing it," Devine changed her demeanor as if she had an epiphany. "I must go. Can you find her?"

"Wait, what?" Kameron was taken back a bit. "I just can't. Where are you going?"

"Can you take Komptin?" Devine had determination in her eyes.

"Of course, where are you going?" Kameron asked.

"To seek answers," Devine told him.

CHAPTER ELEVEN

Alex had been to family meals before but nothing like this. It was much more formal; where the women mainly served the men. It worked for them. Alex wasn't judging. It just wasn't her type of thing. There wasn't much talking about anything until the attention turned to Alex.

"Alex, are you married?" Leroy's wife, Eliza, asked her as she was holding a small baby.

Alex choked on her food because she wasn't expecting such a question. "Sorry, no."

"Family is very important. It is what God asks of us," Leroy started lecturing her. "The problem with townspeople is that they ignore the direction from God." He took a bite of the bread in front of him.

"Yes, some of them have lost faith. Others have not; free will was his gift, wasn't it?" Alex was going to show him she wasn't dismissive.

The table now turned their attention to Alex and Leroy's conversation. "What will you teach your children?" Leroy asked in an arrogant tone as he continued to challenge Alex.

Alex glared right into his eyes. "I'm unable to have children."

All the women gave Alex a sympathetic look. Eliza spoke, "I'm sorry you won't know the blessing from God of children."

Leroy got up and put his hands on his wife's shoulders. "To love them, protect them, to teach them, that is what is important. When you find that person to love, you will know."

Alex didn't say much else for the rest of the night. The ride home in the buggy was quiet. Her mind was thinking about how safe she'd felt with the warmth of the Lite. Her favorite moments were when Kameron would hold her in the church congregation. She had the best of both worlds. The warmth of the Lite and the security of Kameron.

The woods appeared empty as they passed each tree in the carriage. How would she know what's out in those trees? There was no way she could sense the Dark. She didn't know if they were out there. A pair of eyes glowed in the field that got Alex's attention. Her nerves skyrocketed and she prepared to ignite her Lite. She stood up and was about to lunge into action when she realized it was just a coyote.

"Are you all right, Alex?" Uri asked her.

"I'm fine." Alex sat back down.

When they got back to the house, Dorothy went to get the children into their pajamas. Uri and Jeremiah went to do the nightly chores. Alex sat in the rocking chair, staring out the window. Thoughts of her life were racing through her mind.

"Alex," Eli came up to her, placing his hands on the arm of the rocking chair.

Alex had her bonnet off and her hair was down. "Yes."

Both Samuel and Eli jumped on her lap. Alex gave a little laugh as she got them situated on her lap. "Children," Dorothy came to get them off.

"It's okay, really," Alex got herself situated. "I kind of need the company."

"Okay, but when I'm done bathing, it is time for bed." Dorothy smiled as she put her hands on both of her son's cheeks.

"Yes, mama," Samuel said.

Both boys put their heads on Alex. "Tell us a story, Alex."

"Let's see. Let me think of one. I got one. Long before man would walk the Earth, there was a start of a battle. A battle between the Dark and Lite had ignited. The winner would have the authority to mold the newly developing humans. The Lite wanted to give love and freedom, while the Dark wanted to rule with an iron fist. To protect the balance in man, to allow humans to have free will, God asks special people to become Lite Sentries. They battle the Dark, when it tries to enslave the human race. One day, a young seventeen-year-old girl was asked to become a Sentry to battle the Dark," Alex continued with the story.

"What happened to her?" Eli asked as he snuggled into her chest.

"Well, when she became a sentry, she quickly learned about what she was asked to do. She had lost her best friend and later on her brother. The only thing that kept her going in the fight were her relationships and the warmth of the Lite. One day, her connection to the Lite was taken, which sent her on a spiral journey downward. She lost the only one she truly loved and everything else she held dear."

Samuel was almost asleep. "Sounds like she needs a hug. I always feel better when I get a hug."

Alex smiled, "Maybe that is what she needs."

Jeremiah and Uri were on the other side of the room listening. Alex tried to hide that single tear dropping from her face. Dorothy joined them from the washroom. "Come Jeremiah; let's get the children to bed." The two of them lovingly grabbed the children from Alex's lap. Alex took this opportunity to wipe the tear from her face.

Uri stayed behind. "Alex, will you escort an old man home?"

"Papa, it is late and not safe," Dorothy told him. "Just stay here tonight."

"Oh, we'll be fine," Uri told her.

"It's okay, really," Alex got up from the chair. "I could use the fresh air. Can I change clothes first?

"Of course," Uri went into the kitchen to sneak a piece of pie.

"Your clothes are in your room, Alex," Dorothy had a worried look on her face. "You

need to get some rest."

"I won't be long." Alex went into the bedroom and put her hunting clothes on. For some reason, it felt good, like a piece of her was missing. Something she hadn't felt in quite a while. She stepped outside of her room, tying her leather coat. "Ready?"

Uri and Alex stepped out onto the deck. "Nice night," Uri observed.

"It is." Alex looked to the stars before extending her elbow. "Shall we?

Uri grabbed her arm. They walked down the road a bit before Uri spoke. "It's just around the bend of the road."

"Sounds good," Alex said, enjoying the night.

"I heard your story you told to the children." Uri picked up a small pebble in the road.

Alex gazed over to Uri. "It was just a story."

"My great-grandfather told me once about how they were approached by a group consisting of many religions. It was a secret group. They asked if we would join them. We declined but agreed to let them know if we knew of someone who had certain abilities," Uri told her.

"Was there ever one?" Alex's interests peaked.

"One. The group came and asked her to go with them. She accepted and they never saw her again," Uri let her know. "But that was long ago and never talked about." Uri stopped and turned to Alex. "You are a Lite Sentry, are you not?" Alex turned to him. She lit her fist and flashed her eyes. Uri smiled, "I would not be going around here doing that. People wouldn't know how to take that."

"Tell me, Uri," Alex started. "Who else knows about the council upon your...you know?"

"When I go with God?" Uri laughed. "I shall tell Jeremiah when he is ready. Perhaps you coming here is a sign from God that he is."

***

It was nice having Komptin staying with him. Kameron was up sitting on the couch with Komptin's head on his lap. It was relaxing having him to pet while sipping on a glass of sparkling apple juice. "You want a little secret, boy?" He started talking to the dog. "I would have left the agency for Alex. Hell, I pretty much made up my mind before she broke up with me." Kameron softly scratched his ears. "Here's the secret that you may not know. I still would if she'd take me back." Komptin opened his eyes with sadness as he stared out the window. "Do you think she still loves me?" Komptin turned to him and flashed his eyes. Kameron laughed, "I sure wish I knew what that meant."

Komptin started to give a low growl before a knock at the door came. Kameron opened the door to Midnight on the other end. Komptin came up behind Kameron, almost in a protective manner. "What are you doing here?"

"I can't get this out of my mind. It's just wrong for me to think like this," Midnight was obviously upset.

"What is it?" Kameron invited her in.

"The killing of the former F.O.R. members," Midnight clarified. "I wanna know what you think?"

Kameron had his suspicions. "It will sound crazy."

"Mine too. I'll start and you finish," Midnight offered to meet in the middle.

"I'm good with that," Kameron grabbed his drink. "Go ahead."

"Now, I know you were involved in that F.O.R. thing as your office was infiltrated by the group; what if it wasn't limited by that office?" Midnight started to go down a rabbit hole.

"And others were sent to find the other former F.O.R. members who know too much," Kameron concluded.

"Someone who hates religion would make a great ally?" Midnight reluctantly stated.

"That every witness that they came in contact with died?" Kameron added in.

"I don't want to think like that." Midnight was obviously upset. "It's dangerous thinking."

"One could make someone rather upset," Kameron reminded her.

"One could," Midnight agreed.

"No time like the present." He turned to Komptin, "You wanna come?" Komptin barked in agreement.

"The dog, really?" Midnight saw Komptin wagging his tail. Midnight and Kameron made it to Scotty's apartment. Komptin was in front of the door with his ears perked. "Is he a police dog?" Midnight was studying him. "He's very well trained."

"Trust me, there's only one other person I wish I had at my side." Kameron knocked on the door. "Hey, Scotty, it's Kameron and Midnight."

There was movement and commotion on the other end. "Just a minute." He barely opened the door. "What's up?" He was looking at the two of them through a crack in the door.

"Can we talk?" Midnight asked.

"Now's not really a good time," Scotty said, acting suspicious. "How about tomorrow?"

"It's important," Kameron told him.

"Can it wait?" Scotty anxiously tried to get rid of them both. "I'm not free at the moment."

Midnight pushed the door open. "Damn it, Scotty." Kameron followed her in with his hand on his gun. Once inside, they had a sight they were not expecting. "Oh my God." Midnight's mouth was just open from the mere shock of it. "Oh my, I'm so sorry ladies."

Scotty sighed, "Kameron, Midnight, this is Gladis, Deloris, Meg, Sasha, Mary, and Agnes." They were women all over the age of sixty with glasses down to their nose, holding needlepoints. There was an empty spot on the couch with a needlepoint, waiting for it to be completed. Kameron's eyes went wide and Midnight tried everything not to laugh. "It's my week to host our needlepoint group."

"Scotty, I...I don't know what to say," Midnight said with her hand over her mouth.

"How about nothing?" Scotty snapped at her. "Nothing would be good."

"We still need to talk to you." Kameron was still processing this scene. Komptin walked over to the women, being petted.

"Fine, I need to bring out the hors d'oeuvres anyway," he said walking into the kitchen.

The two of them followed Scotty into the next room. "Okay, okay, before we get to why we're here, I have to ask?" Midnight ate one of the little sandwiches on the plate. "These are good."

"This cannot leave the apartment, deal?" Scotty iterated.

"Deal," Kameron agreed.

"It relaxes me, I had a traumatic incident happen to me in junior high, I don't want to talk about that cause it's only going to make me mad, and I needed therapy," Scotty told them. "One day, I was waiting for my mother to get home from work and I picked up one of her needlepoints. I spent the time doing the work while waiting for my mom. Once she got home, we talked all night while doing needlepoint. I find it relaxing, I find it therapeutic, and I would appreciate it if you didn't tell anyone." Scotty was obviously embarrassed.

"If you are honest with us, this will never leave the apartment," Kameron assured him.

"Oh Scotty, this is a big favor," Midnight laughed. "But we need to ask."

"We need to know if you're involved with the F.O.R. and the murders of the former members," Kameron flat out asked.

Scotty laughed, "What?"

Midnight chimed in, "I'm just asking to clear my conscience."

"No, and honestly, I thought Kameron was involved, until I read that report. He wanted that girl's name in there," Scotty gave them both his impression of the situation.

"Why did you want that report closed so badly with no record of conversation?" Kameron was now trying to put this puzzle together.

"Paige didn't want any record of former F.O.R. members." Scotty took a bite of his little sandwich. "She was adamant about it."

Midnight and Kameron both looked as if they had a revelation. "She had complete knowledge of our actions," Kameron sighed. "Oh, this is not good."

Scotty chimed, "She'd be the one to cover everything up."

Midnight included, "She said she was working late tonight."

"I guess we can go see what she is doing." Scotty grabbed a sandwich. "Damn it and I was almost done with the sailboat, too." He grabbed a set of keys from the wall as he peeked into the living room. "Hey Agnes, can you lock up for me?"

***

Anne was laying down in her bed. She moved a bowl next to her in case she couldn't make it to the bathroom. All day was back and forth to the bathroom, sometimes not making it in time. The only thing that was comfortable was sitting in the dark, where she belonged.

A knock on the door was her mom checking up on her. "Honey, are you okay?"

"I'm fine, Mom, I just don't feel well." She just wanted this to be over and done.

"Do you want me to get you anything?"

"A ginger ale would be great," Anne said, holding her stomach.

She noticed she got a call from Father Richard. "Father? I haven't seen or heard from anyone yet. Things at the church are at stand still until I feel better. Just a mild flu, I haven't been able to keep food down. Thank you. Bye."

Anne quickly grabbed the bowl and threw up what little food she had in her system.

**

It felt good to be in her hunting clothes, walking down the road with the darkness of the forest surrounding her. It felt right; it felt as if at least a part of her returned. The stroll she was most enjoying was giving her a choice at the bend. The left was Jeremiah's farm, but to the right was the village square.

She decided to see the part of town where the village met. By the time she got into the town, everything was locked up. From her understanding, they only opened up the markets to tourists on Saturdays. For the life of her, she didn't know what day it was. She just enjoyed the town late at night. It was peaceful, but she was still on guard with no ability in sensing the Dark.

She came across the church they were talking about renovating. It was a very little church. It needed help but not in that bad of shape. The walk around the church didn't take long. From what she could tell, there wasn't much that needed to be done. The fenced-in backyard was well kept. She almost wished she could go into the little building. Not because it was a sanctuary, or because of any hope to feel the Lite, but just because she wanted to remember what it felt like. Alex wanted to take in the rest of the night by sitting on the church step.

She felt like she disappointed Him again. Alex was human, she was also Lite, and she was handicapped in her fight against the Dark. Why did this happen? She was a Lite Sentry; she was a protector of the Balance. There was nothing to stop her from hunting but herself. She needed to sense the Dark to find it. She was a fighter, a survivor. On some level though; she knew she wasn't going to survive much longer. Her relationship with the Lite was suddenly taken away from her. With no connection to the Lite, it was nothing but cold.

Alex had the sudden surge of energy come to her. She wanted to go hunt. She wanted to do anything to get her life back. All she could think of was fighting a Demon or Infiltrator. It was as if she was trying to convince herself. There was still something missing from her. All she did know was that she needed to get home.

The stars shined above her, with Osiah's star shining bright and purple. She smiled at it remembering the last time she saw him. It was so magical in that diner where The Cook helped her get refocused. She then looked to Ariel's star, which was one of strength. She lost so much. She felt that she just couldn't handle anymore.

"Excuse me," a voice said behind her.

Alex rolled her eyes. "Leroy?" Alex turned around to see him with a lantern. "What are you doing here?"

"The elders asked me to check the church tonight before the tourists come tomorrow." Leroy was curious as to why she was sitting here all alone.

"So that would make today Friday," she sarcastically pointed and winked at him.

"What are you doing here?" Leroy asked her.

"Just trying to figure things out." Alex wished she could go inside the church, even if she had no warmth from the Lite.

Leroy blew out the lantern. "It is bright enough out here. What light did you use to walk all the way over here?"

Alex just looked around for an answer. "My eyes just adjusted enough. Well, I guess I should get back."

"Do you want a ride? My carriage is behind the church," Leroy offered.

"Sure," she said with no emotion.

Alex walked to the back of the church to the carriage. They got into it and started to travel back to Jeremiah's farm. "It looked as if you had a lot on your mind," Leroy said, controlling the carriage.

"I just feel empty," Alex told him.

Leroy stopped the carriage. "What do you want?"

"To feel the warmth inside of me." Alex put her guard down just for a moment. She turned to Leroy because he wasn't saying anything. The next thing Alex felt was Leroy kissing her with force. Alex pushed him off her. "Ah, what the hell are you doing?"

"I know you townspeople are fluent in relations, and I know you wanted to do that. Since you are not able to bear children, no one will know," Leroy told her. "We can do this quickly."

Alex was just dumbfounded, "Ah, Leroy, I, ah, your wife, baby." She hopped off the carriage to walk away. "Look, honestly, not going to happen." Alex turned around and shivered. "Yuck."

***

Kameron, Midnight, and Scotty stood outside the back of the federal building. "How do you want to do this?" Komptin, who seemed to be on edge, made sure not to leave Kameron's side.

Scotty scouted the area, "Do you think we should leave that dog in the car?"

"No, I think he'll be fine," Kameron rubbed his fingers behind Komptin's ears.

Midnight checked around. "We shouldn't split up, whatever we do."

Kameron saw Paige's light on in her office. "What are we going to ask her?"

Scotty took out a piece of gum. "We can just say we forgot something and we were all at the pub or something."

Midnight took in a deep breath. "Let's get this over with."

Scotty and Midnight started towards the building. Kameron stayed behind to talk to Komptin. He knelt down, "Can you tell me if the Dark is around?"

Komptin flashed his eyes.

"I'll take that as a yes." Kameron was starting to form a pit of worry in his stomach. "If we go up there, can you tell if Paige is a Demon?"

Komptin again flashed his eyes.

"Okay, let's go." Kameron caught up with the other two.

The three of them were in the elevator with Komptin sitting in front. "Ever get the feeling that something bad is about to happen?" Midnight asked.

"Yep, the day I got shot," Kameron calmly replied. "Routine security sweep and the F.O.R. decided to attack. Woke up that morning with some weird feeling. Later on, got shot. How about you?"

"Had a bad day at work. Not motivated to do anything. Couldn't explain it but I just wanted to go home to crawl underneath the covers and not come out. So, I decided to take a personal day. Came home to find my husband getting a warm front from the weather girl," Midnight answered. "Scotty, your turn."

At first he didn't answer, "Woke up, had a weird feeling, that feeling was crabs," he told her. Kameron and Midnight both turned their heads to Scotty as he just stared forward.

Kameron then asked, "Has anyone hit the button to the office floor?"

The three of them just moved their eyes looking at each other. "I thought you did, Midnight?" Scotty asked.

"You're the one next to the buttons," she replied.

"You were the first one in," they quietly were yelling at each other.

Kameron leaned over the two of them and pressed the button.

"I could have done that," Scotty told his partners.

"You couldn't find the button if you tried," Midnight said to him.

Kameron saw that Komptin was getting a bit tense. "Easy boy." The doors opened. "Okay, let's go." The three of them walked into the office where all the lights were off except Paige's office. "Who's going to ask her?"

"I'm not going to ask her. Midnight should ask her," Scotty offered her up.

Midnight hit Scotty in the arm. "It's your case."

"You're a woman, you have that woman bond thing," Scotty argued.

They walked into Paige's office who had the door open. She was sitting at her desk with a man behind her reading a report. "What are you guys doing here?" Paige asked them.

"Weston? I thought you weren't coming in until tomorrow?" Midnight asked him.

"Are they clean?" Kameron turned his head behind him. The massive German shepherd came out from behind the three of them. They followed him into the office and stood in front of Paige's desk.

"Komptin?" Weston asked. "What are you doing here?"

"You know who Komptin is?" Kameron asked.

"Yes, and I know who you are," Weston let him know. "What's he doing here?" Weston was pointing to the dog. "Why isn't he with the Sentry?"

"The what?" Scotty asked.

Kameron was on guard, "How do you know about Alex?

Paige had enough, "Wait, wait, everyone just stop. What are you guys doing here?"

"Well, we thought you were working for the F.O.R. killing off the former members," Scotty gave away the reason they were here.

"Funny, I thought that of you," Paige pointed to Scotty.

"If you aren't with the F.O.R., why did you not want Lana in the reports?"

"To protect her, I didn't know where the leak was. If she died, then I knew it was either Midnight or you," Paige said out of frustration.

"Why not Kameron?" Scotty asked.

Weston rolled his eyes. "Cause he was cleared by the Council and his dealings with the Sentry."

"The what? What the hell is going on?" Midnight was trying to grasp on things.

"If Paige isn't the leak and neither of us are; then who is?" Kameron was thinking of suspects.

Komptin flashed his eyes and started barking with fury towards the door. In the doorway, Lane stood much bigger than he normally was with glowing red eyes and sharpened teeth. Komptin lunged at the Demon but Lane grabbed him to throw him across the room into a bunch of cubicles.

Scotty and Midnight started shooting the Demon. "Stop firing, you idiots!" Weston yelled. "You're only going to piss it off."

"We're so dead," Paige said, gathering up her files.

Lane rushed in and tackled all three of the agents into a pile. Kameron put up his arm to protect his face as the Demon was biting his arm. "I hate these things," Kameron complained.

Weston jumped on the back of the Demon to pull its neck back to get it off the three of them. "I can't hold this forever." The three of them rolled out of the way, as the Demon flipped Weston onto his back onto the office floor.

The group of them all shoulder blocked the Demon through the drywall of the office, landing on the floor. They all got up to start pounding on the Demon when they heard a growl. A black bear-like creature with glowing red eyes walked out of the conference room. "Oh shit," the three of them said simultaneously.

It growled before it roared and lunged at the three of them but was suddenly stopped. The Infiltrator saw he was grabbed by a purple-skinned gargoyle by the back of the leg. Komptin flashed his eyes before throwing the black beast into the office cubicles.

The Demon regained a fighting stance towards the gargoyle. Komptin roared at it as they both charged it. They collided in mid-air, crashing into the floor. Scotty and Midnight got up. "What the hell is going on?" They stood up and turned to Paige who was trying to get into her safe. "We have to get these files out of here."

"What files?" Scotty was covering Paige.

The Infiltrator jumped onto Komptin's back and bit into his neck. He gave a howl of pain as he jumped into the air, smashing the Infiltrator into the drop ceiling. Weston ran full sprint out of the office to jump on the Demon's back. The Demon flipped him over onto his back. The Demon went to punch Weston while he was down. Kameron and others jumped onto Lane's back, trying to prevent it from happening.

Paige got the files out of the safe and secured them in a briefcase. She ran besides the Demon to see Komptin with his foot on the Infiltrator's back. He grabbed the back of the black beast's neck and ripped it's head off. The creature disappeared forever.

The Demon flung the three agents off, causing Kameron to fall onto Paige's desk. Scotty and Midnight collided with each other against the wall. The Demon went after Paige. Luckily, the Demon was met with Komptin leaping in the air tackling him. The Demon scratched Komptin's shoulders, causing neon blue blood to drip. The sound of the Demon's head getting torn off by Komptin made Scotty and Midnight stop in their tracks.

"That's gross," Midnight thought she was going to vomit.

"Paige!?" Weston yelled from the ground covered in debris.

"I'm good, so are the files." She patted the briefcase.

Kameron rolled over off the desk, crashing onto the floor. The ceiling tiles were all he saw as he decided to lay there for a second to check his forehead. Scotty and Midnight helped each other up. "Oh, did that suck," Scotty said as he checked to see how bad his nosebleed was.

Midnight's blonde hair was out of her tight bun. She checked her eye to see how bad it was bleeding. "Okay, what the hell?"

"Pretty accurate." Weston got up and checked on Paige who was holding the briefcase.

"I never thought I would see an Infiltrator." Paige saw the destruction of the office cubicles. "This is going to be a lot of paperwork." The group of people all gathered in what was left of the doorway. They all looked to Komptin, who was now a German shepherd, licking his paw in the center of the destroyed office.

CHAPTER TWELVE

Alex snuck into her host's house without making a noise. The thought of Leroy kissing her sent shivers down her spine. It wasn't just the fact that he was married, with a baby, and so-called devoted to his faith. It was that his breath was really bad. The thought of it made Alex want to vomit.

"Alex is everything, okay?" Dorothy was taking in some quiet time as her family was sleeping soundly. The bonnet was on the table next to her that allowed her blonde hair to be draped over shoulders. This was the first time Alex had seen her without it.

At first Alex was going to tell Dorothy what happened, but she figured it would do more harm than good. Leroy was respected, he was on path to be an elder, and he had a sweet family. It didn't really matter since she was going to be gone come tomorrow morning anyways. "Everything is fine. I just tried to figure some stuff out."

Dorothy smiled, "I am glad to hear that. Jeremiah said that he would bring you to town the day after tomorrow. We have the tourists coming tomorrow."

"I could probably get a ride with one of them when they come in. That way it's not any trouble," Alex offered another option.

"If that is your wish. We are going to be sad to see you go." Dorothy gave Alex a nice smile.

Alex replied, "I'm going to miss your family as well."

Then Dorothy whispered, "Sit with me, please." Alex sat down in the common room with her. "I may be an Amish wife, but I know people, Alex. There is much that you are hiding from." Dorothy gave some insight about herself. "Tell me more about yourself. I get so few female visitors."

"Girl talk." Alex clapped her hands as she sat down. Dorothy looked at her with confusion. "Never mind. So how long have you been married?"

"Going on ten years," Dorothy told her. "I did not get blessed with a child until three years after the ceremony."

"I'm sorry about that," Alex said to her.

"Oh, don't be. It was a very good three years," Dorothy blushed.

Alex's mouth dropped. "Dorothy," she teased.

Dorothy gave a small little smirk while taking a drink of her hot tea. Her attention went back to Alex. "So, tell me about your love. I can tell when you think about him."

"That obvious, huh?" Alex asked her. "Well, he's tall, but then again, anyone is tall compared to me. He is kind, gentle, but very protective, not smothering, but he would die to protect the ones he loves."

"No doubt a handsome man," Dorothy teased back.

"Oh, he's not hard to look at," Alex blushed. "But I'm afraid I blew it. I said things I shouldn't have and now, I'll never see him again."

"Do you think he is thinking of you now?" Dorothy took a sip from her ceramic cup.

Alex didn't know how to answer that. "If I know Kameron, he has completely pushed out anything about me."

***

"I don't know where Alex is," Kameron was with Komptin lying on the couch with him. The massive dog was fast asleep with his head on Kameron's lap. Weston was amazed at how comfortable Komptin was with him. They all migrated over to Weston's apartment. There were old relics and paraphernalia from all decades. Weston sighed, "We need to find her."

"Will someone tell me what the hell all that was?" Scotty finally called out the elephant in the room.

Weston closed the blinds to his windows. He sat back down next to Paige who was looking over some files from the briefcase that she risked her life for. "There's one in the most northern part of Michigan, kind of backed into a corner."

"Not that I like agreeing with Scotty," Midnight started to say. "But I think we deserve some explanation."

Paige eyed Weston. "They haven't been cleared."

"I think they just got a crash course in everything," Kameron said under his washcloth.

"True." Weston was dipping his tea into some hot water. "But I still need to inform the Council of the events that transpired." He dialed his cell phone when he was leaving the room.

"Okay, until he gets back, what's with the dog?" Paige pointed over to Komptin.

"Komptin was given to Alex the night her mentor died," Kameron lifted his head. "Besides the obvious, that's all I really know about him." He scratched the dog's ears.

"What the hell was that black thing back in the office, and what was up with Lane?" Midnight asked. "It looked like he was possessed or something."

"He was," Kameron told her.

"By a Demon?" Scotty asked with caution.

Paige chimed in, "No, that is what Lane became. The black thing you saw is called an Infiltrator. They possess willing humans to become Demons."

"Okay, my turn?" Kameron asked. "Where do you fit in all this?"

Paige stood up and started pulling her shirt up. That caught Scotty's attention quickly. Just under her bra was an upside down four on it.

"You are a member of F.O.R.?" Midnight asked her.

"Officially," Paige shook her head as if she was trying to forget a painful memory.

"What happened?" Scotty asked.

Paige swallowed hard. "I attended a meeting where the F.O.R. promised us absolute power to rid the world of religion. I was all for it because of the lies I thought religion preached. Anyway, I wanted to attend this meeting at an abandoned hospital. We all claimed we wanted absolute power to destroy religion." Paige started reading something in the file. "Then, when I told my F.O.R. supervisor that I was pregnant, I was told I wasn't allowed to go. I had a choice, get rid of my baby so I could go, or leave the F.O.R." Paige wiped a tear from her eye.

"What did you do?" Midnight asked.

"I told him I always wanted a child, but then he said I wasn't serious enough about the cause, that absolute power wasn't achievable," Paige started to talk again after gaining strength. "I told them I didn't know what to do, so they decided for me and they ripped my baby out of my body." Paige pulled out some napkins that were on the coffee table. "I sat there crying on the table and my F.O.R. Supervisor just told me, 'Now you can have absolute power'.

"I left there being all cold and shivering. I was crying so hard when I ran into a Rabbi who was walking with a Cardinal of all things. They took me in, comforted me, and they didn't judge me. The Cardinal was called away for an emergency, but the Rabbi continued to talk to me. Long story short, he was part of the Jewish Council and he offered me a chance to help battle the F.O.R., and I took it."

"So, what do you do for this council, then?" Scotty wanted more information.

"She goes undercover," Kameron said. Paige nodded. "Dangerous if you get caught."

"Death wouldn't come fast enough," she told them.

"So, does that make you Jewish now?" Scotty asked her. Midnight grabbed a couch pillow to smack him across the head.

"Actually, I'm Baptist," Paige watched Weston come in. "Well?"

Weston walked in. "They weren't happy, but they weren't mad, either." Weston sat down.

"How are you involved in this?" Midnight asked him.

Paige was curious how he was going to answer this question.

"My dad is an alma mater," is all he said. "The council would like to know if you would like to accept a task."

"What is this Council?" Midnight asked them.

"The Council of the Religions, all religious sanctions that contribute to this organization," Weston told them.

"All religions?" Scotty was admiring some needlepoint that was hanging on the wall.

"All the major ones," Weston said. "Except LDS, they are being considered."

"Why aren't they?" Midnight saw Scotty at the craft. "Taking notes?" Scotty turned to her and playfully hissed.

"The religion is too new," Weston told her. "My wife made that when our son was born."

"I've never seen a thread like this," Scotty told him.

"What's this mission they want us to do?" Kameron asked under his cold washcloth.

Weston looked to Kameron. "Find the Sentry."

Kameron lifted his head along with Komptin flashing his eyes.

***

Alex was escorted by Dorothy and Uri into the village for tourist time. There weren't many people but Uri said it was normal. Alex got a couple of weird looks from some tourists as she got off the buggy. Dorothy showed her the store they managed. The quilts were amazing and soft with intricate designs. They would be nice to be under on a cold night, watching some movies in Kameron's arms.

"Thinking of Kameron?" Dorothy asked her with a soft tone to her voice.

"You must be psychic," Alex told her. Then she realized what she just said. "I'm sorry. I didn't mean to refer to you as a witch. It's just an expression we use."

"Don't worry," Dorothy played it off. "I know you didn't mean anything by it. I'm sure going to miss you, Alex."

"I'll come back and visit," she told her.

"I would like that." She gave Alex a hug. "Come. Let's go find you a ride."

There was a group of guys with a couple of girls laughing while congregating over by the wood crafting shop. They would have been the best way for her to get back to a town. All she wanted was to get to a town with a phone to call Father Richard. The group of them were admiring the woodcrafts as Alex approached. "Excuse me."

The group stopped laughing when they saw Alex approaching. "Yes," the tallest one asked. The others suddenly became quiet.

"I was wondering if you could give me a ride into town." Alex was feeling vulnerable asking strangers for help. It was a means to an end.

A girl with a nose ring chimed in with a bit of an attitude. "Where did your ride go?"

Alex tried to lighten the situation. "That's kind of a long story. I can pay you, just not right away."

Two of the boys made eye contact with each other. "We don't have any room. Good luck." The group of them kept quiet as they went to their car.

Alex watched the group leave. There was something not right with these people. It was probably her just being paranoid because she still hadn't gotten used to not having the ability to sense the Dark. Still, Alex wasn't too heartbroken that she couldn't find a ride to town for the rest of the afternoon.

It was nearing the end of time when the tourists would leave. Alex decided to go for a walk around to view the different shops. The walk was peaceful, almost tranquil, but Alex was still on edge when she jumped onto the buggy with Uri and Dorothy. "I guess you're stuck with me," Alex joked.

"The children will be happy," Dorothy told her.

***

Kameron left Scotty and Midnight at the hotel in Alex's hometown of Copper Top Mountain. He thought this was something that should be done alone. Komptin had gone off into the woods, hopefully to find a trace of Alex or maybe a location. Kameron knocked on the door to the house where Anne was staying. A woman answered with a natured-hippy look.

"Can I help you?" she asked with caution.

"I'm Special Agent Kameron Dutcher," he told her as he showed his badge and credentials. "Is Anne around? I stopped by the church but it was locked up."

"She isn't feeling well. Perhaps I could give a message," she coldly told him.

"Please just tell her I stopped by." He handed her a business card.

"Kameron Dutcher? Are you Alex's boyfriend?" She studied the government employee in front of her.

"I was. We decided to end things when I got transferred to San Diego." Kameron never really knew how much that made him upset until someone connected to Alex asked him about her.

"So, what brings you here?" She asked out of curiosity. "I'm Willow, Anne's mother."

Kameron shook her hand. "Kameron. I'm working on a case and I just need some input from Anne."

She didn't really believe him. "Hang on. I'll let Anne know you are here."

Kameron waited outside for a bit before Anne came to the door in a bathrobe. She now had jet-black hair and her skin was pale. Not Alex pale, but pale enough to notice a difference. Dark circles underneath her eyes proved to Kameron that something wasn't right. She smiled at Kameron but he knew it wasn't genuine. Anne was definitely not herself. "Hey Kameron." She gave him a hug.

Kameron was shocked at how bad she looked. "Anne, are you okay?"

"Are you looking for Alex?"

Kameron nodded, "Have you seen her?"

"No." Anne sat down on a porch bench. She held her stomach as if something was wrong.

"Anne, what's wrong?" Kameron asked her.

"Kameron, I don't want to be rude, but I'm really tired," Anne told him.

Kameron put his hand on her shoulder, "If there is anything you need…"

"I'll let you know if I hear from Alex," Anne told him. "I need to get back to bed."

"Thank you." Kameron got to his car and sat there. Anne slowly went back into the house in her bathrobe. There was no doubt something was going on with her. He texted Midnight and Scotty to meet him at a local supper club for dinner.

Kameron arrived at the dinner club where he recognized the larger man greeting them. "Welcome," he said. "How many in your party?"

"Three," he told him. "Preferably booth against the wall." The man escorted him to a booth. "Thank you."

The big guy pointed a finger at Kameron, "I apologize, but you look familiar."

Kameron reminded him. "I was good friends with Kale. I met you at the funeral. Kameron."

The big man put out his hand, "Dan. Nice to meet you, again."

"Likewise," Kameron told him.

"I was told you were there when it happened." Dan showed him the table. "He was a good man."

"Yes he was." Kameron sat down in the booth.

"Well, I'll get your waitress. Want something to drink?" Dan asked.

"Water, for now, thank you." Kameron peeked at the menu.

Kameron started going over in his mind the route he was going to take to find Alex. The problem would be, if she didn't want to be found, she wasn't going to be. On the off-chance he did find her, what would her reaction be when they saw each other. A tall, blonde male came up to Kameron as if he wanted to talk. "Can I help you?"

"You the one dating Alex?"

"I'm sorry, I didn't catch your name," Kameron said.

"Merik," he told him.

"You know Alex?" Kameron asked him.

"A lot of guys know her at least once," Merik told him.

Kameron was resisting the urge to confront the guy, but he had no reason to be upset. Alex wasn't with him. "Have you seen her lately?"

"So, she is still missing, thanks." Merik turned away. He got on the phone as he left the supper club.

"Shit." Kameron followed him out of the restaurant. He ran into Midnight and Scotty as they were coming into the supper club from the parking lot.

"You okay?" Midnight asked.

"Stupid, stupid, stupid," he started beating himself up. "How could I do something so dumb?"

"What?" Scotty asked.

"Did you happen to see a tall, blonde athletic man coming out of here on a phone?" Kameron asked.

"No, but I guess we are going to go look for one." Midnight buttoned up her jacket. "I was getting hungry."

Scotty scratched his eyes, then looked in the direction again.

"See something?" Midnight asked him.

"Must be brake lights or something," Scotty told them. "Hey, if we don't find this guy in an hour, can we eat?"

The three of them covered the area but didn't find the man that'd talked to him.

"This place is a dead-end. She isn't here. We need to start back in DC," Kameron told them.

***

Gron got a little annoyed with Merik on the phone, "No, you can't kill him. Because if you kill him before Alex comes back it will be holy hell. Just make sure nothing happens to the key." Gron hung up the phone, annoyed. "He's so stupid, even in high school he wasn't running on all cylinders."

Misluna was in a miniskirt sitting sideways with her legs crossed. "But he's so cute, can I?"

Gron looked over to her with a drink in his hand. "I don't care but to let you know, while in high school, the sentry and him…"

She frowned. "He's tainted."

"This is a gamble not sending more Hosts or Infiltrators," Gron told her. He sat down on the couch next to her. The two of them shared a drink.

"If we concentrate all the Infiltrators and Demons in one spot, the Lite will counteract by activating more Sentries," Misluna was admiring her red and black streaked hair in her compact makeup mirror.

"There are already four more being activated," Gron told her. "Once this little mission is complete, we will deal with them."

"Can I kill one?" Misluna asked.

"I don't see why not," Gron let her know. He got another phone call. "Right now, we need to think how we are going to get our hands on the Conduit Key when they arrive."

***

Alex was helping Dorothy wash the dishes after dinner. Out of respect for their household, Alex put the outfit Dorothy gave her back on. "You are quiet," Dorothy said to her.

"Just thinking," Alex told her. "I really should get back home."

Jeremiah looked out the window. "It is going to storm tonight."

Alex included, "I heard one of the tourists talk about how bad it is supposed to storm tomorrow."

Jeremiah's mouth tightened, "If that is true, then we should wait until we take you to town."

Alex sighed, "I understand." They finished their dishes and sat down at the table.

Uri came in from the common room. "Leroy and his family are coming over tonight for cards."

"Oh yes, I forgot about that." Dorothy got some lemons. "I will make some lemonade. There are some pies I can serve."

Alex got annoyed at having to see Leroy again. What he did to her was unacceptable. He betrayed his wife and family. During the game, Leroy was acting as if he was holier than anyone in the room. It was making Alex nauseous. Thunder and lightning started roaring in the distance. Jeremiah saw the storm coming from out the window. "Storm is coming. Should make sure everything is secure in the barn."

Uri got up. "Let's go, son. There is something I would like to talk to you about, anyway." He gave Alex a little wink before leaving for the barn.

Alex smiled at him and then caught Leroy staring at her. She shivered at the thought of him. "I'm going to go help Uri and Jeremiah."

Uri was in the barn securing the stables. Some of the animals were starting to get agitated by the thunder coming in. "Easy girl," Jeremiah calmed the horse. "What did you want to talk to me about, Papa?"

"Something that maybe something hard for you to understand. My great-grandfather had once told me about a group of people from different religions," Uri started to stay.

"The Council of the Religions, yes, you told me this story," Jeremiah told him.

"I did?" Uri asked out of confusion.

"Yes, last year," he told him. "If anyone shows up with special gifts, then I should take a pilgrimage to contact this council. They are used to fight evil."

"My old age must be getting to me," Uri started rubbing his head.

"You are fine, Papa," he smiled as he petted the horse. "Have you ever heard of anyone with such abilities?"

"Alex." Uri turned to see her in the doorway of the barn. "What are you doing here?"

"I needed to get some fresh air." She saw she was standing next to the manure bin.

"We are just finishing up," Jeremiah told her.

Out of nowhere, a big crack of thunder came. The sound vibrated the barn. The animals started to become restless as the bull was bucking in its stable. His immense body smashed against the wall causing it to break.

"Papa, I'll get the bull. Take care of the horses," Jeremiah grabbed a chain. He ran over to the bullpen to secure the gate. The bull busted through the gate, knocking over Jeremiah. It started running towards Uri who was pinned against the horse gate.

Alex lit her fists and with her eyes glowing, she stepped in front of the bucking bull. She grabbed it by the horn and punched it straight into it forehead. There was a sound of the bull's skull cracking rippled down it back, killing the bull instantly. The bull stood still for a moment before crashing to the ground. Alex stood over her kill with her eyes still lit with her hand stinging from the hit. "Ow, that hurt." She shook her hand as she turned to Uri. "You okay?"

Uri nodded his head. He turned to Jeremiah who was looking at Alex with his mouth open. "Yes, son, I have heard of someone with such abilities."

Jeremiah continued to lay on the ground when Alex offered her hand in help. Her eyes returned to normal. Jeremiah grabbed her hand and Alex lifted him up with ease. "You are strong."

Alex smiled, "I'm still Alex."

"Who else knows?" Jeremiah asked.

"Just the people in this barn," Uri said, calming down the horse.

Jeremiah smiled, "Thank you for saving Papa. Your secret is safe with me." He gave her a hug.

The three of them looked over the carcass of the bull. Uri was the first to say, "I guess we will butcher tonight."

***

Leroy fell onto the ground when he saw the townswoman manhandle a bull with her bare hands. The witch's eyes glowed blue as she cast a spell with her hands. He thought he was just coming out to help Jerimiah with locking up the barn. Now he sees that a slave of the Devil is walking among them. This family has suffered from her evil ways. This explains why he was watching her from the bushes performing actions that are not in line with God's wishes. This just confirms that the witch had tried to cast a spell on him, but Leroy was too righteous to fall for it.

The way she acted with Uri and Jeremiah only cemented that they had fallen for the witch's magic. He could only assume Dorothy and the children had fallen for the same. He needed to get his family away from this land of evil before they fell into her power. The noise from him barging into the house startled his wife and children. "We must go."

"What's wrong?" his wife asked him.

"Listen to me, we must go." Leroy was trying to hide his nerves. The witch and her minions had walked into the house behind him. He went to protect his family from that black hearted harlot.

"The bull died," Jeremiah walked into the house. "We must butcher it tonight."

"I'll get the supplies. Children, we must butcher," Dorothy got up. "Wasn't expecting to do this tonight."

Excitement from the children's voices carried throughout the house.

"We must go," Leroy insisted to his family. The witch must have been trying to cast the spell on him while he was watching Alex as she bent over to pick up a knife that fell to the ground. His face was getting hot. "We must leave to check on our stables."

"Yes, Leroy," his wife gathered up her bag for their child. "I shall come by in the morning to help with what I can."

Dorothy turned, "Thank you."

"May God protect you," Leroy said as they left in haste.

Alex watched Leroy leave. "What a tool."

Dorothy looked at the butcher's knife. "It does make it easier to cut the meat."

Leroy had gathered the entire elders together near the communal church. There was much talk among them. "Why did you call us here, Leroy?" one of them asked.

"I'm afraid we lost the souls of Jeremiah and his family," Leroy whispered in confidence.

"Why would you say such a thing?" Reuben was shocked at the words coming from Leroy.

Leroy jumped in, "The witch, Alex, she has them under her spell."

"Witch?" one of the elders said, almost laughing. "There hasn't been a witch claim with our people since…" He couldn't think of a date.

"She is. I saw her glowing blue eyes and I saw her cast a spell with her glowing hands to kill a bull as a sacrifice to Satan," Leroy frantically explained.

"Leroy, are you sure you didn't see something else?" one of the other elders asked.

Leroy stood up with frustration. "I wouldn't believe it either, but she tried to cast her spells on me, but my faith kept me pure."

The elders spoke among each other before facing him. "We will need proof."

**

The three agents had to catch an overnight flight back to DC. They decided to go to the spot where Komptin was kidnapped. The German shepherd sniffed around the train tracks for Alex but there was no trace of her. Kameron was getting irritated. "Where is she?" There was no hope in sight. He sat down on the bench, defeated. Midnight and Scotty returned with no luck. They both knew Kameron was upset, especially when all he said was, "This sucks."

"We'll find her," Midnight tried to support him. She knew he took work seriously but this was something different. It was probably because of the

301

severity of this fight she suddenly found herself immersed.

"I'm a realist. I don't even know where to begin. If she doesn't want to be found, we're not finding her." Kameron got up with his flashlight in his hand. "We'll look around for an hour before we head back to the hotel." There was no motivation in his voice. All hope he once had was fading quickly.

Scotty and Midnight watched him go across the tracks with hopelessness. Scotty commented, "Why is he taking this so hard?"

"Don't know." Midnight shook her head. "Come on, let's go see if there are any signs that someone was here."

Kameron got to the other side of the tracks. His team stayed back, no doubt giving him some space to think things through. The night sky was clear with the stars twinkling. "Hi there," he started to pray. "I'm assuming You have no contact with her and can't see her either? I'm not asking for a handout. I just need strength to keep on looking. I have no idea how I'm supposed to find her if You can't even do it." The sound of a train caught Kameron's attention in the background. "I just feel hopeless. Give Kale my best and let Michelle know I always think of her." Komptin was alongside Midnight and Scotty; they just shook their heads with regret of no news. "I think we should call it." Kameron admitted his defeat.

The both of them just nodded with agreement.

Kameron started to walk towards them when his foot was caught in a gopher's hole. He fell face first into the dirt. Midnight and Scotty were trying not to laugh. "You okay?" Midnight asked.

"I'm fine." He turned over to check his ankle quickly when he saw something reflected in the moonlight. He leaned over to see the necklace he got her for Christmas laying in the dirt. The sapphire angel was an instant hope of inspiration that she was alive. He ran over to Scotty and Midnight with a renewed sense of inspiration. "Hey, look!" He was like a child in a theme park. He crossed the tracks just before the train went by.

"It's a train. Yes, Kameron," Midnight thought her friend had lost his mind.

"No, not that. Her necklace," he showed them. As the train went by, Kameron stepped next to the two of them. He turned to Midnight. "Do you think?"

"It's worth a shot," Midnight thought it wasn't, but she knew he was going to continue the search regardless.

They went to the map near the transfer station. "There isn't much in between here and there." Scotty was pointing to the map. "Once it crosses the river, it's got a while before coming to a town."

"What if she got off before the next town," Midnight said.

"Why would she?" Scotty asked.

"If she was fighting something, got injured…" Kameron started to look. "Here, what if she got knocked off into the river? The current could have taken her down river."

"But where?" Midnight asked. "She could be on the bottom of the river. It's a good possibility that she's dead."

"No, I would know," Kameron told them.

"How?" Scotty asked.

Kameron tried not to laugh. "No, her Godmother would let me know." He studied the map. "That bridge is pretty far from here."

**

Ekaterina and Oleg were walking up the hill. "How much further?" Ekaternia asked. "You said it was a short hike."

"I lied. Otherwise, you wouldn't have come," Oleg teased. "It will be worth it anyways."

They were both on a scouting mission to find a place to shoot their music video for their class project. The band they were shooting wanted a setting where they could write their song about the death of the religion. Oleg had heard about this church but it was off limits due to the path to it being engulfed by the forest. He thought it would be perfect.

"Carrying the equipment up here is going to be impossible," Ekaternia commented. "We'll have to spend a couple of nights up here."

Oleg's eyes peeked opened, "That wouldn't be so bad." He turned around to put his hands on Ekaternia's waist.

"Oleg," she smiled. "I'm still with Dima." She put her hands around his waist. "If he were to find out, it would be bad for the both of us." She kissed him.

"You're such a tease," Oleg told her. He spanked her as he laughed into the woods.

She followed after him and had chased him for a bit, but then noticed he had stopped in his tracks. "What's wrong?"

Oleg just pointed. "I found it." Just ahead of them was an old church. The shutters were hanging off the hinges with no sign of light inside. The moss had been growing on the shingles of the roof. The weather-torn wood added to the gothic artistic atmosphere.

Ekaternia had shivers run down her spine. "Okay, we found it. We can go now."

Oleg turned to her. "You're scared."

"No," she defended. "It's just that it is far and we won't be able to carry the equipment up here."

"Let's at least go check it out." Oleg started to walk ahead. The two of them started to head to the church when Oleg turned to Ekaternia. "What did you say?"

Ekaternia looked around, "I didn't say anything."

Oleg scoured his surroundings. "Oh, well. Come on."

They continued to walk when Ekaternia stopped. "You're the one who said we should go in there."

"What?" Oleg asked her.

"Didn't you just say that we should leave?" she asked him.

"No," he told her.

They walked into the church where the musty air was mixing with the smell of rotting wood. "The band wanted spooky, this is it." Ekaterina continued to walk into the congregation hall. She held Oleg's hand tight as they continued to walk slowly into the church.

"See me," a voice came out of nowhere. They both looked up to the front of the church where a pair of red eyes emerged followed by a dark, living shadow.

Oleg and Ekaternia turned around and took off running into the woods. They stumbled into each other before heading back to the trail.

The Dark Myst watched the two primates run from the church. He turned back to go to his perch in the darkest corner he could find, when he sensed someone else in the room. In the doorway stood half of the former Guardians to the Conduit. The purple-haired angel stood in battle armor with her misty wings and halo showing. Her Lite Bo was gripped in her hand, ready to use in a moment's notice.

"I wish not to be disturbed, Lite Sow," Salamor perched himself on the mantle of the fireplace inside the church. He covered himself with his misty, black wing only showing his eyes.

"I do not wish to be here any more than you wish me to be, but something has happened and answers are needed," Devine stated.

Salamor floated to another Dark corner. "Why should I answer?"

"You helped before," Devine studied the creature.

"And my punishment is severe." Salamor disappeared into the shadows and appeared in front of the face of Devine. "Every moment pains me to be here. I have betrayed my Master, and if he is ever to return, I shall throw myself at his mercy."

"I thought you said he would show you none," Devine asked.

"Anything is better than this," Salamor admitted his pain.

"The Sentry is missing. She has lost her sense of the Lite and Dark," Devine told him, backing away. "Other things are going on which there are no answers to."

"Doesn't concern me, Lite Sheila," Salamor snapped back.

Devine's facial expression tensed with anger. "There is something else-"

"LEAVE ME ALONE!" Salamor flashed his red eyes.

Devine bowed her head, "As you wish."

Salamor floated out of the church for the first time since his self-banishment from the Dark. At first, the energy in the air was polluted by the Lite from the former Guardian, but when that dissipated, something caught his attention. The coldness of the energy was growing, hiding from the Lite senses. They wouldn't see this coming. This opportunity was unexpected. He would have to make sure his true intentions were hidden. No one would know that this would be his key to get home. Once the twins are born, he could slip in without detection just as they open the Conduit to the Dark.

***

Anne came out of the bathroom after throwing up what little dinner she had left. She wrapped a bathrobe around her body. After wiping her face, she flopped back into bed face down. Her mother knocked before entering. "Anne, honey."

"Yes, Mom?" Anne said, speaking into the bed.

"You wanna talk about it?" her mom asked.

"Not really," Anne told her. She rolled over to crawl back under the covers of her bed.

Her mom sat next to her to put her arm around her daughter. Anne moved up to her mother to nestle into her body. She stroked her daughter's hair trying to comfort her. Willow got comfortable as Anne snuggled up next to her mother. She felt so useless to see her daughter in so much pain. Nothing she could do would comfort her child. Willow ran her fingers through her daughter's now jet-black hair. She didn't understand why her hair was now so dark. This wasn't the daughter she knew. This wasn't Anne.

CHAPTER THIRTEEN

Gron got off the plane onto the private tarmac located on the other side of the airfield. His hometown was always something that had a particular smell. It was enough for him to realize how much he hated it here growing up. His classmates treated him like an annoying flea in their small little paradise of a school. Now, he was Gron, Leader of the F.O.R. He was about to change this town forever. Merik was greeting him outside the plane with a grin on his face. "How was it?" Gron asked.

"Just as I imagined it would be," Merik bragged about his accomplishment. "Everything is all set. The house is located outside the town's limit. We will be secluded."

Misluna joined Gron. "And the Conduit Key facilities are all set?"

"Yes, they are," Merik motioned for the bags to be put into the trunk. "When are they due?"

"Ironically, at the end of October," Gron told him. "Has there been any sign of the Sentry?"

Merik shook his head, "All I know is that her boy toy is still looking for her."

"Well, she isn't here. That's all I care about," Gron said, walking to the limo. The three of them got into the stretched-out car with maroon seating. Misluna sat next to Gron as Merik sat across. The cell phone in Gron's pocket started to ring.

Sometimes it would seem his phone never stopped ringing. "What? She's where? No wonder no one could find her." He sat there and listened. "Kill her."

***

The agents were walking on the train tracks. Midnight and Scotty were making small talk about how they found themselves immersed in an unbelievable religious war. The three of them had to search along the tracks to ensure Alex didn't fall off the train. Komptin had his nose constantly on the ground, hoping to smell Alex if she was lying in a ditch somewhere.

Kameron was in the middle while Midnight and Scotty scoured the edge. It was nice that it was a clear night and the moon was full. It provided a much-needed light source. They had their issued flashlights, but, at continuous use, they wouldn't last more than four hours. Of course, Kameron was hoping it wouldn't take that long to find her.

Up ahead a bit, Komptin's body language seemed to be alerted to something, but he then continued his search. Kameron's heart stopped every time he did that. The night was starting to get a chill to it with all three of them getting tired. "We should take a break," Midnight told them. "Who knows how long this is going to take."

Kameron wanted to keep on going, but she did have a point. The group sat on a downed tree off to the side of the tracks. Midnight and Scotty both

310

gave Kameron a facial expression as if something was on their minds. "What?" He asked them.

"Are you going to tell us about her?" Midnight asked him.

"The Sentry?" Kameron tried to play dumb. "She was asked to maintain the balance between good and evil."

Scotty rolled his eyes. "Right."

Komptin's eyes flashed to the three of them. His barking got them all startled as to see what was coming next. Then, radiating confidence, Devine dropped from the sky, landing in front of them. Both Midnight and Scotty drew their weapons on her. The angelic entity viewed their sudden actions with confusion combined with a hint of arrogance. "I have been watching your progress. You move rather slowly," she told the three of them.

"Do we shoot this one?" Midnight asked Kameron.

"You would regret it," Devine told her. She generated her Lite Bo and took a fighting stance in front of her. Komptin greeted Devine as she knelt down to scratch his ears. "It is good to see you."

"No, she's a good one," Kameron told them. The two of them holstered their guns. "Midnight and Scotty. Guys, this is Devine."

"And how are you involved with all this?" Midnight asked her.

"The Sentry must be found," she confidently answered. "How is she to be found if we do not look?"

Scotty put his weapon away. "Can't argue with that logic."

Midnight pointed her finger at Devine. "You were in San Diego with Komptin. Who are you?"

"She's one of the former Guardians of the Conduit," Kameron told them. Scotty and Midnight both had blank expressions on their faces. Kameron didn't feel like getting into it, so he broke it down to the simplest answer that would get them back on the search for Alex. "She's an angel."

"There is no sign of the Sentry from above," Devine told them.

"Kam, there is a good chance that she is dead," Midnight tried to break the news. "The next town is only about thirty to forty miles from here. Considering how long she has been gone, she should have come across some way to contact the church."

Kameron's face told the group he was thinking about giving up.

"Kameron, her body still lives," Devine told him.

"How do you know?" Kameron asked her.

"Because she is not in Heaven, and she is not represented in the stars," Devine informed him.

Kameron got a fearful revelation. "What if her losing the connection to the Lite prevents her from becoming a star or entering Heaven? She could be dead, and we wouldn't know." Kameron sat back down on the log.

"You may be correct," Devine flat out said. "There are things happening that have never been dealt with before." The angel could see that this pure heart was in pain. "But that does not mean we give up."

"Kameron, if she is still alive, we will find her," Midnight told him.

Kameron got up with no enthusiasm. "Let's find her."

The tracks sent them to a long bridge that seemed like the darkness of the forest engulfed on the other end. The group just stared at the crossing. Scotty asked the question, "Ever see that movie with those kids looking for a dead body, and they almost get run over by that train?"

Midnight answered him, "Stand by Me."

Devine interjected, "I am right here, there is no fear you should have."

Kameron with his two friends tilted their heads in Devine's direction and then all four looked below the bridge. "What would happen if she fell off of the bridge?"

"The river current leads deeper into the woods." Midnight pulled up a map on her phone. "It's a long way down."

Kameron said, "We could walk the bank a bit."

Midnight chimed in, "There's an Amish town a couple of miles down the river."

The group looked down at the water below them. Scotty turned to Devine, "So, angel, huh?"

Devine just stared down at the water. "Yes."

"Why aren't there any dinosaurs in the Bible?"

"I did not write it," Devine replied quickly.

313

Kameron got a text message from Paige. "Hey, it looks like the leader of the F.O.R. has gone to Copper Top Mountain."

"I should go," Devine informed them. "The Pure of Heart is not protected. He could seek revenge for her escaping from their clutches."

Kameron stopped her. "Before you go, do you mind?" He pointed down.

"Of course." Devine allowed Kameron to put his arm around her. The two of them walked to the edge of the bridge and jumped off.

Midnight and Scotty's eyes widened. They looked at each other and simultaneously said, "You're next."

***

Those three boys and girls Alex had asked for a ride were stuck in her mind. They almost were shocked to see her, as if they knew who she was. There would be no reason the F.O.R. would be all the way out here. Perhaps she lost all trust among people. Besides, tomorrow she would take the long buggy ride into town to get ahold of Father Richard.

Jeremiah and Uri went back into town to lock up the shops. Alex was helping Dorothy with some of the chores outside. They both were back in the barn to ensure everything was secure. "Thank you for your help, Alex." Dorothy put the plank on the barn door.

"No biggie." Alex watched as some of the animals started to get a little spooked. There wasn't evidence of a storm coming. The sky was clear as she automatically checked to see if Osiah's star was still with her. To her surprise, it was Ariel's star that got her attention. How she missed the late Guardian.

"Animals seemed a little agitated." Dorothy tried calming down the horse

"Yes." Alex just stared out onto the field. "Where are the kids?"

Dorothy locked up the stable. "In the house."

"I thought I heard them call for you," Alex continued to survey the field.

Dorothy tried to listen. "I didn't hear them, but I should go check on them. Quiet children usually means a big mess." Dorothy went back into the house carrying the lantern. "Samuel? Eli?"

"Yes, Mama," Eli was showing Samuel his wooden horse.

"Did you call for me?" she asked them.

"No, Mama," Samuel answered. "Who's your friend behind you, Mama?"

Dorothy's eyes widened as her nerves heightened. Behind her was a slender man with clean cut hair. "Children," she moved together and placed them behind her.

"Where's the Sentry?" he said, grabbing some apple pie off the table.

"I don't know what that is," Dorothy told the man.

"Of course, you don't." The man showed her the apple pie. "This is really good." He licked his fingers.

"You can take it with you as long as you don't hurt my children." Dorothy was in need of something to defend her children.

"Mama, I'm scared," Eli cried out.

"There's nothing to be scared of," Dorothy tried to ease their worries. "God will protect us."

"Not this time." The man's eyes flashed a bright red, and his teeth became sharp. "This is going to hurt a lot."

The boys screamed as Dorothy held her children backed into a corner. "What do you want?"

He started to walk towards the three of them with his glowing red eyes. His fingernails grew in preparation to shred their bodies. "I want the Sentry," he started getting irritated.

"Careful what you wish for." Alex grabbed the monster from the back. She lifted him up and slammed him into the ground. The blue from her eyes and fists illuminated the common room. The Demon tried to get up but Alex quickly countered by grabbing his hair and kneeing him in the face a couple of times before throwing him out the window. There was no evidence he was making a quick counter attack. Alex turned to Dorothy and the kids. "Are you okay?"

"Yes," Dorothy checked her children. "Are you going to hurt us?"

"No. I'm still the Alex you know." Alex smiled as she walked up to them. "We need to get you to the church. You'll be safe there until I can figure out how many of them there are."

"It will be some time to get the horses ready." Dorothy was getting worried about the children.

"We don't have time for that." Alex made sure she wasn't going to be jumped from behind. "We'll walk."

"That monster is out there." Eli buried himself into his mother.

"Don't worry, Eli, I've got this," she gave him a wink. The four of them walked out of the house. The kids stayed close to their mother, and Dorothy close to Alex.

"Do you think we should go through the woods?" Dorothy asked her.

"No, we'd be too vulnerable in the woods. I want to see them coming," Alex told her.

They continued to walk down the road. The woods didn't have a sound to them. Even though Alex didn't have her sense of the Dark, she knew they were out there. Her main goal was to get them to church. They would be safe there; the Dark could not harm them.

Alex saw a pair of red eyes stare at her in the thickness of the woods. "Dorothy, listen to me," she whispered. "I cannot protect you if you take off running with the children. I need you to stay close."

"The children?" Dorothy was becoming frantic.

"Will not be harmed if you listen to me," Alex instructed.

"Those monsters are going to get us." Samuel was obviously scared.

"No they won't," Alex assured. "I will die before they touch you. Trust me; they are more scared of me than you are of them."

"Why?" Samuel held tight to his mother.

"Because," Alex stood up with confidence with her eyes lit with her fists. "I am a Lite Sentry."

***

Kameron watched as Midnight, followed by Scotty were brought down by Devine. Komptin decided to take the long way around. The angel said her goodbyes before taking off to ensure the Pure of Heart was protected from the Dark. "How far do you want to go down?" Midnight asked him.

"I don't know," Kameron saw the length of the river. "This is like looking for a needle in a haystack."

"Funny thing is, one time I actually found a needle in a haystack," Scotty light-heartily said. "I was investigating an OD near the border. Dead girl in a stack of hay…a couple feet from her, I found the needle."

"I just wish I knew I was heading in the right direction," Kameron told them. He saw that he barely had one bar on his cell phone but he got a text from Paige. It told him the F.O.R. spotted Alex in a small Amish town down the river.

"Where's that dog?" Scotty asked.

"He'll catch up," Kameron said. "Midnight, where's that town?"

"It would be faster if we follow the river than jump up on the road into the town," she told him.

***

Anne couldn't sleep because her stomach was still hurting. The only thing she wanted to do was feel better. Perhaps the church would give her strength. For some reason she felt as if she needed to go there. She parked the car in front of the church, just by the steps. The steering wheel wasn't comfortable when she laid her head on it, but she just felt miserable altogether. Even though it was a safe refuge, the church looked so creepy, all dark with no electricity.

"Pure of Heart," a voice said behind her.

Anne turned around to see Devine. Anne immediately went to the worst. "Alex?"

"We still do not know where she is," Devine told her.

"Then what are you doing here?"

Then it seemed to come from the shadows. Gron appeared with a group of Demons which meant that Infiltrators weren't far behind. "Anne," he said to her. "Long time."

Devine made sure that Anne was behind her on the stairs to the church. Devine formed her Bo staff while staring down the group of Demons. "You cannot harm her on holy ground."

Gron rolled his eyes. "Thanks for the update on that one, wow, didn't know that," he sarcastically said. "Just wanted to check up on something."

Gron looked up to the stars, "Which one is she?" He winked at Devine.

"Roger, what are you doing in town?" Anne stayed behind Devine. She couldn't manage to look at him. The image of Kale being killed was continuously entering her mind.

"Oh, Anne, we didn't really get to say goodbye the last time we saw each other," he told her. "How've you been? You don't look well. Something happened?" He winked at her. A black limo pulled up to pick up Roger. There were some other people in the limo but Anne couldn't make out any of them.

Devine guarded Anne as they watched Roger leave with the group of Demons. Devine stared down the limo before turning to Anne. She was crying as she sat down on the stairs to the church. Devine sat down next to her. "You should go home and rest. When we find the Sentry, we will send her to your domicile."

"How am I going to tell Alex what I did?" Anne pleaded to Devine. "She will never forgive me for how I betrayed Kale."

Devine was confused. "What was it that you did that was so shameful?" Anne could barely whisper it in Devine's ear. The angel stood up. "You feel violated. You feel as if something was taken from you." The angel stood over Anne as she cried on the church steps.

***

"Satisfied?" Misluna asked Gron as they drove off leaving the church.

"Actually, I am. They seem to be healthy and growing," Gron told her. "Everything is falling into place." Gron sat back in the chair. "Merik, is everything done out at the house?"

"It's coming together. By the time of their arrival, we'll have everything set," Merik concurred.

Gron's phone got a message. "It looks like they encountered the Sentry." Gron got irritated. "That means she's alive and she knows we're onto her." He got another message that the Sentry's ex-boyfriend is coming close to finding her. "How would he know where she is?"

"Someone is feeding him information," Misluna was looking through her phone. "Any ideas?"

"Not as of yet, but we'll find that person," Gron said. "We need to stop her boyfriend from finding her." He sat and thought for a moment. "Get me, Tomix."

***

Alex cracked her neck as she stared down another pair of eyes that appeared out of the darkness of the forest. She lit her fists and her eyes were glowing in preparation of the imminent attack. "Come on, I'm right here!" she yelled at them.

With a flash of red eyes, the Dark answered her call. Two Infiltrators started to run at Alex. She shot one with a Lite Beam, causing it to roll into the ditch. The other jumped at her with its bear-like mouth and claws. It was met with a punch underneath the jaw. It went flying backwards, landing on the ground. Alex immediately followed by jumping in the air and landing on its chest with her knee. A flurry of punches from Alex followed on the black beast.

The Infiltrator she shot with her beam got up with a massive roar before running towards Alex. This challenge was not ignored as Alex returned the scream while heading right for it. She shot another Lite Beam at it but it dodged out of the way. The Infiltrator tackled Alex causing the two of them to land on the ground and roll into the ditch. She flipped the Infiltrator that was on top of her into the other one as it tried to get up.

Alex got up to make sure that Dorothy and the kids were staying safe. Dorothy felt secured when Alex lifted her finger up to tell her it would be just a moment. Alex approached the monsters that were just then untangling from each other.

One of them started to charge at Alex. Confidently and with determination, Alex met it with a fist on top of the head. She was able to drive its chin into the ground. The second Infiltrator leaped over the downed body. Its sharp claws swung at Alex's face. Her arms got up in time to protect her face, however, she was still knocked to the ground. Blood dripped from the sleeve of her jacket. The black beast went for her neck but she managed to put her arm up in time. The Infiltrator bit down on her arm. With her other arm, she punched it on the side of the head. It broke the hold with its mouth and then Alex head-butted it. She punched it again, causing it to roll onto its side.

She shot another beam at the other one to give her some room to maneuver. She punched the Infiltrator until it was weakened to the point she could destroy it. A knife formed from her Lite and she stabbed it in the side of its head. It disappeared into the ground. She turned her attention to the second who was charging her. With one-step to the side, she was able to grab it in a headlock. She screamed as she leaned back. The Infiltrator's neck started to rip. She formed another knife and jabbed into the side of its neck. After it disappeared into the earth, Alex checked her nose for blood. Of course, it was bleeding.

She walked over to Dorothy and the kids, still checking her nose. "You okay?"

"Are you?" Dorothy asked her.

"I'm fine, I've had worse," Alex told her. "Come on, let's get to the church."

***

Komptin caught up rather quickly to take point once they got to the road. He seemed a bit more alert than before. He morphed into his gargoyle state and took off into the woods.

"Where the hell is he going?" Midnight watched the dog take off.

"Do you think he knows Gozer, you know that hot chick from Ghostbusters?" Scotty asked, pointing to Komptin.

Midnight put her finger to her mouth, "Shhh, something is up." She unbuckled her coat.

"Damn it, I don't want to go another round with those things." Scotty checked to see if something was coming from the woods.

Kameron stopped. "We have an issue."

Qawi was leading a group of young men and women, all made up of his community activists. "See I told you," he yelled. "The government-sent spies were following us as we scouted for a new meeting location. This is because it fears us. They don't want us to unite."

"This is not good." Scotty took a deep breath.

"Nope, we are in some serious trouble." Kameron decided to approach the community activist. They could see several people in front of them. "I would like no to speak to Qawi." He turned to Midnight and Scotty. "Let me see if I can talk our way out of this."

"Good luck with that one," Scotty surveyed the situation.

Kameron walked ahead with his hands out to his sides showing his hands were empty. Qawi told the group to stay put so he could see what this agent wanted from him. "I'm Agent Kameron..." where he started to say.

"I know who you are, Agent Kameron Dutcher," Qawi interrupted.

Kameron was caught a little off guard but he hid his surprise. "Look, we are on a missing person investigation. We just want to continue to that little Amish town. I can assure you that this encounter will not be in the official report."

Qawi leaned into him. "She's not missing. We know exactly where she is." Kameron's nerves shot up. Qawi turned back to his group. "He said he is here to arrest us, to bring down our rights to assemble. They want to shut us up and have no justice for Darius King!"

Kameron stared at Qawi, "They have no idea why they are here." Kameron looked into his eyes. "What's your name?"

"You will not shut us up!" Qawi yelled.

Kameron turned to Midnight and Scotty to join them. "They are not going to let us pass. I think Qawi is a Demon, but the others, I think they are being played."

"We could back track," Scotty suggested.

Midnight turned to see what was coming behind them. "Nope."

They turned around to see a group of people moving quickly in their direction.

"Oh damn." Scotty and Midnight backed into each other.

"Here we go," Kameron commented.

***

The four of them made it to the church where Uri and Jeremiah were ensuring all the shops were locked up. The kids ran to their dad giving them a big hug. "What is going on?" he asked.

"Monsters tried to eat us," Samuel said.

"But Alex fought them off," Eli told them. "With her lite eyes."

Jeremiah and Uri both looked at Alex. She just shrugged her shoulders. The low sound of growls was heard in the background. Alex put her hands on the family. "Come on, I think it's time for you to get into the church." Alex got them into the church. Dorothy got the kids some blankets from a closet. "I have to go."

"Alex!" the boys yelled.

She turned around. "Don't worry, you'll be safe."

Jeremiah walked Alex to the door. "God is with you."

"I hope so," Alex told him. "You'll be fine. They are here for me and I'm going to answer them."

Alex walked outside the church to see Osiah's star shining bright. She smiled at the purple speckle in the sky and gave a thumb's up. She took off to hide in the shadows of the building. Alex watched two Demons come out with two Infiltrators. They started to head towards the church. She lit her hands and shot a Lite Beam at one of the Demons. It hit him in the head causing him to knock over into the Infiltrator next to him. She stepped out of the shadows and blew a kiss at the group before taking off into the shadows of the town.

The Demon motioned for the Infiltrators and other Demons to spread out. Alex ran to the quilt shop. A lattice was available that Alex used to get on top of the roof. Below her, the Infiltrator was stalking her. She hopped down on the Infiltrator's back to drive her knee into it. The creature tried to howl for help but Alex held its mouth shut. The black beast stood up and flew itself back, crashing Alex into the ground.

Alex never broke her hold of the Dark creature. She was able to roll over the Infiltrator onto its stomach with her on top of it. She grabbed its head and smashed it on the ground. It got up again with her on its back but this time she wrapped her leg around its own, tripping it to the ground. It landed on a stick that was imbedded in the ground. It weakened enough for Alex to eliminate the dark beast.

"One down." Alex got up to see where the other one was. She peaked around the corner to see the other Demon trying to find her. Alex thought she could probably take the two demons at once, but, with the Infiltrator, she would not survive. Alex had sight on the Infiltrator; she was watching what route it was going to take as it went by the mercantile.

Alex was hoping she could get the advantage over this Infiltrator as well. She saw there was an outhouse next to the building on the route it was going. It wasn't the most exciting place to hide, but she could get the drop on it. She could see the Demon still searching in the opposite direction of the Infiltrator. She maintained her silence as she moved from shadow to shadow. The door to the female side of the outhouse didn't make any sound as she shut the door. She kept quiet as she was watching the Infiltrator move about the sides of the building from a small hole in the wall. The two Demons caught up with each other in front of the bathroom.

"She's not here," the bigger Demon complained.

The slenderer Demon looked around. "She may have joined the others."

Alex's attention peaked. "Others?" She couldn't help but think of who was all here. There was no way for anyone to know where she was.

"I think the harridan did us more harm than good," the big Demon was looking around. "Taking away her sense to detect the Dark is preventing us from smelling her Lite."

"There are bigger reasons for her actions than just taking the Sentry's senses away," the slick one reminded him.

Alex couldn't believe what she just heard. Her senses were stolen from her. They weren't taken away for any other reason than the Dark doing something to her. Now, there was more she needed to think about with the hope of getting it back; who took away her sense and how? The other thing she needed to find out was why? What were those bigger reasons?

"So, what do we do?" The big one asked.

"The Infiltrator is off doing his thing. Go and make sure others don't screw it up," the skinny one said. The big one went off to the woods.

The skinny one started to head towards Alex. Her nerves heightened. Did he detect her? He went into the men's side of the outhouse. "Do Demons really use the bathroom?" Alex thought to herself. The Demon went into the bathroom next to her as he let out the foulest sound and smell. There was no way she could handle this torture any longer.

She blasted a Lite Beam through the wall, pushing the Demon out the other side.

He rolled on the ground with pants down to his knees. He tried standing up again but Alex shot another beam at him to knock him back down. She ran up to him and started to smash his face with the bottom of her foot. He tried to defend himself but Alex had the upper hand. She picked him up to wrap her arms around his head. She then dropped to the ground to drive the Demon into the ground. With her arms still wrapped around his head, she leaned back feeling the neck of the Demon break. She figured this was a weakened state of the Demon and jabbed a knife made of Lite through the head. The Demon disappeared into the ground.

Alex got up from the ground and wiped herself off. She took a whiff of her hands. "Yuck." She went to the water pump and washed her hands. As she was washing her hands, she felt a hand on the back of her head that forced her into the handle of the pump. The blood started to drip from her forehead as she fell to the ground. She turned over to see the big Demon standing over her.

CHAPTER FOURTEEN

"I say we shoot them," Scotty suggested as he put his hand on his weapon. The group started to get closer with more anger in their yelling.

"There's no doubt in my mind we are being videotaped somewhere," Midnight pointed out. "If you look, none of them have guns or weapons out."

Kameron surveyed the situation. "We could run for it." The river was to the left of them and the thickness of the woods was to the right. Whatever got Komptin to get into the woods was still in there because he had not returned. "I think we should holster our weapons."

"What?" Midnight and Scotty both said.

"Look, we are going to have to fight our way out this one way or the other," Kameron told them. "I'm sure some of them have guns too. If we draw, they will draw, and we are vastly out-numbered. I don't feel like getting shot today."

"So you want to get the crap beat out of you instead? Good plan." Scotty put his thumb up.

"If we maintain a defensive posture, then they can't use it to escalate the hate relations in the city," Kameron told him.

Midnight took her hand off her weapon. "I hope you're right."

The group surrounded the three of them. Kameron felt Scotty and Midnight get closer to him.

The biggest of the group walked up to Kameron. "I'm a federal agent, please don't do anything rash."

"You're not going to draw your weapon?" he asked Kameron.

"Do I need to?" Kameron stared at him in the eye.

The crowd started to taunt the federal agents. "We are not going to let you pass."

"Why?" Kameron asked him.

"Because you are spies for the government who keep our people down!" the man yelled in Kameron's face.

Kameron stepped up. "We are strictly here for a missing person case."

"Right," he didn't believe him. "Who are you looking for?"

"Alexandria Johnson, about yay tall," he put up his hands to show her height. "Petite, pale white skin, long black extensions."

One of the girls with a nose ring turned to Kameron. "Got a scar down her face, wears a collar?"

Kameron perked up, "You've seen her?"

"Tamela?" the big man harshly said to her.

The young girl submitted to the man. "No, I haven't."

"Please, we really need to find her," Kameron approached the girl as he was met with fist across the face knocking him down.

Midnight blocked a punch meant for her and followed suit with a knee to the man's side. She pushed him out of the way so she could defend herself from her next attacker.

Scotty wasn't as fortunate as he was met with a punch in the nose and then a strike across the face. He didn't fall to the ground though; he was able to regain his footing and kicked the knee of one of his assailants. It was evident that he broke the man's leg. He stood up quickly to move onto the next person who attacked. He blocked a punch and swiveled to the side to send a punch into the armpit of the individual, and then punched him across the face to knock him down.

Kameron was being kicked. He grabbed the foot of the person, twisted it, and used it to push the man back as Kameron got up. Another person came to attack him but he stepped out of the way. Being off-balance threw the person off and Kameron pushed him into some others as another came in for an assault.

Midnight was knocked to the ground just before Scotty got pushed back into Midnight. He crashed to the ground by tripping over her. Kameron turned to see if they needed help, in that instance Kameron was knocked down with a bat into the chest. He joined his companions on the road.

"This has gotten out of hand!" Tamela yelled. She got in front of them. "They didn't fall into the trap. Our tape is useless. We look like we are at fault."

Another spoke up. "That means we're going to jail. I'm too pretty to go to jail."

The leader of the group spoke with hate in his eyes. "We'll have to kill them, dump the bodies in separate locations." Kameron sat there stone faced as Midnight and Scotty were showing legitimate fear as they sat there listening about their executions. The leader of the group turned to one of the followers. He was handed a gun and pointed it at Kameron. Two others from the group had their guns pointed at Scotty and Midnight. "Any requests before we get this over with?"

"Just two. One, most important, go to the town and find Alexandria Johnson. Tell her that she is needed back home. Second, I want to see it coming," Kameron told him.

"I will deliver your message, but I will not give you the privilege of your death in your terms. You government slimes kill our people without remorse, and you shall receive the same," the big man said. "Turn them over."

They all were flipped around so their stomachs touched the ground. "I wonder if it will hurt." Scotty said as he felt the barrel on the back of his head.

Midnight closed her eyes as she was praying under her breath. Kameron just remained emotionless. He made it a point to lock eyes with one of the group. He just stared.

She looked away. "I can't watch this."

From the depth of the woods was a massive roar, enough to vibrate the air. The group turned to the sound coming from the woods as a pair of neon blue eyes of a German Shepard came running with lightning speed. The assailants tried shooting the dog but it was as if the bullets had no effect on him. Komptin attacked the man holding a gun to Scotty's neck by biting him on the hand. He bit so hard that his hand was barely attached to his body.

Kameron flipped over and knocked the gun out of the big man's hand. He then kicked the man in the groin. The big man fell over and then Kameron kicked him in the face from the ground.

Komptin finally let go of the man's hand and jumped to Midnight's executioner. The big dog knocked him to the ground and was about to go for the man's neck. "Komptin!" Kameron yelled. Komptin snapped his massive jaws at the face of the individual. The dog had blood and saliva dripping from his mouth. The man on the ground fainted from fright.

The crowd went running and dispersed from the three of them. Komptin made sure everything was all right before turning to Kameron. "Thanks boy," Kameron scratched the ears of the blood-soaked head of Komptin.

"I'm sure glad he's on our side," Scotty said, wiping the dirt off his clothes.

"You guys okay?" Midnight silently thanked God.

"I've been better," Scotty checked himself over. "You?"

"Well, there's no doubt I will be attending more church," Midnight told him. "Kameron?"

"I'm fine," he said with no emotion. He got up from petting Komptin. "Come on, let's go find Alex."

***

Alex's body was thrown against the wall of a building that was in front of the outhouse. She landed on the ground causing dust to rise. The big Demon confidently walked up to her. He went to kick her but she caught the foot of the Demon. "I'm tired of getting kicked on that side." She stood up with the Demon's foot in her hand. She kicked the Demon's crotch, then in the leg, and finally she spun him around. She shot a Lite Beam in the back of the Demon's head causing him to fall on the ground.

She followed the Demon's body as it rolled on the ground. The Demon stood and Alex punched it across the face. It held up its hand as if telling her to wait a minute. He opened up his mouth and pulled out a loose tooth. He saw what Alex did and then gave a facial expression to scare the darkest of evil as he threw the tooth to the ground.

"Ah, my bad," she softly said.

The Demon ran and football tackled her. The two of them fell to the ground in the center of the village square. The Demon continued to punch Alex in the face. He held her down, raised his fist to punch her, and gave her the opportunity to jab her lit thumb into the Demon's eye. He got up screaming in pain. He refocused with a bit of blood dripping from his eye.

Alex ran up and jumped in the air, but the Demon caught her midair. Alex punched him in the face with fury before he slammed her onto the ground. Her head spun from being dizzy combined with the feeling of weightlessness. Then she realized she'd been tossed in the air just before landing back on the ground. Alex got up with her eyes lit and fists off to her side.

"Why won't you die!?" the Demon yelled.

The two ran at each other full tilt, before the two met for a collision, Alex stepped to the side in a slide. She stuck out her leg tripping the Demon to the ground. She jumped in the air and landed her knee on the back of its head. The sound of the Demon's neck cracked. She formed a knife and jammed it in the back of the head of the Demon. The body of the Demon melted into the ground below. Alex got up with her eyes glowing. She scanned the area before making sure that Jeremiah and his family were safe in the church.

***

"I told you she was a witch," Leroy told the others. He was hiding the darkened forest outside the town village.

"What do we do?" One of them asked.

"She must be destroyed," Leroy said. "To ensure she doesn't eat the souls of others."

"She just killed that poor man in the center of town, how do you expect us to handle her?" Reuben asked.

"God will protect us," Leroy told him.

"Look, Samuel and Eli are meeting her at the door," the elder leader pointed out.

"The evil will have no power in the church of God. If we do this, we have to do this now," Leroy told them.

Another elder spoke up, "If we kill her, then hopefully her spell over Jeremiah and his family will be lifted."

"Leroy, you are the strongest of us. This burden will be on you." The leader of the elders entitled Leroy with the dirty task of disposing the witch. "God will protect you."

"I will do the Lord's work," he accepted his duty.

***

Alex walked into the church. She sat down on the pew with Eli and Samuel at her sides. "I suppose you don't have any ice?"

"Not in the summer," Eli told her.

"You are bleeding," Samuel said.

Dorothy came running with Jeremiah and Uri. "Alex, are you okay?"

"I think so." She put her head back on the wall. "I really could use some ibuprofen, got any?"

"I don't know what that is." Dorothy told her. "But I can get you some water from the back." Dorothy stopped and turned around. "Is it safe?"

"I'm pretty sure there aren't any more out there. The Dark doesn't like fair fights," Alex told her. She saw that Dorothy was a bit hesitant. "Is the pump on church land?"

"Yes, it is in the fenced-in backyard," she told Alex.

"You're safe, trust me," Alex smiled at her.

"I will go with you, Dorothy," Jeremiah told her. "Papa, children, get Alex anything she needs." He joined his wife to go in the back.

Uri looked to Alex, "How do you feel?"

Alex smiled. "Honestly, I hurt."

"Thank you for protecting us," Samuel said as he snuggled up to Alex. She put her arm around the two boys.

"No problem," she smiled at them. They waited a couple of minutes before Alex got up. "They've been gone awhile." Alex walked outside to the back of the church to see Jeremiah on the ground, bleeding from his forehead and Dorothy with her mouth covered with a rag. They were surrounded by the elders. "What the hell?"

Alex was met with a shovel in the back of her head. She fell down the stairs onto the ground. Leroy dragged her body to a lantern pole in the middle of the church's backyard. Leroy stood her up and tied her body with ropes and leather horse reins. Alex tried fighting her way out but couldn't do it.

"Alex!" Uri yelled. "What are you doing?" he asked the elders.

"Uri, this for your family's own good," Reuben proclaimed. "Please my friend, if you are still with us, this must be done."

"She's not evil, she is chosen by God," Uri pleaded.

"You are under her spell!" one elder yelled. "You are blind to see all that is going on!"

Uri ran over to Leroy, trying to take the shovel away from him. He punched the old man across the face and he landed into the group of the elders. "I am protecting this village from the witch's spell," Leroy told him.

"Papa, Mama," Eli ran over to his mother trying to set her free.

"What are you doing!?" Samuel cried.

One of the elders grabbed the children. "You should not see this."

"They have to see this. The burning of the witch will release them," the elder cried.

Alex tried to break free as some of the elders were putting firewood and branches at her feet. "Ah, what are you doing?"

"Witches need to be burned at the stake," he told her. "If you had a soul, I would pray for it."

"What is this, Salem? I'm not a witch!" she yelled.

"You are casting spells over the people of this town!" Leroy said. "Causing them to do things they normally wouldn't do."

"You kissed me, you psycho! You asked me to have sex with you!" she yelled at him.

"Liar!" Leroy smacked her across the mouth. "Now the witch spreads lies as part of her power to deceive." They poured lantern kerosene over the wood.

"Look, you are making a very bad mistake," Alex told them. "A very, very, bad mistake."

Leroy lit the match and walked up to her. Alex blew out the match before he could drop it. Leroy's face was one of shock before anger. He slapped her again across the face. He quickly lit the match and released it into the sticks. "Burn, like you will in hell, harlot. No God would give you such power. You are a soulless whore who is incapable of good. You do not deserve to walk among us." He came up to her so only she could hear what he said. "You are incapable of having anyone love you."

The ground beneath her started to burn when he stepped back to watch the fire start to spread. The smoke started to get into Alex's lungs and the heat was starting to burn her clothes. In what seemed like an eternity, she had concluded that he was right. She was unworthy. For the first time, she was in a life and death situation, and she had no will to fight. The failures as a Sentry, all the men she used, and the one love she pushed aside; she deserved this fate. Blackness started to overtake her when a force exploded in the fire beneath her. Pieces of wood and burning branches flew through the air. A massive roar from her purple-skinned companion startled the elders. Komptin walked towards the

341

elders in his gargoyle state ensuring they didn't move.

Kameron came running behind Komptin with his pistol drawn at Leroy who was now holding a shovel. "Don't you move," Kameron told him. Another man and a blonde woman came in behind Kameron.

"We got you covered," the blonde woman told him.

Kameron ran over to Alex and quickly untied her. She fell to the ground, breathless. "Alex, Alex," Kameron started to shake her a bit. He quickly calmed himself down before starting CPR on Alex. "Come on, come on, Alex," he started to give her mouth-to-mouth resuscitation.

Alex put her arms around his neck as she turned it into an instinctive kiss before coughing up smoke. She opened up her eyes to see Kameron holding her. She took a second to realize who was holding her. There was no control of emotion from her as she cried as he held her tight. "It's okay, Alex, I'm here." He kissed her on top of her head.

The elders stood and watched Alex cry in the man's arms. Leroy screamed, "She's a witch!"

"No witch would cry with that much emotion," the old man said. "The only thing I hope is that God will forgive us for what we have done."

"No, no, she's a witch," Leroy gripped the shovel and ran after Alex. "That's the only explanation!"

All three of the agents pulled their weapons at Leroy to shoot him but Komptin jumped in front of the bullets, protecting him from being shot. Komptin growled at the man, who now was trembling in fear.

"Help me. This creature of Hell is going to eat me!" Leroy cried.

"No, he just saved your stupid ass," Scotty said putting his weapon away. He joined Midnight in watching their friend comfort the Lite Sentry, but now they both knew she was much more important to him than that.

***

Gron was walking through the hallway with Misluna at his side. "I've always hated this town." His view from the hallway window had the town in the far distance.

"I can see why," she told him. "Though, Marty's makes a pretty good burger." She continued to walk down the hall of their new mansion. The sound of her licking her fingers and footsteps was all that heard down this dark hallway.

"My leader," a young girl came running down the hall.

"What?" he asked as he turned around.

"Qawi is on the phone for you," she handed him a cell phone.

"Tell me good news," Gron commanded. He waited a minute. "That isn't good news. No, we can still use the plan. Come back here, find yourself a volunteer." Gron hung up the phone. He turned to

Misluna, "Apparently, Alex is still alive. Not only that, she is heading here."

Misluna looked worried. "We will have to stall for time until they arrive."

Gron nodded. "We're all set for their arrival." He opened the door behind him to a room with two black cribs next to the wall.

***

Alex watched the sun come up over the farm field. The mixture of the bright colors with the warmth of the sun reminded Alex of how she once felt the Lite. Komptin was still in his gargoyle state next to her. She put her arm around him and leaned her head onto his. "Thank you," she told him. He snuggled her head into him.

Kameron was on the deck watching her. Midnight and Scotty joined behind him. "Are you going to tell us about her?" Midnight asked him.

"She's the Lite Sentry," Kameron told them.

"You know what we mean," Midnight told him.

Kameron just watched her stare into the field, "Excuse me." He stepped off the porch to join Alex. He slowly walked up to her to join her overlooking the field. Komptin morphed down as a dog. After getting a scratch from Kameron, he joined Midnight and Scotty on the porch.

The two of them didn't say a word to each other. Each of them not knowing how to start. Finally, Alex was the first to speak. "Thank you."

"You're welcome," Kameron softly replied.

The two didn't say anything as a pair of doves flew by. "What now?"

"We need to get you to Anne, there's something not right going on over there," Kameron told her. He kept his hands in his coat.

"I wasn't talking about Anne." Alex just continued to stare.

"I don't know," Kameron told her. "You hurt me, Alex. You pushed me away when I tried to be there for you."

Alex swallowed hard. "I know. Will you ever forgive me?"

"Of course, I forgive you," he assured her.

"Do you still love me?" Alex asked him, still staring forward at the field.

"I will always love you, Alex," Kameron told her. He stared out to the field with her, before turning around to the house. He grabbed her hand and put the necklace in it. "But trusting you...only time will answer that one." Kameron joined Scotty and Midnight on the porch.

Alex was rushed with emotion as she saw the necklace back in her hand. She closed her eyes as tears fell down her cheeks.

CHAPTER FIFTEEN

Alex had better plane rides than the one she was just on. Kameron was being friendly but she knew him too well. He definitely had a wall up. Alex got a rental car from the airport and drove to go see Anne. Kameron told her that there was something wrong and she needed to go see for herself. Kameron was going to meet her at the church with Midnight and Scotty, who are now for some reason deep in this fight.

Alex parked in front of the church. She walked around the church to see if she could get in, but Anne had it boarded up. It looked as if it was locked. Alex walked around back to see Devine staring up at the stars. "Devine?" she softly said.

"Alexandria," Devine turned around.

Alex wasn't sure but it looked as if she was crying. "I didn't know you were going to be that happy to see me," she joked. Then she saw the star she was looking at. Ariel's star was shining so bright and bold, just as she was. "I'm sorry, do you want to be left alone?" Komptin joined Alex by her side after coming back from the woods. Alex knelt down to pet him after returning from a perimeter sweep.

"No, what are you doing here?" Devine asked her.

"I was looking for Anne," Alex told her.

"She is not here," Devine let her know.

Alex gave a look of disappointment. "She might be at home." Alex was hoping Devine had some insight that was going on with Anne. "Do you know what is wrong with her?"

"It is not my place," Devine told her.

Komptin's eyes flashed as he started barking out of anger. Alex was on guard as she turned in the direction where Komptin was barking but there was nothing. "Excuse me," Alex told Devine.

Devine told her, "It is the Dark. Their presence here is growing."

"Come on, Komptin. We will hunt tonight, but first, I need to talk to Anne," Alex told him. "Do you want to come with me?"

"No, I will stay behind." Devine turned back to Ariel's star.

"Suit yourself." Alex walked back to the car. Komptin looked back at the woods but then followed Alex back to the car.

Devine watched the Lite Sentry walk away to visit her friend. She made sure she left before turning to look out in the woods. "Why are you here?"

Salamor approached out of the woods. "She does not know?"

"No," Devine turned to the shadow. "And she will not know from your words."

***

Alex arrived at Anne's house just as Kameron was coming in behind her. She had texted him to

347

meet there. Alex got out of her car with Komptin at her side. "Go and secure the perimeter while I talk to Anne." Komptin agreed by flashing his eyes. He took to the woods to hunt for the Dark. The porch seemed to creek as Anne's mom greeted her outside the porch. Alex touched the spot where she almost punched Anne back in high school, but hit the corner of the house instead.

"I'm so glad you are here," her mom hugged Alex. "How are you doing, Kameron?"

"I'm fine, Mrs. McClure, I wish it wasn't under these circumstances," Kameron answered her.

Alex didn't know why Willow being nice to Kameron irritated her. Willow never cared for government officials. Anne's dad came out from the hallway when Alex and Kameron came into the room. "Hey, I don't know if she will see you. She's still pretty out of it," he told her. "She is refusing to go to the doctor."

Alex walked down the hallway with Kameron behind her. She knocked on the door, "Anne?" She slowly walked in. "Can I come in?"

"Leave the light off," Anne muffled in the darkness.

Alex walked in with Kameron. Having him behind her was comforting, but hurtful as she knew it wasn't what it was. He moved to the corner of the room and stood completely still. Alex softly sat down on the bed next to Anne. "Anne, how are you doing?"

"Alex," was all she could answer.

"I'm right here," Alex sat down on the bed next to her.

"I'm a horrible person," Anne started to cry.

"You are the kindest person I know." Alex patted her hand.

Anne tried to fight back tears. "No, I betrayed Kale."

Alex fought back a lump in her throat at the mention of her brother. "How, Anne?"

"No, I can't." Anne put her head underneath the covers so she wouldn't have to look at Alex.

Alex turned on the lamp next to Anne's bed.

"I said to leave it off," Anne commanded but Alex didn't oblige.

Alex started to get irritated. She grabbed the covers and pulled them down to uncover Anne's head. "Your hair is really black." Alex said, lifting it up looking at it.

"I know." Anne started to cry harder.

"Oh, Anne, we can change it back. Is that why you are crying? It's no big deal; we might even put some streaks in it." Alex was trying to pretend she liked the color.

"Alex, please forgive me," Anne begged.

"For what?" Alex asked.

"Oh, Alex, I ran into Shawn," Anne started to explain.

"Okay," Alex was on guard fearing the worst.

"I was so lonely, hurting… he said such nice things, and then he just got up and left," Anne cried.

"What happened, Anne?" Alex knew the answer to this question.

"I betrayed Kale," Anne cried. "Shawn and I had…" Anne couldn't finish the sentence out of shame. "And then he just got up and left me on the ground at the lake."

Alex hugged Anne and opened her eyes in a glow. "I understand. This isn't your fault. Get some sleep." Alex got up. "Love you, Anne." Alex kissed her on top of her head as she embraced her surrogate sister.

"Will Kale forgive me?" Anne begged.

"Of course, Anne, he loves you," Alex reassured her. "Get some sleep."

Alex watched Anne rollover onto her bed to get some sleep. Alex walked by Kameron and headed straight for her car. As soon as she got outside, she whistled loudly for Komptin. He came running out of the woods. Kameron, as well, came running out behind her.

"Alex, where are you going?" Kameron demanded.

"I'm going to go have a talk with Shawn. This has been a longtime coming." Alex's determination meant that there was no changing her mind. She opened the car door to let in Komptin. "Can you stay here with Anne until I get back?"

"Of course," Kameron said. "Don't do anything stupid."

"You know me," Alex said, getting into her car.

"Yes, yes I do," he said to himself.

***

Alex got Shawn's address from the white page and found the house with ease. She walked up to the little house to start pounding on the door. "Shawn!" Alex yelled. She continued to knock. "Shawn! Open up, you piece of crap!" Each knock was getting harder and harder, almost to the point Alex was going to knock the door down.

Alex was banging loud enough that the neighbors came out from next door. "Will you please keep it down?" a man in his forties said. "I have to work in the morning."

"Have you seen him?" She pointed to the door.

The man had a disappointed look on his face. "Look, you're not the first girl to go knocking on that door in anger. Do yourself a favor. Get yourself checked out for STDs and a pregnancy test. Pray to God they both come back negative."

"Ugh," Alex rolled her eyes. "Thanks." She walked down the driveway and stopped herself. "Pregnant," she said to herself. She thought back to Anne feeling ill. She noticed there was a smell of her vomiting. Alex got more infuriated. She turned around to the neighbor.

"What is it, young lady?" the man asked her.

"Do you know where he hangs out?" Alex was now more than determined to find Shawn.

"I've heard him talk about bowling on Thursdays," he told her.

"Thanks." Alex drove to a bowling alley where there were many cars. Alex told Komptin to stay by the car while she went inside. Inside the bowling alley was a sea of cigarette smoke and the smell of stale beer. There were a crowd of people but she spotted Shawn with ease on the other side of the room.

Shawn was laughing with a girl while drinking a beer when he saw Alex in the doorway, "I gotta go!" Fear entered his face when he saw Alex with the look of death planted on her face.

Alex walked through the crowd with a sense of purpose.

One guy approached Alex. "Hey baby."

She just pushed him out of the way causing him to fall over the side of the table. Once she got outside to the parking lot, she couldn't see Shawn. A shadow across the parking lot caught Alex's attention. There were cars between them, but that didn't stop Alex from running after him. "Shawn!"

He stopped in his tracks. "Alex?" He watched her approach. Her small stature was nothing compared to her confidence. "Alex?" he questioned again. The air thickened with tension but there was no doubt that she didn't sense the Dark in him.

"Shawn, you have about two seconds to defend yourself. How you could do that to Anne?" She got up right to his face.

"No problem. She was so sweet and innocent. I just had to take it." Shawn winked at her. "What are you going to do, Alex?" Shawn unzipped his bowling bag before opening his trunk.

Alex was amazed at how cold he was about it. "How could you just leave her like that? How could you be so callous?"

Shawn turned around in anger. "My name is Merik, not callous."

Alex's eyes widened from seeing Shawn's eyes glow red. Next thing she felt was a punch come across her face, followed by a knee connecting on her nose. She was lifted in the air and thrown onto the pavement.

The sound of broken glass caught Shawn's attention as Komptin came running up to the fight. He morphed into his hunting form while bellowing a massive roar. Shawn threw the bowling ball at Komptin but he caught it with his mouth. He broke it into many pieces with his jaw.

Shawn felt a sharp pain in his crotch when Alex kicked him. She got up while punching him underneath the chin that sent him flying over the car. Shawn, who now called himself Merik, got up to brush himself off. "I'll be back for my keys," Shawn told her before taking off running into the woods.

Alex didn't see that he dropped his keys anywhere on the ground. Blood dripped a little from her nose. "Didn't see that coming." She checked how bad it was bleeding. Komptin morphed back down to a dog, licking Alex. "Come on. Let's go see how Anne is doing." Komptin walked in front of Alex. The massive dog turned around to see Alex deep in thought. "Wait a minute, Shawn is a Demon, and if he got Anne pregnant?" Alex feared the worst as she ran to the car.

Alex stopped by the church, hoping that Devine was still there. "Devine? I need your help!" she yelled. She ran back to Devine to see she was talking with Salamor. "What are you doing here?"

"Sentry?" he hissed.

"I thought you were in hiding." Alex didn't really care why he was here. "Devine, do you know where Anne is?"

"I can find her with ease." Devine got up rather slowly. "Why?"

"I need both your help in verifying something," she started back to the car. She turned around back to Devine and Salamor. "Come on!"

***

"You okay?" Anne asked Kameron as he stayed in the corner of the room. The bed squeaked a little as she adjusted herself to sit up. The room was still dark but there was enough light to see her friend at a distance. It was so hard to read his body language at times. As he stared out the window, this was no exception.

"I should be asking you that." Kameron turned his attention to Anne as he got up from his seat. "Can I get you anything?"

"No." Anne reached over to her tea. "Yuck, it's cold."

"You've been sleeping really hard since Alex left. Let me get you some hot lemon water with honey." He left the room.

Anne could hear him tell her parents that she was up. They both came in to check on her while Kameron was getting her drink. The water was hot but it felt good. "Thanks Kameron."

"No problem, Anne," he told her. "Glad to do it."

Anne smiled. "Could you open the window? The room feels a bit musty."

When he opened the window, the fresh air started pouring in. "Better?" he asked.

"Much," Anne got out of bed. The room was dirty and filthy. It was comfortable but she wanted to get out of it.

Her mom came in with new sheets and covers. "How about you go get some fresh air so I can switch out your linen?"

"Thanks, Mom." Anne got out of bed, slowly still holding her stomach. "Kameron, do you mind taking me for a drive?"

"Not at all." Kameron left the room so she could get herself ready.

Anne didn't really say a word except giving directions to the lake. The two of them walked up to the cliff overlooking the water. The night was so clear and the stars were bright. The moon's reflection on the lake was like one from a painting. Kameron just kept Anne company without saying a word.

"This is where Kale and I started our relationship," Anne finally spoke out.

"It's a nice spot," Kameron commented. "Very peaceful."

Anne thought back to that night. "It's amazing how events turned out."

Kameron nodded. "Yes."

Anne turned to her somber-faced friend. "Are you going to move on?"

Kameron swallowed hard. "I will, if you will."

"It's hard with these constant reminders, isn't it?"

Kameron got up to look around. "Come on. Let's go for a walk on the beach." Kameron extended his hand to help Anne up from the ground. The two of them platonically walked down the lakefront together.

"Can I ask you something?" Anne asked Kameron. "You don't have to answer if you don't want to."

"Go ahead." Kameron picked up a rock and threw it in the lake.

"You think you and Alex are done?" Anne asked as she sat on a log.

"We broke up." Kameron saw a fish jump in the lake.

"Doesn't mean you're done." Anne shivered from the night air. Kameron took off his jacket and gave it to Anne. "Thank you."

"Just between us?" Kameron asked her.

"I won't say anything," Anne assured.

"I'm not going to close the door on us, but I'm not walking through it either. If that makes any sense," Kameron explained.

"It does." Anne played with some of the rocks with her feet.

Kameron could tell Anne was in deep thought. "What about you?"

"What I did was bad," Anne told him.

"What you did wasn't your fault," Kameron retaliated. "He took advantage of you. There may not have been alcohol or drugs involved, but there is no doubt in my mind that what he did was a violation. It was not your fault."

"I accepted him willingly." Anne started to cry.

"By the mere cold facts, maybe. But what he did, as far as I'm concerned, was evil and vile. And I hope Alex will talk to him about that." Kameron tried to formulate his words.

Anne chuckled. "I have a feeling it will be a short conversation."

"Probably." Kameron gave a small laugh as well. "Anne, you have nothing to be ashamed of. It was all on that guy. No decent human being would take advantage of a person in the state you were in. There is no doubt in my mind that Kale understands that. If anything, how much pain you are in is just a testament on how much love you have for him."

Anne turned her head to the sky to see a falling star. It was almost as if Kale was telling her that it was okay. She started to cry. Kameron slowly walked over to her with his arms open. "Come on. It's okay not to blame yourself."

Anne accepted his embrace as she broke down crying harder than she ever had. She cried so hard that her legs went limp. Kameron gently brought her down to the beach as she continued to release her pain.

***

Alex raced over to the lake where Kameron and Anne were on the beach. The two of them were sitting on a log. Anne looked as if a weight was lifted off her. She wiped her eyes and blew her nose.

"What are you guys doing here?" Alex asked them.

Kameron was stoic as he talked to Alex. "She wanted to show me where her and Kale first started their relationship."

"What's going on, sweetie?" Anne asked, holding her stomach. She put her tissue into Kameron's coat pocket that he let her use.

"Anne, oh Anne." She hugged her. "We'll figure this out."

"I know." Anne wiped her eyes. "I'm feeling much better now." She turned and smiled at Kameron. "Thank you."

Devine landed on the ground next to Alex as Salamor rose out of the ground.

Alex didn't know how to tell her that Shawn was a Demon. She didn't know what would happen if someone who was pure of heart got pregnant by a Demon. "The baby, we'll make sure to find out what's going to happen."

"Baby?" Anne's eyes opened.

"Your hair turning suddenly black, your sickness, and you not wanting to come out during

358

the day?" Alex was putting the pieces together for her.

"What does that have to do with being pregnant? I felt horrible so I made a mistake by getting my hair dyed down at that hair salon on Main Street. I was making myself sick by my guilt over what I did to Kale," Anne explained. "I was in a depressed state, but Kameron and I talked, that made me feel a lot better. I could never repay him for that."

"Anytime." He gave her a brotherly smile of support.

Alex looked at Kameron as she just admired is true nature. He was so kind-hearted, such a good person. How could she push him away the way she had? Now wasn't the time for self-pity. She needed to ask Anne flat out. "You're not pregnant?" Alex bluntly asked.

"What? No." Anne was not expecting that question.

"You sure?" Alex wanted verification.

"Not to go into details, but pretty much verified this morning, sweetie," Anne let her know.

Alex was confused. "This makes no sense on what Merik said."

Kameron's eyes widened. Anne turned to Alex with a look of confusion. "Who?"

Salamor was listening to the group talk as they tried to figure out what was going on. His head then turned to the former Guardian of the Conduit of Lite staring at her reflection in the lake with fear, holding her stomach.

POST END

"Scarlett!" A deep voice from down the hall came echoing into the room.

Scarlett switched computer screens and brought up the F.O.R. Recruitment video. The video she was watching of her in a bikini at the beach back in Los Angeles talking about the benefits the F.O.R. did for her. The hope was to influence others in the freedom from religion. Aside from the fact she was focus and that her light brown skin emphasized the black and green bikini that matched the green streaks in her hair, the video was a piece of crap. They were going to have to reshoot it. Which meant she needed to go back on a stricter diet.

The big man who was screaming her name from down the hall came into the video editing room. "Scarlett."

"What?" She said looking up from the screen with her big brown eyes.

"Is that how you address a Provisionary?" The tall, dark man with deep voice addressed her.

"To his command,...dad," she said with sarcasm.

"I swear, I can only protect you for so long." He shook his head. "When are you going to realize that without the F.O.R., your nothing. You need to achieve absolute power."

360

"Dad, I know what the F.O.R. has to offer. I'm well aware of that." Scarlett told him.

"Then stand up when a Provisionary talks to you." He angrily pointed the folder that was in his hand at her.

Scarlett stood up while giving her dad a look of death. "What is it that you command of me?"

"I fired your assistant," her dad dropped the bombshell.

"You did what!" Scarlett yelled out.

"The F.O.R. will assign you one that is more suitable for you. Scarlett Roberts cannot be seen with a white boy as your assistant if we are to bring more diversity into the organization." Her dad handed her the folder. "You can pick any of these girls as your assistant."

"Let me guess, all attractive and young." Scarlett skimmed the potentials.

"Get the girls, the guys will follow." He told her.

Scarlett shook her head. "Can I at least talk to Steven?"

"No." Her dad said. "But that is not why I'm here."

"What then?" She asked him. That question earned her a slap across the face from her dad. Scarlett fell into the wall of her desk as she held her face. She was in shock as she regained her stature.

"Do not talk to a Provisionary like that," he said calmly.

"To your command," she softly said as she tried not to shed a tear.

"I don't give a shit who you think you are. Just because you have over a six million followers on some media platform, doesn't make you special on the Roadmap to Power." Her dad handed her a form. "Sign this."

She grabbed a pen and signed her name. "What is it?"

"You just handed me control of all your assets and funds. The F.O.R. will give you everything you need." Her dad turned around another member of the F.O.R. standing nervously in the entryway.

"To his command," the young man said as her dad walked out of the room. He waited a couple of minutes before he spoke. "You okay?"

"I don't think I will be. Even if it works." Scarlett told him.

The young boy closed the door to the room and stood in front of the camera in the corner of the room. "I'm sorry for this." He grabbed her from the back of neck and forced her into the chair. He wasn't holding her tight as it was just for show. He was using both their bodies to cover the computer screens. "You should be good, pull up the screen."

The screen enlarged to a page of alarm codes for the sensors along the fence line. "What time will the truck be here?"

"About eleven at night. The driver usually isn't F.O.R. related so he won't be on the lookout for anything suspicious. This will be the opportunity to escape. How are you getting into town?"

"Steven, my assistant, will be in a car waiting for us, right here, right next to the woods." There was a noise coming from the hallway. Both their hearts stopped until they realized they were safe.

"I can put the sensors on sleep mode from this point to this one. The only way they will notice the sensors aren't actually transmitting is if they actually go into the program." Eric stood closed the sensor grid down.

"What about the key?" Scarlett whispered.

"You'll have to break into the HS Office and grab it. I'll make sure it's clear. The key to the key box is in his top drawer. He has it hidden under some nude magazines." Eric closed the program down. "The guy is a pig."

"I'll be careful," Scarlett told him.

"You grab that key, get Kaylee, and get the hell out of here. I'll be able to follow-up in two days." Eric let go of Scarlett's neck. He moved to the front of the desk in stance to show the camera as if he was scolding her.

"How are you going to escape?" Scarlett asked him.

Eric was in fear as he whispered, "Don't worry about that, the less you know, the better it is. Just get Kaylee and my baby to a safe location."

Without them knowing, there was a short middle-aged blonde woman with freckles staring at

363

the two of them. "What are you guys talking about?"